9.95
7/21/09

SEVENTEEN SYLLABLES

and other stories

SEVENTEEN SYLLABLES

and other stories

Revised and Expanded Edition

Hisaye Yamamoto

Introduction by King-Kok Cheung

Rutgers University Press
New Brunswick, New Jersey, and London

Original edition first published by Kitchen Table: Women of Color Press in 1988;
published by Rutgers University Press in 1998

Revised and expanded edition published by Rutgers University Press in 2001
Fourth paperback printing, 2006
Library of Congress Cataloging-in-Publication Data

Yamamoto, Hisaye.
　　Seventeen syllables and other stories / Hisaye Yamamoto ;
introduction by King-Kok Cheung.—Rev. and expanded ed.
　　　p.　cm.
Includes bibliographical references.
ISBN 0-8135-2953-0 (alk. paper)
1. Japanese Americans—Evacuation and relocation, 1942–1945—
Fiction.　2. United States—Social life and customs—20th century—
Fiction.　3. Japanese Americans—Fiction.
I. Title.
PS3575.A43 S4 2001
813′.54—dc21　　　　　　　　　　　　　　00-067362

British Cataloguing-in-Publication information is available from the British Library.

Manufactured in the United States of America

For Paul, Kibo, Yuki, Rocky, and Gilbert.

TABLE OF CONTENTS

INTRODUCTION

I first met Hisaye Yamamoto at a conference in Irvine, California in 1987. Long an admirer of her short stories, I asked which was her favorite. "None of them is any good," said the recipient of the Before Columbus Foundation's 1986 American Book Award for Lifetime Achievement, with a seemingly straight face. But her words, like her stories—often told by unreliable narrators and laden with irony—cannot be taken literally.

Born in 1921 in Redondo Beach, California, Yamamoto "had early contracted the disease of compulsive reading" and started writing as a teenager (for a time under the pseudonym Napoleon). She received her first rejection slip at fourteen and her first acceptance by a literary magazine at twenty-seven.[1] Much of her work is intimately connected with the places and the events of her own life; to borrow her own felicitous compliment about Toshio Mori's writing, she "shapes the raw dough of fact into the nicely-browned loaf of fiction." For instance, she reveals that "Seventeen Syllables" (her most widely anthologized piece) is her mother's story, though all the details are invented.[2] During World War II Yamamoto was interned in Poston, Arizona (the setting for "The Legend of Miss Sasagawara"). There she served as a reporter and a columnist for the *Poston Chronicle* (the camp newspaper) and published "Death Rides the Rails To Poston," a serialized mystery. It was also in Poston that a lasting friendship between Yamamoto and Wakako Yamauchi began to develop. (A painter then, Yamauchi has since become an accomplished writer and playwright.) Like many of the Nisei[3] who left the camps to seek work or education in the Midwest and the East, Yamamoto worked briefly as a cook in Springfield, Massachusetts, an experience recounted in "The Pleasure of Plain Rice." She went back to Poston upon receiving the news that one of her brothers had been killed in combat in Italy. After the war she worked for three years from 1945 to 1948 for the *Los Angeles Tribune,* a Black weekly; "A Fire in Fontana" is an artful memoir of her job as a reporter.

A John Hay Whitney Foundation Opportunity Fellowship (1950-1951) allowed Yamamoto to write full time for a while. Drawn to the pacifist and selfless ideals advocated in the *Catholic Worker,* she lived from 1953 to 1955 as a volunteer, with her adopted son Paul, in a Catholic Worker rehabilitation farm on Staten Island, where "Epithalamium" is set. She then married Anthony DeSoto, returned to Los Angeles and became mother to four more children. She confides that when she has to fill out a questionnaire, she must "in all honesty list [her] occupation as housewife."[4] Yet her best stories are equal to the masterpieces of Katherine Mansfield, Toshio Mori, Flannery O'Connor, Grace Paley, and Ann Petry.

Our appreciation of Yamamoto's fiction and achievement will be enhanced by knowledge of Japanese American history, of which only a glimpse can be given here.[5] Most Japanese immigrants came to the U.S. between 1885 (the year the Japanese government permitted the emigration of Japanese nationals) and 1924 (the year the Asian Exclusion Act was passed). The first waves of immigrants consisted mainly of single young men who saw North America as a land of opportunity. Only after establishing themselves in the new country did they contemplate starting a family. Some returned to Japan to seek wives; others arranged their marriages by means of an exchange of photographs across the Pacific. Hence a large number of Japanese "picture brides" came to this country after the turn of the century to meet bridegrooms they had never seen in person. By 1930 the American-born Nisei already outnumbered the Issei, and about half of the Japanese American population lived in rural areas in the western U.S. Japanese was the language generally spoken at home, so that many Nisei (including Toshio Mori and Yamamoto) spoke only Japanese until they entered kindergarten.

Interest in literature was strong among Japanese Americans. Despite the strenuousness of survival in the New World, a number of Issei maintained their interest in Japanese poetry. There were literary groups engaged in the traditional forms of haiku, tanka, and senryu, and numerous anthologies and magazines (e.g. *Tachibana* and *Remoncho*) devoted to Issei poetry. Nisei with a literary bent, on the other hand, mostly expressed themselves in the English sections of Japanese American newspapers such as *The New World, Kashu Mainichi,* and *Nichibei Shimbun* (Yamamoto contributed regularly to *Kashu Mainichi* as a teenager.) In the 1930s and 1940s, there were magazines such as *Reimei* and *Current Life* that published fiction and poetry by Nisei. *Yokohama, California,* a collection of short stories by Toshio Mori, probably the first Nisei writer read outside of the Japanese American community, was scheduled for publication by Caxton Printers (Caldwell, Idaho) in spring, 1942, but did not appear until 1949 because of the war.

The life of just about every person of Japanese ancestry living in the U.S. was drastically altered by World War II. Within four months of the bombing of Pearl Harbor on December 7, 1941, over 110,000 Japanese Americans (two-thirds being American-born citizens) were forced to abandon homes, farms, and businesses throughout the West Coast and were detained in various internment camps as potential enemies despite overwhelming evidence to the contrary. Besides dislocating Japanese Americans physically, socially, and psychologically, the internment also disrupted their nascent literary tradition. The creative activities of most, if not all, Issei were arrested. Many destroyed all traces of their own writing in Japanese to avoid being suspected of disloyalty. But a few Nisei writers persisted in writing, even while in camp. Poems and short stories appeared in camp magazines such as the *Poston Chronicle*, *Trek* (Topaz, Utah), and *Tulean Dispatch Magazine* (Tule Lake). Almost every interned Nisei who wrote after the war—notably Miné Okubo, Monica Sone, John Okada, Yoshiko Uchida, Jeanne Wakatsuki Houston— sought to express the bewilderment of massive uprooting.[6] It is also significant that "The Legend of Miss Sasagawara," Yamamoto's haunting story about derangement, is set in camp. Looking back on the internment, Yamamoto writes:

> Any extensive literary treatment of the Japanese in this country would be incomplete without some acknowledgement of the camp experience.... It is an episode in our collective life which wounded us more painfully than we realize. I didn't know myself what a lump it was in my subconscious until a few years ago when I watched one of the earlier television documentaries on the subject, narrated by the mellow voice of Walter Cronkite. To my surprise, I found the tears trickling down my cheeks and my voice squeaking out of control, as I tried to explain to my amazed husband and children why I was weeping.[7]

Yamamoto was one of the first Japanese American writers to gain national recognition after the war, when anti-Japanese sentiment was still rampant. Four of her short stories found their way to Martha Foley's yearly lists of "Distinctive Short Stories." (These lists are included in Foley's annual *Best American Short Stories* collections.) They are "Seventeen Syllables" (1949), "The Brown House" (1951), "Yoneko's Earthquake" (1951), and "Epithalamium" (1960); "Yoneko's Earthquake" was also chosen as one of the *Best American Short Stories: 1952*. Because of her extensive reading of American and European writers and her own cultural background, Yamamoto writes out of both an Anglo-American and a Japanese American literary tradition. But all her protagonists are Japanese Americans, and her sympathy is invariably with those who are on the fringes of American society.

All the same, her writing encompasses a wide range of subject matter, from vignettes of sexual harassment in "The High-Heeled Shoes," her first major publication, to an Issei odyssey that spans Japanese

American history in "Las Vegas Charley." Several themes, however, recur in her work: the interaction among various ethnic groups in the American West, the relationship between Japanese immigrants and their children, and the uneasy adjustment of the Issei in the New World, especially the constrictions experienced by Japanese American women. Intent on depicting human complexity, Yamamoto seldom casts her characters as heroes or villains, and rarely presents personal interaction in simple black and white terms. Discernible in her treatment of all three themes is a voice that is at once compassionate and ironic, gentle and probing, one that can elicit in rapid succession anger and pity, laughter and tears.

Having lived among both whites and non-whites, Yamamoto captures both the tension and the rapport among people from diverse ethnic backgrounds. Like Ann Petry, she can portray instances of racism in realistic and galling detail. Like Flannery O'Connor, she can do so without explicit accusations but with incisive irony. The white protagonist of "Underground Lady," for example, betrays her own bigotry while complaining about her Japanese American neighbors to a Nisei listener. In "Wilshire Bus," a story set in postwar Los Angeles, a drunk white man on a bus heaps racist slurs on a Chinese couple who are fellow passengers and demands that they return to where they came from. Soon the couple (one of whom is carrying a plant) get off at the veterans hospital—most likely to visit a son who is an American veteran injured in the war. "Life Among the Oil Fields" shows the insolence of a neighboring white couple who run over a Japanese American child in their car but who refuse to apologize or make compensation. By framing the incident with allusions to F. Scott Fitzgerald and his wife Zelda, and by linking this couple to the heartless one in the story, Yamamoto insinuates that the callous racism exposed in her story also characterizes the attitudes and work of some celebrated white writers.[8]

There are, however, touching instances of cross-cultural bonding as well. In "The Eskimo Connection" a friendship develops through the exchange of letters between a middle-aged Japanese American housewife and a young Eskimo prisoner. In "Epithalamium," we are privy to the thrills and heartaches of a Nisei woman who has fallen in love with an Italian alcoholic. "A Fire in Fontana" tracks the growing political consciousness of the narrator, whose inner self turns "Black" in empathy after reporting on a fire that has "accidentally" killed a Black family residing in a hostile white neighborhood. In each of these stories, a Nisei woman is drawn to persons who are marginalized as members of other ethnic groups.

Yamamoto's inter-ethnic encounters contain not just sober reflections but also funny touches. "The brown house"—the gambling establishment in the story of the same name—does not discriminate among races. During a police raid, its "windows and doors. . . began to spew out all kinds of people—white, yellow, brown, and black." A Black man seeks refuge and is granted shelter in the car of a Japanese woman, Mrs. Hattori, who with her five children is waiting for her husband. Before long Mr. Hattori joins them and drives away without knowing that his car carries an extra passenger. When the Black man reveals his presence and asks to be let off, the driver receives a shock:

> Mrs. Hattori hastily explained, and the man, pausing on his way out, searched for words to emphasize his gratitude. He had always been, he said, a friend of the Japanese people; he knew no race so cleanly, so well-mannered, so downright nice. As he slammed the door shut, he put his hand on the arm of Mr. Hattori, who was still dumfounded, and promised never to forget this act of kindness. (page 42)

Once the fugitive is gone, Mr. Hattori reproaches his wife for offering sanctuary to a Black person, and Mrs. Hattori retorts that her husband has no misgivings about mixing with men of other colors when he is inside the brown house.

The episode is interwoven with humor, pathos, and irony. Besides presenting a comic sketch of "one minority stereotyping another,"[9] it plays on the discrepancy between appearance and reality. Mr. Hattori, whom the Black man thanks profusely, has performed an act of charity against his will. Assumed to be "well-mannered" and "downright nice," he refers to the thankful man derogatorily as "*kurombo*," which is somewhere between "Blackie" and "Nigger" in its connotation. The ensuing argument about what Mrs. Hattori has done culminates in Mr. Hattori beating his wife later that night. Finally, one must reflect sadly on the irony that it is a gambling den that embraces people of various hues, and that it is only there that the inmates are above racism. Unlike overtly political statements that can be abstract and one-sided, Yamamoto presents race relations with an eye to nuances and resonances. The author, who identifies strongly with other people of color, satirizes both white and Asian prejudices. Yet her satire is ever so subtle. She exposes human narrowness not with the biting sarcasm of Joan Didion or the pungent rhetoric of John Okada, but with the acerbic wit of Grace Paley and the piquant understatement of Toshio Mori.

Another theme that Yamamoto explores repeatedly is the precarious relationship between Issei parents and Nisei children. While generational differences are by no means unique to Japanese Americans, in their case the gap between the old and the young is aggravated by language barriers and disparate cultural values. Rosie in "Seventeen Syllables" cannot appreciate her mother's haiku, though she pays lip service to its beauty:

"Yes, yes, I understand. How utterly lovely," Rosie said, and her mother, either satisfied or seeing through the deception and resigned, went back to composing.

The truth is that Rosie was lazy; English lay ready on the tongue but Japanese had to be searched for and examined and even then put forth tentatively (probably to meet with laughter). It was so much easier to say yes, yes, even when one meant no, no. (page 8)

The mother and daughter in "Yoneko's Earthquake" likewise talk at cross purposes. Out of guilt Mrs. Hosoume, who has undergone an abortion and then lost her younger son, envisions a causal link between the two premature deaths:

"Never kill a person, Yoneko, because if you do, God will take from you someone you love."

"Oh, that," said Yoneko quickly, "I don't believe in that, I don't believe in God."...She had believed for a moment that her mother was going to ask about the ring (which, alas, she had lost already, somewhere in the flumes along the cantaloupe patch). (page 56)

The mother's cryptic moral is entirely lost on Yoneko. Mrs. Hosoume is thinking of the abortion when she admonishes Yoneko against killing, but "someone you love" could refer either to the son who has recently died or to Marpo, her lover who has disappeared on the day of the abortion.[10] None of these possibilities occur to Yoneko, who merely balks at the very idea of God. She is more nervous about having lost the ring given to her by Mrs. Hosoume, who in turn has received it from Marpo. The daughter's loss of the ring symbolizes the mother's bereavement at the loss of her lover. A mere trinket in the eyes of the daughter, the ring is associated in the mother's mind with an inner tumult as intense as the earthquake that has unnerved Yoneko.

Despite difficulties and failures, these mothers at least attempt to impart their hard earned wisdom to their daughters, but the fathers, either preoccupied by material survival, bent on spiritual enlightenment, or shackled by vice, communicate even less effectively, if at all, with their children. Mr. Hayashi in "Seventeen Syllables" and Mr. Hosoume in "Yoneko's Earthquake" are earthbound men oblivious to the artistic or romantic inclinations of their wives and daughters. On the other hand, the Buddhist father in "The Legend of Miss Sasagawara" is too absorbed in his spiritual pursuit to notice that his sensuous daughter is disintegrating mentally right under his saintly nose. Then there are Mr. Hattori and Charley (the title character of "Las Vegas Charley"), inveterate gamblers unfit to set examples for their children.[11] None of these men is evil, but each is severely limited. Noriyuki's mixed reaction to his deceased father at the end of "Las Vegas Charley" is illustrative. The doctor has just said of Charley, "At least he enjoyed himself while he was alive."

And Noriyuki—who, without one sour word, had lived through a succession of emotions about his father—hate for rejecting him as a child; disgust and exasperation over that weak moral fiber, embarrassment when people asked what his father did for a living; and finally, something akin to compassion, when he came to understand that his father was not an evil man, but only an inadequate one with the most shining intentions, only one man among so many who lived from day to day as best as they could, limited, restricted, by the meager gifts Fate or God had doled out to them—could not quite agree.[12] (page 85)

Noriyuki's reflections on his Issei father can be connected to the third theme concerning the aspirations and difficulties of the Japanese immigrants, and the temptations and frustrations that await them in America. As Dorothy Ritsuko McDonald and Katharine Newman aptly observe, "all those who seek but lose are of interest to Yamamoto."[13] Ineffectual as the Issei fathers may be in her stories, they are never reduced simply to stereotypes. Perhaps it is because Yamamoto can understand so well the hardships that beset the newcomers to American soil that she can afford tender strokes even while painting incorrigible souls such as Charley and Mr. Hattori. Once a successful farmer, Charley turns to gambling in his lonely hours after the death of his beloved wife. Twice he tries to kick the habit, but renews his addiction when the monotony of camp life and his isolation in Las Vegas become unbearable. By delineating the circumstances that turn this well-meaning man into a compulsive gambler, Yamamoto gives us insights into a life that is otherwise all too easily condemned. Mr. Hattori, who gambles in the hope of making a quick fortune after losing money on his strawberry crop, has less claim on our sympathy. Yet even this gambler disarms us with his sincere though short-lived resolutions to reform.

But if Yamamoto portrays the failings of Mr. Hattori with tolerance, she extends the strongest sympathy to his long-suffering wife, who does not have the heart to leave her reckless husband permanently. At the end of the story, her family is mired in debt and she is pregnant again. Looking at Mrs. Hattori, Mrs. Wu (the Chinese proprietess of the brown house) "decided she had never before encountered a woman with such bleak eyes." (page 45) Whether or not one sees the author as a feminist ahead of her time, Yamamoto does reveal through her fiction the sorry plight of many female immigrants caught in unhappy marriages. What made the lives of these Issei women especially bleak was that unlike Black women, for example, who in similar situations often turned to other women for support, rural Issei women were not only separated by the Pacific from mothers, and grandmothers, but were often cut off from one another as well. Having to take care of children and to work alongside their husbands on isolated farms, they had little time and opportunity to cultivate friendships with other women. The only members of the same sex to whom they could unbosom their thoughts were their own daughters, who all too often had engrossing problems of their own.

Mrs. Hayashi in "Seventeen Syllables" is a haunting portrait of a repressed Issei who struggles to express herself through poetry. Notwithstanding her long hours of work at home and on the farm, she takes to writing haiku. But her husband, a farmer who is indifferent to her creative endeavors, expresses disapproval and resentment whenever she engages in long discussions of poetry with people who share her interests. The conflict comes to a head when she wins a haiku contest sponsored by a Japanese American newspaper. On the day the editor comes in person to deliver the award, a Hiroshige print, the family is busy packing tomatoes. Mr. Hayashi becomes increasingly impatient while his wife discusses poetry with the editor in the main house, and finally stalks inside in anger and emerges with the prize picture. What follows is the most wrenching passage in the story, told from the daughter's point of view:

...he threw the picture on the ground and picked up the axe. Smashing the picture, glass and all (she heard the explosion faintly), he reached over for the kerosene that was used to encourage the bath fire and poured it over the wreckage. I am dreaming, Rosie said to herself, I am dreaming, but her father, having made sure that his act of cremation was irrevocable, was even then returning to the fields.

Rosie ran past him and toward the house. What had become of her mother? She burst into the parlor and found her mother at the back window, watching the dying fire. They watched together until there remained only a feeble smoke under the blazing sun. Her mother was very calm. (page 18)

This haunting description attests to Yamamoto's genius at creating scenes that are powerful on both a literal and a symbolic level. The external calmness of the mother, almost frightening at this point, seems only to suggest the depth of her anguish. Although we are not immediately told of her inner reaction to her husband's outrage, the incinerated picture speaks for her: we feel that she, too, is consumed by seething rage and smoldering despair. More effective than registering a host of angry screams or plaintive wails, the tableau sears into our consciousness the husband's cruelty and the wife's desolation.[14]

Another striking use of a symbolic scene (analogous to a near epiphany) to convey repressed emotions occurs in "Yoneko's Earthquake," when Mr. Hosoume drives his wife to the hospital to abort an illegitimate child. On the way the father hits a beautiful collie, but drives on as though nothing has happened. The unblinking killing of the animal enables us not only to perceive the father's intense anger and his total indifference to the life about to be destroyed but also to imagine the mother's contrasting psychological state. She must cringe inwardly as she witnesses the act that foreshadows the fate of her unborn child. The harrowing silence that accompanies the brutal burning in "Seventeen Syllables" and the unfeeling and unacknowledged killing in "Yoneko's Earthquake" heightens the horror of both episodes. We can almost feel the lifeblood slowly seeping from the two hurt women.

Two other narrative techniques contribute to the exquisite telling of "Seventeen Syllables," "Yoneko's Earthquake," and "The Legend of Miss Sasagawara": the use of limited point of view and the juxtaposition of a manifest and a latent plot.[15] These two strategies are interconnected: the limited point of view allows the author to suspend or conceal one of the plots of a given story.[16] Though narrated in third person, "Seventeen Syllables" is told from young Rosie's point of view. While we are informed of Mrs. Hayashi's poetic interest from the beginning and are reminded of it periodically, the first part of the story revolves around Rosie's adolescent concerns, especially her secret rendezvous with Jesus, the son of the Mexican couple who work for her family. Only two thirds into the story does Yamamoto begin to unfold the submerged plot—the tragedy of the mother, whose artistic aspirations come to an abrupt halt in the wake of her jealous husband's fury. The burning of the award signals the end of Mrs. Hayashi's poetic career. As mother and daughter watch the dying fire together, their lives—separate strands at the outset—begin to intertwine. Rosie, who has newly experienced the thrills of her first romance, is made to look squarely at her mother's chastening marriage. Her "rosy" adolescent world must now be viewed through the darkening lens of Mrs. Hayashi's hindsight.

The counterpoint emotions of mother and daughter are deftly superimposed in the dramatic last paragraph of the story:

Suddenly, her mother knelt on the floor and took her by the wrists. "Rosie," she said urgently, "Promise me you will never marry!" Shocked more by the request than the revelation, Rosie stared at her mother's face. Jesus, Jesus, she called silently, not certain whether she was invoking the help of the son of the Carrascos or of God, until there returned sweetly the memory of Jesus' hand, how it had touched her and where. Still her mother waited for an answer, holding her wrists so tightly that her hands were going numb. She tried to pull free. Promise, her mother whispered fiercely, promise. Yes, yes, I promise, Rosie said. But for an instant she turned away, and her mother, hearing the familiar glib agreement, released her. Oh, you, you, you, her eyes and twisted mouth said, you fool. Rosie, covering her face, began at last to cry, and the embrace and consoling hand came much later than she expected. (page 19)

As an expression of the mother's cynical wisdom, the shocking request reveals her thorough disillusionment with her past and present relationships with men. Deserted by her lover in Japan and stifled by her husband in America, Mrs. Hayashi has abandoned all hopes for herself; she can only try to prevent her daughter from repeating her mistakes. Her sudden kneeling and anxious clutching, however, oddly and ironically correspond to the posture and gesture of an ardent suitor proposing marriage. One suspects that the ironic correspondence flashes across Rosie's mind as well. Though not deaf to her mother's plea, Rosie drifts into a romantic reverie at the very moment Mrs. Hayashi implores her to remain single. Rosie's reaction to the entreaty is couched in words that recall her recent sexual awakening. "Jesus" is both a spontaneous exclamation and a conscious invocation of her beau, whose arousing grip contrasts with Mrs. Hayashi's tenacious clutch. "Yes, yes" recalls not only the double affirmative at the beginning of the story, when Rosie pretends to understand the workings of haiku, but also her first kiss with Jesus in the shed, when she can only think of "yes and no and oh...." The affirmative answer also extends the proposal analogy: it is an answer many a suitor wishes to hear and many a woman in love longs to utter.[17] In the present context, however, it is a hollow acquiescence extorted by the mother and given grudgingly by the daughter. As a desperate plea against marriage and as a travesty of a proposal, the passage conflates the mother's disenchantment and the daughter's dampened but inextinguishable hopes.

The degree of Mrs. Hayashi's embitterment and the extent of Rosie's transformation are conveyed in the delicate understatement of the last sentence. Taking umbrage at Rosie's insincere reply, the disconsolate mother cannot bring herself to hug her sobbing daughter immediately.

Although Rosie's "glib agreement" as well as Mrs. Hayashi's unspoken reprimand and temporary withdrawal hark back to the story's opening, when the mother treats Rosie as a child too young to grasp the intricacies of Japanese poetics, the last sentence also bespeaks Rosie's growth from a carefree child to a perplexed adult. As Stan Yogi observes, the image of delayed embrace "suggests the maturity that Mrs. Hayashi now expects of her daughter, who has been initiated into the excitement, pain, and disillusionment of adult life."[18]

Rosie's story and Mrs. Hayashi's story are inexorably enmeshed at the end. But in "Yoneko's Earthquake," one of the plots remains hidden throughout. Also told from a daughter's point of view, the seemingly light-hearted tale ostensibly describes ten year old Yoneko's crush on Marpo, the twenty-seven year old Filipino farmhand who works for her family. Yoneko confides to us matters of utmost concern to *her* while reporting in passing the daily occurrences in her family, such as getting a ring from her mother one day and being driven by her father to a hospital another day. But her random digressions are in fact pregnant hints dropped by Yamamoto. These hints allow us to infer that Yoneko's mother is also in love with Marpo and that their liaison leads to an abortion. Just as we must unravel these secrets by piecing together Yoneko's haphazard observations, so must we gauge the emotional upheaval in the adult world by monitoring Yoneko's changing moods. Her passing crush on Marpo and fleeting sorrow after his departure at once parallel and contrast with the mother's passionate affair and unremitting sorrow at being deserted.

Because the story operates on multiple levels of consciousness—those of the young girl, the reader, and the author—there are unlimited occasions for dramatic irony. For instance, it is through Yoneko's separate admiration for Marpo and for the mother that we learn the likelihood of mutual attraction between the two adults. After Marpo's disappearance Yoneko only notes as a matter of fact that the new hired hand is "an old Japanese man who wore his gray hair in a military cut and who, unlike Marpo, had no particular intersts outside working, eating, sleeping, and playing an occasional game of *goh* with Mr. Hosoume." But the reader can appreciate the humor and the pathos behind the replacement: this time the father has taken precautions. The new worker is Marpo's antithesis in every way, devoid of youth, industry, and talents. Instead of being a constant companion for the mother, he is the father's playmate.

In "The Legend of Miss Sasagawara," we are presented not so much with two plots as with shifting perspectives. The word "legend" nicely calls into question the veracity of the information provided in the story, in which we are often misled into looking at a character or an event in a certain way, only to have our perceptions radically altered by the end. The title character is introduced to us through various secondhand reports, made up of gossip and rumors, the gist of them being that Miss Sasagawara is highly eccentric, if not downright crazy. As for her family, we know only that her mother is dead and that her father is a devout Buddhist priest. At the end of the story, however, the narrator discovers a poem written by Miss Sasagawara in which she intimates the torment of being tied to someone "whose lifelong aim had been to achieve Nirvana, that saintly state of moral purity and universal wisdom." The poet continues:

> But say that someone else, someone sensitive, someone admiring, someone who had not achieved this sublime condition and who did not wish to, were somehow called to companion such a man. Was it not likely that the saint, blissfully bent on cleansing from his already radiant soul the last imperceptible blemishes...would be deaf and blind to the human passions rising, subsiding, and again rising, perhaps in anguished silence, within the selfsame room? The poet could not speak for others, of course; she could only speak for herself. But she would describe this man's devotion as a sort of madness, the monstrous sort which, pure of itself, might possibly bring troublous, scented scenes to recur in the other's sleep. (page 33)

This revealing poem, the veiled record of a passionate daughter's anguished remonstration with an ascetic father, not only gives us new insight into Miss Sasagawara's tragedy but forces us to revise our earlier judgment of who is sane and who is not. The daughter, who feels circumscribed emotionally and aesthetically in the presence of her father, is also literally incarcerated. Because of the internment, father and daughter are condemned to live "within the selfsame room." Her mental illness seems an unconscious act of resistance against the chilling influence of her father and against the senseless decree of the U.S. government. By contrast, the other internees conduct their lives in camp as though they were at liberty. Miss Sasagawara's father, who "had felt free for the first time in his long life" during this confinement, offers the most bizarre example. The line between sanity and insanity is a hard one to draw in this story.

Though Yamamoto persistently confronts religious and moral issues, she is never dogmatic or moralistic in her judgment. Instead she can find fault with the seemingly divine and perceive redeeming grace among erring humanity. Her characters are often caught in circumstances that render unqualified approval or condemnation difficult. Thus Miss Sasagawara's father, so close to sainthood, is yet hopelessly oblivious and insensitive. By contrast, Charley the gambler and Mrs. Hosoume in "Yoneko's Earthquake" engage us not despite but because of their susceptibilities to vice and passion. Whether Yamamoto uses a Buddhist or a Christian frame of reference, her overriding tone is one of human questioning accompanied by understanding rather than of moral certainty coupled with religious complacency.

Not given to effusive rhetoric and militant statements, Yamamoto appeals to us in another way.[19] Reminiscent of the verbal economy of haiku, in which the poet "must pack all her meaning into seventeen syllables only," Yamamoto's stories exemplify precision and restraint. We must be attentive to all the words on the page to unbury covert plots, fathom the characters' repressed emotions, and detect the author's silent indictment and implicit sympathy. Many of her stories give added pleasure with each new reading, but some may actually have to be read at least twice to be fully appreciated. Then may we find ourselves echoing Rosie by saying, without glibness, "Yes, yes, I understand. How utterly lovely."

King-Kok Cheung
University of California, Los Angeles

King-Kok Cheung is Professor of English and Asian American Studies at University of California, Los Angeles. She is author of *Articulate Silences: Hisaye Yamamoto, Maxine Hong Kingston, Joy Kogawa* (1993); editor of *An Interethnic Companion to Asian American Literature* (1996), *"Seventeen Syllables"* (1994), and *Words Matter: Conversations with Asian American Writers* (2000); and co-editor of *The Heath Anthology of American Literature* (2000–2005) and *Asian American Literature: An Annotated Bibliography* (1988).

Notes

1. Hisaye Yamamoto, "Writing," *Amerasia Journal* 3.2 (1976): 127, 128, 130. Yamamoto said that she hid under the pseudonym "as an apology for [her] little madness" (i.e. her immense zeal to write; 128).

2. Yamamoto, "Introduction," *The Chauvinist and Other Stories* by Toshio Mori (Los Angeles: UCLA Asian American Studies Center, 1979), p. 12; Susan Koppelman, ed. *Between Mothers and Daughters: Stories Across a Generation* (Old Westbury, NY: Feminist Press, 1985), p. 162.

3. Nisei are second generation Japanese Americans, children of the Issei, or Japanese immigrants. Sansei are the third generation.

4. "Writing," 126.

5. For a fuller discussion of the relationship between Japanese American history and literature, see Elaine H. Kim, *Asian American Literature: An Introduction to the Writings and their Social Context* (Philadelphia: Temple Univ. Press, 1982), 122-72. For a detailed study of Issei history, see Yuji Ichioka, *The Issei: The World of the First Generation Japanese Immigrants, 1885-1924* (New York: Free Press, 1988).

6. Miné Okubo, *Citizen 13660* (New York: Columbia Univ. Press, 1946; Seattle: Univ. of Washington Press; 1983; Monica Sone, *Nisei Daughter* (Boston: Little Brown, 1953); John Okada, *No-No Boy* (Vermont: Tuttle, 1957; Seattle: Univ. of Washington Press, 1977); Yoshiko Uchida, *Desert Exile: The Uprooting of a Japanese American Family* (Seattle: Univ. of Washington Press, 1982); James Houston and Jeanne Wakatsuki Houston, *Farewell to Manzanar* (Boston: Houghton Mifflin, 1973).

7. "...I Still Carry It Around," *RIKKA* 3.4 (1976): 11.

8. I want to thank Barbara Smith for this suggestion.

9. Robert Rolf, "The Short Stories of Hisaye Yamamoto, Japanese-American Writer," *Bulletin of Fukuoka University of Education* 30.1 (1982): 75.

10. The ambiguous reference is noted by Charles Crow in "Home and Transcendence in Los Angeles Fiction," in *Los Angeles in Fiction: A Collection of Original Essays*, ed. David Fine (Albuquerque: Univ. of New Mexico Press, 1984), p. 202.

11. Not surprisingly, Charles Crow argues that Yamamoto's portrayals of Issei fathers are uniformly unflattering; see "The *Issei* Father in the Fiction of Hisaye Yamamoto," in *Opening Up Literary Criticism: Essays on American Prose and Poetry* (Salzburg: Verlag Wolfgang Neugebauer, 1986), pp. 34-40. Yet interestingly enough, unlike Maxine Hong Kingston and Alice Walker, who have been attacked by critics for reinforcing the negative stereotypes of respectively Chinese American men and Black men, Yamamoto has not had to answer similar charges. I believe this is due to Yamamoto's ability to soften her critical vision by rendering the vulnerabilities of Japanese American men sensitively, as in "Morning Rain" and "My Father Can Beat Muhammad Ali." Although the father figures in these stories are not of heroic mold, they are too human to be judged as caricatures.

12. The poignancy of this ending recalls the ending of Hemingway's "My Old Man," but Yamamoto is closer to Steinbeck and Mansfield in her uncanny ability to shift imperceptibly from a comic to a tragic key. As in her presentation of interracial contact, her juxtaposition of Issei and Nisei can be funny as well as sad.

13. "Relocation and Dislocation: The Writings of Hisaye Yamamoto and Wakako Yamauchi," *MELUS* 7.3 (1980): 28.

14. The cremation scene reminds me of the many poignant accounts about Issei who burned everything associated with their country of origin after Pearl Harbor, so as to avoid being suspected by the War Relocation Authority. Yamamoto herself must have witnessed actual incidents whereby family heirlooms and literary manuscripts were turned into ashes, and the experience might have added to the graphic and heart-rending quality of her description.

15. For a detailed analysis of the technique of the double-plot, see Stan Yogi, "Legacies Revealed: Uncovering Buried Plots in the Stories of Hisaye Yamamoto and Wakako Yamauchi," MA thesis, Univ. of California, Berkeley, 1988. To Yogi I owe many insights; in particular, his thoughtful reading of "The Legend of Miss Sasagawara" (pp. 117-28) informs my own interpretation of the story.

16. Although experimentation with limited as well as shifting points of view is common among both Modernist writers (e.g. James, Faulkner, Conrad, and Durrell) and women of color writers (e.g. Toni Morrison, Louise Erdrich, Leslie Silko), Yamamoto might have been inspired by the communication pattern characteristic of Nisei. According to Stanford Lyman, "conversations among Nisei almost always partake of the elements of an information game between persons maintaining decorum by seemingly mystifying one another. It is the duty of the listener to ascertain the context of the speech he hears and to glean from his knowledge of the speaker and the context just what is the important point" ("Generation and Character: The Case of the Japanese Americans," *Roots: An Asian American Reader* [Los Angeles: UCLA Asian American Studies Center, 1971], p. 53). Similarly, both "Yoneko's Earthquake" and "The Legend of Miss Sasagawara" engage the reader in information games.

17. Perhaps the most famous literary example is Molly Bloom's reverie of her proposal that concludes Joyce's *Ulysses*: "...I asked him with my eyes to ask again yes and then he asked me would I yes to say yes my mountain flower and first I put my arms around him yes and drew him down to me so he could feel my breasts all perfume yes and his heart was going like mad and yes I said yes I will Yes."

18. "Legacies Revealed," p. 52.

19. Yuri Kageyama considers Yamamoto's style (and that of Issei and Nisei writers in general) to be superior to the polemical style of some Sansei ("Hisaye Yamamoto—Nisei Writer," *Sunbury* 10:41). I tend to agree.

The High-Heeled Shoes
A Memoir

In the middle of the morning, the telephone rings. I am the only one at home. I answer it. A man's voice says softly, "Hello, this is Tony."

I don't know anyone named Tony. Nobody else in the house has spoken of knowing any Tony. But the greeting is very warm. It implies, "There is a certain thing which you and I alone know." Evidently he has dialed a wrong number. I tell him so, "You must have the wrong number," and prepare to hang up as soon as I know that he understands.

But the man says this is just the number he wants. To prove it, he recites off the pseudonym by which this household, Garbo-like, goes in the directory, the address, and the phone number. It is a unique name and I know there is probably no such person in the world. I merely tell him a fragment of the truth, that there is no such person at the address, and I am ready to hang up again.

But the man stalls. If there is no such person available, it appears he is willing to talk to me, whoever I am. I am suddenly in a bad humor, suspecting a trap in which I shall be imprisoned uncomfortably by words, words, words, earnestly begging me to try some product or another, the like of which is unknown anywhere else in the world. It isn't that I don't appreciate the unrapturous life a salesman must often lead. And I like to buy things. If I had the money, I would buy a little from every salesman who comes along, after I had permitted him to run ably or ineptly (it doesn't really matter) through the words he has been coached to repeat. Then, not only in the pride of the new acquisition, but in the knowledge that he was temporarily encouraged, my own spirits would gently rise, lifted by the wings of the dove. At each week's end, surrounded knee-deep by my various purchases—the Fuller toothbrush, the receipt for the magazine subscription which will help a girl obtain a nine-week flying course which she eagerly, eagerly wants, the one dozen white eggs fresh from the farm and cheaper than you can get at the corner grocery, the first volume in the indispensable 12-volume Illustrated Encyclopaedia of

Home Medicine, the drug sundries totalling at least two dollars which will help guarantee a youngish veteran a permanent job—I could sigh and beam. That would be nice. But I don't have the money, and this coming of ill temper is just as much directed at myself for not having it as it is at the man for probably intending to put me in a position where I shall have to make him a failure.

"And just what is it you want?" I ask impatiently.

The man tells me, as man to woman. In the stark phrasing of his urgent need, I see that the certain thing alluded to by the warmth of his voice is a secret not of the past, but, with my acquiescence, of the near future. I let the receiver take a plunge down onto the hook from approximately a one-foot height. Then, I go outside and pick some pansies for Margarita, as I had been intending to do just before the phone rang. Margarita is the seven-year-old girl next door. She has never known any mother or father, only *tias* and *tios* who share none of her blood. She has a face that looks as if it had been chiseled with utter care out of cream and pale pink marble. Her soft brown hair hangs in plaits as low as her waist. And these days, because the Catholic school is full and cannot take her, she wanders lonesomely about, with plenty of time for such amenities as dropping in to admire a neighbor's flowers. The pansies I pick for her, lemon yellow, deep purple, clear violet, mottled brown, were transplanted here last year by Wakako and Chester, a young couple we know who have a knack for getting things wholesale, and they are thriving like crazy this spring, sprawling untidily over their narrow bed and giving no end of blooms.

Later, there is a small, timid rat-tat-tat at the door. It's Margarita, bearing two calla lilies, a couple of clove pinks, and one tall amaryllis stalk with three brilliant brick-red flowers and a bud. She dashes off the porch, down the steps, and around the ivy-sprawled front fence before I can properly thank her. Oh, well. Taking the gift to the service porch, I throw out the wilting brown-edged callas she dashed over with last week, rinse out the blue potato glass, fill it with water, and stick in the new bouquet. But all the time the hands are occupied with these tokens of arrived spring and knowing Margarita, the mind recalls unlovely, furtive things.

When Mary lived with us, there was a time she left for work in the dark hours of the morning. On one of these mornings, about midway in her lonely walk past the cemetery to the P-car stop, a man came from behind and grabbed her, stopped her mouth with his hand, and, rather arbitrarily, gave her a choice between one kiss and rape. Terrified, she indicated what seemed to be the somewhat lesser requirement. He allowed her to go afterwards, warning her on no account to scream for help or look back, on penalty of death. When she arrived at her place of work, trembling and pale green, her office friends asked whether she was ill, and she told them of her encounter. They advised her to go to the police immediately.

She doubted whether that would help, since she had been unable to see the man. But, persuaded that a report, even incomplete, to the police was her duty to the rest of womankind, she reluctantly went to the nearest station with her story. She came back with the impression that the police had been much amused, that they had actually snickered as she left with their officially regretful shrug over her having given them nothing to go on. She told her boss and he called the police himself and evidently made his influence felt, for we had a caller that evening.

It was I who answered the knock. A policeman stepped in, and, without any preliminaries, asked, "Are you the girl that was raped?"

Making up with enough asperity for a sudden inexplicable lack of aplomb, I said, no, and no one had been raped, *yet*, and called Mary. She and the officer went out on the porch and talked in near whispers for a while. After he left, Mary identified him and his companion as the night patrol for our section of the city. He had promised that they would tell the dawn patrol to be hovering around about the time she left for work each morning. But Mary, nervously trying the dim walk a couple of more times, caught no sign of any kind of patrol. Thereafter, she and the rest of the women of the household took to traveling in style, by taxi, when they were called on to go forth at odd hours. This not only dented our budgets, but made us considerably limit our unescorted evening gadding.

There were similar episodes, fortunately more fleeting. What stayed with me longer than Mary's because it was mine, was the high-heeled shoes. Walking one bright Saturday morning to work along the same stretch that Mary had walked, I noticed a dusty blue, middle-aged sedan parked just ahead. A pair of bare, not especially remarkable legs was crossed in the open doorway, as though the body to them were lying on the front seat, relaxing. I presumed they were a woman's legs, belonging to the wife of some man who had business in the lumberyard just opposite, because they were wearing black high-heeled shoes. As I passed, I glanced at the waiting woman.

My presumption had been rash. It wasn't a woman, but a man, unclothed (except for *the high-heeled shoes, the high-heeled shoes*), and I saw that I was, with frantic gestures, being enjoined to linger awhile.

Nothing in my life before had quite prepared for this: some Freud, a smattering of Ellis, lots of Stekel, and fat Krafft-Ebing, in red covers, were on my bookshelves, granted; conversation had explored curiously, and the imagination conjured bizarre scenes at the drop of a casual word. But reading is reading, talking is talking, thinking is thinking, and living is different. Improvising hastily on behavior for the occasion, I chose to pretend as though my heart were repeating Pippa's song, and continued walking, possibly a little faster and a little straighter than I had been, up to the P-car stop. When I got to the print shop, the boss said, "You look rather put upon this morning." I mustered up a feeble smile and nodded, but I couldn't bring myself to speak of the high-heeled shoes. This was nothing so uncomplicated as pure rape, I knew, and the need of the moment was to go away by myself, far from everybody, and think about things for awhile. But there were galleys and page proofs waiting to be read, and I set to with a sort of dedicated vengeance, for I had recently been reprimanded for getting sloppy again. When the hectic morning of poring over small print was over and my elbows black, letting my thoughts go cautiously but wholly back to the time between leaving the house and boarding the P-car, I found there was not much to think about. I had seen what I had seen. I had, admit it now, been thrown for a sickening loop. That was all. But the incongruity of a naked man in black high-heeled shoes was something the mind could not entirely dismiss, and there were times afterwards when he, never seen again, contributed to a larger perplexity that stirred the lees around and around, before more immediate matters, claiming attention, allowed them to settle again.

There was a man in the theatre with groping hands. There was a man on the streetcar with insistent thighs. There was a man who grinned triumphantly and walked quickly away after he trailed one down a drizzly street at dusk and finally succeeded in his aim of thrusting an unexpected hand under one's raincoat.

I remembered them as I plucked the pansies, took them over to Margarita's house, came back home, answered the door, received the amaryllis, the callas, the pinks, and arranged them in the blue potato glass on top of the buffet. I remembered another man, Mohandas Gandhi, probably a stranger to this company, not only because I had been reading on him of late, but because he seemed to be the only unimpeachable authority who had ever been called on to give public advice in this connection. When someone had delicately asked Gandhi, "What is a woman to do when she is attacked by miscreants?," naming the alternatives of violent self-defense and immediate flight, he had replied, "For me, there can be no preparation for violence. All preparation must be for non-violence if courage of the highest type is to be developed. Violence can only be tolerated as being preferable always to cowardice. Therefore I would have no boats ready for flight...." Then he had soared on to the nobler implications of non-violence, reproaching the world for its cowardice in arming itself with the atomic bomb.

I understood. When I first read these words, I had said, "Why, of course," smiling at the unnecessary alarms of some people. But I had read the words at a rarefied period, forgetting Mary, forgetting the high-heeled shoes. I decided now that the inspiration they gave to his probably feminine questioner was small potatoes. Of all the men suspected of sainthood, Gandhi, measured by his own testimony, should have been able to offer the most concrete comfort here. But he had evaded the issue. In place of the tangible example, vague words. Gandhi, in face of the ubiquitous womanly fear, was a failure. All he had really said was: don't even think about it. Then (I guessed), holding up his strong, bony brown hand, he had shaken his white-fuzzed, compactly-shaped head slowly back and forth and declined to hear the ifs and buts. The rest, as they say, was silence.

But could I have momentarily borrowed Gandhi's attitude to life and death, what would I have done as the man who called himself Tony rang my number? With enough straining, with maybe a resort to urgent, concentrated prayer, could I have found the gentle but effective words to make Tony see that there were more charming ways to spend a morning? I practiced this angle for awhile:

"I'm afraid you *do* have the wrong number." Soberly, hang up. Disconcerting enough, but rather negative.

"It's a nice day for the beach, sir. Why don't you go swimming?— might help you cool off a little." The voice with a compassionate smile. Too flippant.

"There are many lonely women in the world, and there are more acceptable ways to meet them than this. Have you tried joining a Lonely Hearts club? Don't you have any kind of hobby?" Condescending, as though I were forever above his need. Ambiguously worded, too, that last, fraught with the possibility of an abrupt answer.

"Listen, you know you aren't supposed to go around doing things like this. I think I know what made you do it, though, and I think a psychiatrist would help you quite a bit, if you'd cooperate." The enlightened woman's yap. Probably'd hang up on me.

Anyway, it was too late. And, after all, Gandhi was Gandhi, an old man, moreover dead, and I was I, a young woman, more or less alive. Since I was unable to hit on the proper pacifist approach, since, indeed, I doubted the efficacy of the pacifist approach in this crisis, should I, eschewing cowardice, have shouted bitter, indignant words to frighten Tony? Not that, either. Besides, I hadn't gauged his mood. He had spoken casually enough, but there had been an undertone of something. Restrained glee? Playfulness? Confidence? Desperation? I didn't know.

Then, to help protect my sisters, should I have turned toward the official avenues? Was it my responsibility to have responded with pretended warmth, invited him over, and had the police waiting with me when he arrived? Say I had sorrowfully pressed the matter, say Tony were consequently found guilty (of abusing his communication privileges, of course) —the omnipotent they (representing us) would have merely restricted his liberty for a while, in the name of punishment. What would he have done when he was let go, his debt to society as completely repaid as society, who had created his condition, could make him repay? Telephones in working order abound, with telephone books conveniently alongside them, containing any number of women's names, addresses, and numbers.

And what did Tony do when the sound of my receiver crashed painfully in his ear? Did he laugh and proceed to some other number? His vanity bruised, did he curse? Or perhaps he felt shame, thinking, "My God, what am I doing, what am I doing?" Whatever, whatever—I knew I had discovered yet another circle to put away with my collection of circles. I was back to what I had started with, the helpless, absolutely useless knowledge that the days and nights must surely be bleak for a man who knew the compulsion to thumb through the telephone directory for a woman's name, any woman's name; that this bleakness, multiplied infinite times (see almost any daily paper), was a great, dark sickness on the earth that no amount of pansies, pinks, or amaryllis, thriving joyously in what garden, however well-ordered and pointed to with pride, could ever begin to assuage.

The telephone rings. Startled, I go warily, wondering whether it might not be Tony again, calling perhaps to avenge the blow to pride by anonymous invective, to raise self-esteem by letting it be known that he is a practical joker. I hold my breath after I say, "Hello?"

It is the familiar voice, slightly querulous but altogether precious, of my aunt Miné. She says I am not to plan anything for supper. She has made something special, ricecakes with Indian bean frosting, as well as pickled fish on vinegared rice. She has also been able to get some yellow-tail, to slice and eat raw. All these things she and Uncle are bringing over this evening. Is about five o'clock too early?

It is possible she wonders at my enthusiastic appreciation, which is all right, but all out of proportion.

(1948)

Seventeen Syllables

The first Rosie knew that her mother had taken to writing poems was one evening when she finished one and read it aloud for her daughter's approval. It was about cats, and Rosie pretended to understand it thoroughly and appreciate it no end, partly because she hesitated to disillusion her mother about the quantity and quality of Japanese she had learned in all the years now that she had been going to Japanese school every Saturday (and Wednesday, too, in the summer). Even so, her mother must have been skeptical about the depth of Rosie's understanding, because she explained afterwards about the kind of poem she was trying to write.

See, Rosie, she said, it was a *haiku*, a poem in which she must pack all her meaning into seventeen syllables only, which were divided into three lines of five, seven, and five syllables. In the one she had just read, she had tried to capture the charm of a kitten, as well as comment on the superstition that owning a cat of three colors meant good luck.

"Yes, yes, I understand. How utterly lovely," Rosie said, and her mother, either satisfied or seeing through the deception and resigned, went back to composing.

The truth was that Rosie was lazy; English lay ready on the tongue but Japanese had to be searched for and examined, and even then put forth tentatively (probably to meet with laughter). It was so much easier to say yes, yes, even when one meant no, no. Besides, this was what was in her mind to say: I was looking through one of your magazines from Japan last night, Mother, and towards the back I found some *haiku* in English that delighted me. There was one that made me giggle off and on until I fell asleep—

> *It is morning, and lo!*
> *I lie awake, comme il faut,*
> *sighing for some dough.*

Now, how to reach her mother, how to communicate the melancholy song? Rosie knew formal Japanese by fits and starts, her mother had even less English, no French. It was much more possible to say yes, yes.

It developed that her mother was writing the *haiku* for a daily newspaper, the *Mainichi Shimbun,* that was published in San Francisco. Los Angeles, to be sure, was closer to the farming community in which the Hayashi family lived and several Japanese vernaculars were printed there, but Rosie's parents said they preferred the tone of the northern paper. Once a week, the *Mainichi* would have a section devoted to *haiku,* and her mother became an extravagant contributor, taking for herself the blossoming pen name, Ume Hanazono.

So Rosie and her father lived for awhile with two women, her mother and Ume Hanazono. Her mother (Tome Hayashi by name) kept house, cooked, washed, and, along with her husband and the Carrascos, the Mexican family hired for the harvest, did her ample share of picking tomatoes out in the sweltering fields and boxing them in tidy strata in the cool packing shed. Ume Hanazono, who came to life after the dinner dishes were done, was an earnest, muttering stranger who often neglected speaking when spoken to and stayed busy at the parlor table as late as midnight scribbling with pencil on scratch paper or carefully copying characters on good paper with her fat, pale green Parker.

The new interest had some repercussions on the household routine. Before, Rosie had been accustomed to her parents and herself taking their hot baths early and going to bed almost immediately afterwards, unless her parents challenged each other to a game of flower cards or unless company dropped in. Now if her father wanted to play cards, he had to resort to solitaire (at which he always cheated fearlessly), and if a group of friends came over, it was bound to contain someone who was also writing *haiku,* and the small assemblage would be split in two, her father entertaining the non-literary members and her mother comparing ecstatic notes with the visiting poet.

If they went out, it was more of the same thing. But Ume Hanazono's life span, even for a poet's, was very brief—perhaps three months at most.

One night they went over to see the Hayano family in the neighboring town to the west, an adventure both painful and attractive to Rosie. It was attractive because there were four Hayano girls, all lovely and each one named after a season of the year (Haru, Natsu, Aki, Fuyu), painful because something had been wrong with Mrs. Hayano ever since the birth of her first child. Rosie would sometimes watch Mrs. Hayano, reputed to have been the belle of her native village, making her way about a room, stooped, slowly shuffling, violently trembling (*always* trembling), and she would be reminded that this woman, in this same condition, had carried and given issue to three babies. She would look wonderingly at Mr. Hayano, handsome, tall, and strong, and she would look at her four pretty friends. But it was not a matter she could come to any decision about.

On this visit, however, Mrs. Hayano sat all evening in the rocker, as motionless and unobtrusive as it was possible for her to be, and Rosie found the greater part of the evening practically anaesthetic. Too, Rosie spent most of it in the girls' room, because Haru, the garrulous one, said almost as soon as the bows and other greetings were over, "Oh, you must see my new coat!"

It was a pale plaid of grey, sand, and blue, with an enormous collar, and Rosie, seeing nothing special in it, said, "Gee, how nice."

"Nice?" said Haru, indignantly. "Is that all you can say about it? It's gorgeous! And so cheap, too. Only seventeen-ninety-eight, because it was a sale. The saleslady said it was twenty-five dollars regular."

"Gee," said Rosie. Natsu, who never said much and when she said anything said it shyly, fingered the coat covetously and Haru pulled it away.

"Mine," she said, putting it on. She minced in the aisle between the two large beds and smiled happily. "Let's see how your mother likes it."

She broke into the front room and the adult conversation and went to stand in front of Rosie's mother, while the rest watched from the door. Rosie's mother was properly envious. "May I inherit it when you're through with it?"

Haru, pleased, giggled and said yes, she could, but Natsu reminded gravely from the door, "You promised me, Haru."

Everyone laughed but Natsu, who shamefacedly retreated into the bedroom. Haru came in laughing, taking off the coat. "We were only kidding, Natsu," she said. "Here, you try it on now."

After Natsu buttoned herself into the coat, inspected herself solemnly in the bureau mirror, and reluctantly shed it, Rosie, Aki, and Fuyu got their turns, and Fuyu, who was eight, drowned in it while her sisters and Rosie doubled up in amusement. They all went into the front room later, because Haru's mother quaveringly called to her to fix the tea and rice cakes and open a can of sliced peaches for everybody. Rosie noticed that her mother and Mr. Hayano were talking together at the little table—they were discussing a *haiku* that Mr. Hayano was planning to send to the *Mainichi,* while her father was sitting at one end of the sofa looking through a copy of *Life,* the new picture magazine. Occasionally, her father would comment on a photograph, holding it toward Mrs. Hayano and speaking to her as he always did—loudly, as though he thought someone such as she must surely be at least a trifle deaf also.

The five girls had their refreshments at the kitchen table, and it was while Rosie was showing the sisters her trick of swallowing peach slices without chewing (she chased each slippery crescent down with a swig of tea) that her father brought his empty teacup and untouched saucer to the sink and said, "Come on, Rosie, we're going home now."

"Already?" asked Rosie.

"Work tomorrow," he said.

He sounded irritated, and Rosie, puzzled, gulped one last yellow slice and stood up to go, while the sisters began protesting, as was their wont.

"We have to get up at five-thirty," he told them, going into the front room quickly, so that they did not have their usual chance to hang onto his hands and plead for an extension of time.

Rosie, following, saw that her mother and Mr. Hayano were sipping tea and still talking together, while Mrs. Hayano concentrated, quivering, on raising the handleless Japanese cup to her lips with both her hands and lowering it back to her lap. Her father, saying nothing, went out the door, onto the bright porch, and down the steps. Her mother looked up and asked, "Where is he going?"

"Where is he going?" Rosie said. "He said we were going home now."

"Going home?" Her mother looked with embarrassment at Mr. Hayano and his absorbed wife and then forced a smile. "He must be tired," she said.

Haru was not giving up yet. "May Rosie stay overnight?" she asked, and Natsu, Aki, and Fuyu came to reinforce their sister's plea by helping her make a circle around Rosie's mother. Rosie, for once having no desire to stay, was relieved when her mother, apologizing to the perturbed Mr. and Mrs. Hayano for her father's abruptness at the same time, managed to shake her head no at the quartet, kindly but adamant, so that they broke their circle and let her go.

Rosie's father looked ahead into the windshield as the two joined him. "I'm sorry," her mother said. "You must be tired." Her father, stepping on the starter, said nothing. "You know how I get when it's *haiku*," she continued, "I forget what time it is." He only grunted.

As they rode homeward silently, Rosie, sitting between, felt a rush of hate for both—for her mother for begging, for her father for denying her mother. I wish this old Ford would crash, right now, she thought, then immediately, no, no, I wish my father would laugh, but it was too late: already the vision had passed through her mind of the green pick-up crumpled in the dark against one of the mighty eucalyptus trees they were just riding past, of the three contorted, bleeding bodies, one of them hers.

Rosie ran between two patches of tomatoes, her heart working more rambunctiously than she had ever known it to. How lucky it was that Aunt Taka and Uncle Gimpachi had come tonight, though, how very lucky. Otherwise she might not have really kept her half-promise to meet Jesus Carrasco. Jesus was going to be a senior in September at the same school she went to, and his parents were the ones helping with the tomatoes this year. She and Jesus, who hardly remembered seeing each other at Cleveland High where there were so many other people and two whole grades between them, had become great friends this summer—he always had a joke for her when he periodically drove the loaded pick-up up from the fields to the shed where she was usually sorting while her mother and father did the packing, and they laughed a great deal together over infinitesimal repartee during the afternoon break for chilled watermelon or ice cream in the shade of the shed.

What she enjoyed most was racing him to see which could finish picking a double row first. He, who could work faster, would tease her by slowing down until she thought she would surely pass him this time, then speeding up furiously to leave her several sprawling vines behind. Once he had made her screech hideously by crossing over, while her back was turned, to place atop the tomatoes in her green-stained bucket a truly monstrous, pale green worm (it had looked more like an infant snake). And it was when they had finished a contest this morning, after she had pantingly pointed a green finger at the immature tomatoes evident in the lugs at the end of his row and he had returned the accusation (with justice), that he had startlingly brought up the matter of their possibly meeting outside the range of both their parents' dubious eyes.

"What for?" she had asked.

"I've got a secret I want to tell you," he said.

"Tell me now," she demanded.

"It won't be ready till tonight," he said.

She laughed. "Tell me tomorrow then."

"It'll be gone tomorrow," he threatened.

"Well, for seven hakes, what is it?" she had asked, more than twice, and when he had suggested that the packing shed would be an appropriate place to find out, she had cautiously answered maybe. She had not been certain she was going to keep the appointment until the arrival of mother's sister and her husband. Their coming seemed a sort of signal of permission, of grace, and she had definitely made up her mind to lie and leave as she was bowing them welcome.

So as soon as everyone appeared settled back for the evening, she announced loudly that she was going to the privy outside, "I'm going to the *benjo!*" and slipped out the door. And now that she was actually on her way, her heart pumped in such an undisciplined way that she could hear it with her ears. It's because I'm running, she told herself, slowing to a walk. The shed was up ahead, one more patch away, in the middle of the fields. Its bulk, looming in the dimness, took on a sinisterness that was funny when Rosie reminded herself that it was only a wooden frame with a canvas roof and three canvas walls that made a slapping noise on breezy days.

Jesus was sitting on the narrow plank that was the sorting platform and she went around to the other side and jumped backwards to seat herself on the rim of a packing stand. "Well, tell me," she said without greeting, thinking her voice sounded reassuringly familiar.

"I saw you coming out the door," Jesus said. "I heard you running part of the way, too."

"Uh-huh," Rosie said. "Now tell me the secret."

"I was afraid you wouldn't come," he said.

Rosie delved around on the chicken-wire bottom of the stall for number two tomatoes, ripe, which she was sitting beside, and came up with a left-over that felt edible. She bit into it and began sucking out the pulp and seeds. "I'm here," she pointed out.

"Rosie, are you sorry you came?"

"Sorry? What for?" she said. "You said you were going to tell me something."

"I will, I will," Jesus said, but his voice contained disappointment, and Rosie fleetingly felt the older of the two, realizing a brand-new power which vanished without category under her recognition.

"I have to go back in a minute," she said. "My aunt and uncle are here from Wintersburg. I told them I was going to the privy."

Jesus laughed. "You funny thing," he said. "You slay me!"

"Just because you have a bathroom *inside*," Rosie said. "Come on, tell me."

Chuckling, Jesus came around to lean on the stand facing her. They still could not see each other very clearly, but Rosie noticed that Jesus became very sober again as he took the hollow tomato from her hand and dropped it back into the stall. When he took hold of her empty hand, she could find no words to protest; her vocabulary had become distressingly constricted and she thought desperately that all that remained intact now was yes and no and oh, and even these few sounds would not easily out. Thus, kissed by Jesus, Rosie fell for the first time entirely victim to a helplessness delectable beyond speech. But the terrible, beautiful sensation lasted no more than a second, and the reality of Jesus' lips and tongue and teeth and hands made her pull away with such strength that she nearly tumbled.

Rosie stopped running as she approached the lights from the windows of home. How long since she had left? She could not guess, but gasping yet, she went to the privy in back and locked herself in. Her own breathing deafened her in the dark, close space, and she sat and waited until she could hear at last the nightly calling of the frogs and crickets. Even then, all she could think to say was oh, my, and the pressure of Jesus' face against her face would not leave.

No one had missed her in the parlor, however, and Rosie walked in and through quickly, announcing that she was next going to take a bath. "Your father's in the bathhouse," her mother said, and Rosie, in her room, recalled that she had not seen him when she entered. There had been only Aunt Taka and Uncle Gimpachi with her mother at the table, drinking tea. She got her robe and straw sandals and crossed the parlor again to go outside. Her mother was telling them about the *haiku* competition in the *Mainichi* and the poem she had entered.

Rosie met her father coming out of the bathhouse. "Are you through, Father?" she asked. "I was going to ask you to scrub my back."

"Scrub your own back," he said shortly, going toward the main house.

"What have I done now?" she yelled after him. She suddenly felt like doing a lot of yelling. But he did not answer, and she went into the bathhouse. Turning on the dangling light, she removed her denims and T-shirt and threw them in the big carton for dirty clothes standing next to the washing machine. Her other things she took with her into the bath compartment to wash after her bath. After she had scooped a basin of hot water from the square wooden tub, she sat on the grey cement of the floor and soaped herself at exaggerated leisure, singing "Red Sails in the Sunset" at the top of her voice and using da-da-da where she suspected her words. Then, standing up, still singing, for she was possessed by the notion that any attempt now to analyze would result in spoilage and she believed that the larger her volume the less she would be able to hear herself think, she obtained more hot water and poured it on until she was free of lather. Only then did she allow herself to step into the steaming vat, one leg first, then the remainder of her body inch by inch until the water no longer stung and she could move around at will.

She took a long time soaking, afterwards remembering to go around outside to stoke the embers of the tin-lined fireplace beneath the tub and to throw on a few more sticks so that the water might keep its heat for her mother, and when she finally returned to the parlor, she found her mother still talking *haiku* with her aunt and uncle, the three of them on another round of tea. Her father was nowhere in sight.

At Japanese school the next day (Wednesday, it was), Rosie was grave and giddy by turns. Preoccupied at her desk in the row for students on Book Eight, she made up for it at recess by performing wild mimicry for the benefit of her friend Chizuko. She held her nose and whined a witticism or two in what she considered was the manner of Fred Allen; she assumed intoxication and a British accent to go over the climax of the Rudy Vallee recording of the pub conversation about William Ewart Gladstone; she was the child Shirley Temple piping, "On the Good Ship Lollipop"; she was the gentleman soprano of the Four Inkspots trilling, "If I Didn't Care." And she felt reasonably satisfied when Chizuko wept and gasped, "Oh, Rosie, you ought to be in the movies!"

Her father came after her at noon, bringing her sandwiches of minced ham and two nectarines to eat while she rode, so that she could pitch right into the sorting when they got home. The lugs were piling up, he said, and the ripe tomatoes in them would probably have to be taken to the cannery tomorrow if they were not ready for the produce haulers tonight. "This heat's not doing them any good. And we've got no time for a break today."

It *was* hot, probably the hottest day of the year, and Rosie's blouse stuck damply to her back even under the protection of the canvas. But

she worked as efficiently as a flawless machine and kept the stalls
heaped, with one part of her mind listening in to the parental murmuring about the heat and the tomatoes and with another part planning the
exact words she would say to Jesus when he drove up with the first load
of the afternoon. But when at last she saw that the pick-up was coming,
her hands went berserk and the tomatoes started falling in the wrong
stalls, and her father said, "Hey, hey! Rosie, watch what you're doing!"

"Well, I have to go to the *benjo*," she said, hiding panic.

"Go in the weeds over there," he said, only half-joking.

"Oh, Father!" she protested.

"Oh, go on home," her mother said. "We'll make out for awhile."

In the privy Rosie peered through a knothole toward the fields,
watching as much as she could of Jesus. Happily she thought she saw
him look in the direction of the house from time to time before he finished unloading and went back toward the patch where his mother and
father worked. As she was heading for the shed, a very presentable
black car purred up the dirt driveway to the house and its driver motioned to her. Was this the Hayashi home, he wanted to know. She
nodded. Was she a Hayashi? Yes, she said, thinking that he was a
good-looking man. He got out of the car with a huge, flat package and
she saw that he warmly wore a business suit. "I have something here for
your mother then," he said, in a more elegant Japanese than she was
used to.

She told him where her mother was and he came along with her,
patting his face with an immaculate white handkerchief and saying
something about the coolness of San Francisco. To her surprised
mother and father, he bowed and introduced himself as, among other
things, the *haiku* editor of the *Mainichi Shimbun,* saying that since he
had been coming as far as Los Angeles anyway, he had decided to bring
her the first prize she had won in the recent contest.

"First prize?" her mother echoed, believing and not believing,
pleased and overwhelmed. Handed the package with a bow, she
bobbed her head up and down numerous times to express her utter
gratitude.

"It is nothing much," he added, "but I hope it will serve as a token
of our great appreciation for your contributions and our great admiration of your considerable talent."

"I am not worthy," she said, falling easily into his style. "It is I who
should make some sign of my humble thanks for being permitted to
contribute."

"No, no, to the contrary," he said, bowing again.

But Rosie's mother insisted, and then saying that she knew she was being unorthodox, she asked if she might open the package because her curiosity was so great. Certainly she might. In fact, he would like her reaction to it, for personally, it was one of his favorite *Hiroshiges*.

Rosie thought it was a pleasant picture, which looked to have been sketched with delicate quickness. There were pink clouds, containing some graceful calligraphy, and a sea that was a pale blue except at the edges, containing four sampans with indications of people in them. Pines edged the water and on the far-off beach there was a cluster of thatched huts towered over by pine-dotted mountains of grey and blue. The frame was scalloped and gilt.

After Rosie's mother pronounced it without peer and somewhat prodded her father into nodding agreement, she said Mr. Kuroda must at least have a cup of tea after coming all this way, and although Mr. Kuroda did not want to impose, he soon agreed that a cup of tea would be refreshing and went along with her to the house, carrying the picture for her.

"Ha, your mother's crazy!" Rosie's father said, and Rosie laughed uneasily as she resumed judgment on the tomatoes. She had emptied six lugs when he broke into an imaginary conversation with Jesus to tell her to go and remind her mother of the tomatoes, and she went slowly.

Mr. Kuroda was in his shirtsleeves expounding some *haiku* theory as he munched a rice cake, and her mother was rapt. Abashed in the great man's presence, Rosie stood next to her mother's chair until her mother looked up inquiringly, and then she started to whisper the message, but her mother pushed her gently away and reproached, "You are not being very polite to our guest."

"Father says the tomatoes..." Rosie said aloud, smiling foolishly.

"Tell him I shall only be a minute," her mother said, speaking the language of Mr. Kuroda.

When Rosie carried the reply to her father, he did not seem to hear and she said again, "Mother says she'll be back in a minute."

"All right, all right," he nodded, and they worked again in silence. But suddenly, her father uttered an incredible noise, exactly like the cork of a bottle popping, and the next Rosie knew, he was stalking angrily toward the house, almost running in fact, and she chased after him crying, "Father! Father! What are you going to do?"

He stopped long enough to order her back to the shed. "Never mind!" he shouted. "Get on with the sorting!"

And from the place in the fields where she stood, frightened and vacillating, Rosie saw her father enter the house. Soon Mr. Kuroda came out alone, putting on his coat. Mr. Kuroda got into his car and backed out down the driveway onto the highway. Next her father emerged, also alone, something in his arms (it was the picture, she realized), and, going over to the bathhouse woodpile, he threw the picture on the ground and picked up the axe. Smashing the picture, glass and all (she heard the explosion faintly), he reached over for the kerosene that was used to encourage the bath fire and poured it over the wreckage. I am dreaming, Rosie said to herself, I am dreaming, but her father, having made sure that his act of cremation was irrevocable, was even then returning to the fields.

Rosie ran past him and toward the house. What had become of her mother? She burst into the parlor and found her mother at the back window watching the dying fire. They watched together until there remained only a feeble smoke under the blazing sun. Her mother was very calm.

"Do you know why I married your father?" she said without turning.

"No," said Rosie. It was the most frightening question she had ever been called upon to answer. Don't tell me now, she wanted to say, tell me tomorrow, tell me next week, don't tell me today. But she knew she would be told now, that the telling would combine with the other violence of the hot afternoon to level her life, her world to the very ground.

It was like a story out of the magazines illustrated in sepia, which she had consumed so greedily for a period until the information had somehow reached her that those wretchedly unhappy autobiographies, offered to her as the testimonials of living men and women, were largely inventions: Her mother, at nineteen, had come to America and married her father as an alternative to suicide.

At eighteen she had been in love with the first son of one of the well-to-do families in her village. The two had met whenever and wherever they could, secretly, because it would not have done for his family to see him favor her—her father had no money; he was a drunkard and a gambler besides. She had learned she was with child; an excellent match had already been arranged for her lover. Despised by her family, she had given premature birth to a stillborn son, who would be seventeen now. Her family did not turn her out, but she could no longer project herself in any direction without refreshing in them the memory of her indiscretion. She wrote to Aunt Taka, her favorite sister in America, threatening to kill herself if Aunt Taka would not send for her. Aunt Taka hastily arranged a marriage with a young man of whom she knew, but lately arrived from Japan, a young man of simple mind, it was said, but of kindly heart. The young man was never told why his unseen betrothed was so eager to hasten the day of meeting.

The story was told perfectly, with neither groping for words nor untoward passion. It was as though her mother had memorized it by heart, reciting it to herself so many times over that its nagging vileness had long since gone.

"I had a brother then?" Rosie asked, for this was what seemed to matter now; she would think about the other later, she assured herself, pushing back the illumination which threatened all that darkness that had hitherto been merely mysterious or even glamorous. "A half-brother?"

"Yes."

"I would have liked a brother," she said.

Suddenly, her mother knelt on the floor and took her by the wrists. "Rosie," she said urgently, "Promise me you will never marry!" Shocked more by the request than the revelation, Rosie stared at her mother's face. Jesus, Jesus, she called silently, not certain whether she was invoking the help of the son of the Carrascos or of God, until there returned sweetly the memory of Jesus' hand, how it had touched her and where. Still her mother waited for an answer, holding her wrists so tightly that her hands were going numb. She tried to pull free. Promise, her mother whispered fiercely, promise. Yes, yes, I promise, Rosie said. But for an instant she turned away, and her mother, hearing the familiar glib agreement, released her. Oh, you, you, you, her eyes and twisted mouth said, you fool. Rosie, covering her face, began at last to cry, and the embrace and consoling hand came much later than she expected.

(1949)

The Legend of Miss Sasagawara

Even in that unlikely place of wind, sand, and heat, it was easy to imagine Miss Sasagawara a decorative ingredient of some ballet. Her daily costume, brief and fitting closely to her trifling waist, generously billowing below, and bringing together arrestingly rich colors like mustard yellow and forest green, appeared to have been cut from a coarse-textured homespun; her shining hair was so long it wound twice about her head to form a coronet; her face was delicate and pale, with a fine nose, pouting bright mouth, and glittering eyes; and her measured walk said, "Look, I'm *walking!*" as though walking were not a common but a rather special thing to be doing. I first saw her so one evening after mess, as she was coming out of the women's latrine going toward her barracks, and after I thought she was out of hearing, I imitated the young men of the Block (No. 33), and gasped, "Wow! How much does *she* weigh?"

"Oh, haven't you heard?" said my friend Elsie Kubo, knowing very well I had not. "That's Miss Sasagawara."

It turned out Elsie knew all about Miss Sasagawara, who with her father was new to Block 33. Where had she accumulated all her items? Probably a morsel here and a morsel there, and, anyway, I forgot to ask her sources, because the picture she painted was so distracting: Miss Sasagawara's father was a Buddhist minister, and the two had gotten permission to come to this Japanese evacuation camp in Arizona from one further north, after the death there of Mrs. Sasagawara. They had come here to join the Rev. Sasagawara's brother's family, who lived in a neighboring Block, but there had been some trouble between them, and just this week the immigrant pair had gotten leave to move over to Block 33. They were occupying one end of the Block's lone empty barracks, which had not been chopped up yet into the customary four apartments. The other end had been taken over by a young couple, also newcomers to the Block, who had moved in the same day.

"And do you know what, Kiku?" Elsie continued. "Oooh, that gal is really temperamental. I guess it's because she was a ballet dancer before she got stuck in camp, I hear people like that are temperamental. Anyway, the Sasakis, the new couple at the other end of the barracks, think she's crazy. The day they all moved in, the barracks was really dirty, all covered with dust from the dust storms and everything, so Mr. Sasaki was going to wash the whole barracks down with a hose, and he thought he'd be nice and do the Sasagawaras' side first. You know, do them a favor. But do you know what? Mr. Sasaki got the hose attached to the faucet outside and started to go in the door, and he said all the Sasagawaras' suitcases and things were on top of the Army cots and Miss Sasagawara was trying to clean the place out with a pail of water and a broom. He said, 'Here let me flush the place out with a hose for you; it'll be faster.' And she turned right around and screamed at him, 'What are you trying to do? Spy on me? Get out of here or I'll throw this water on you!' He said he was so surprised he couldn't move for a minute, and before he knew it, Miss Sasagawara just up and threw that water at him, pail and all. Oh, he said he got out of that place fast, but fast. Mad-woman, he called her."

But Elsie had already met Miss Sasagawara, too, over at the apart-ment of the Murakamis, where Miss Sasagawara was borrowing Mrs. Murakami's Singer, and had found her quite amiable. "She said she was thirty-nine years old—imagine, thirty-nine, she looks so young, more like twenty-five; but she said she wasn't sorry she never got married, because she's had her fun. She said she got to go all over the country a couple of times, dancing in the ballet."

And after we emerged from the latrine, Elsie and I, slapping mos-quitoes in the warm, gathering dusk, sat on the stoop of her apartment and talked awhile, jealously of the scintillating life Miss Sasagawara had led until now and nostalgically of the few ballets we had seen in the world outside. (How faraway Los Angeles seemed!) But we ended up as we always did, agreeing that our mission in life, pushing twenty as we were, was first to finish college somewhere when and if the war ever ended and we were free again, and then to find good jobs and two nice, clean young men, preferably handsome, preferably rich, who would cherish us forever and a day.

My introduction, less spectacular, to the Rev. Sasagawara came later, as I noticed him, a slight and fragile-looking old man, in the Block mess hall (where I worked as a waitress, and Elsie, too) or in the laundry room or going to and from the latrine. Sometimes he would be farther out, perhaps going to the post office or canteen or to visit friends in another Block or on some business to the Administration buildings, but wherever he was headed, however doubtless his destination, he always seemed to be wandering lostly. This may have been because he walked so slowly, with such negligible steps, or because he wore perpetually an air of bemusement, never talking directly to a person, as though, being what he was, he could not stop for an instant his meditation on the higher life.

I noticed, too, that Miss Sasagawara never came to the mess hall herself. Her father ate at the tables reserved for the occupants, mostly elderly, of the end barracks known as the bachelors' dormitory. After each meal, he came up to the counter and carried away a plate of food, protected with one of the pinkish apple wrappers we waitresses made as wrinkleless as possible and put out for napkins, and a mug of tea or coffee. Sometimes Miss Sasagawara could be seen rinsing out her empties at the one double-tub in the laundry that was reserved for private dishwashing.

If any one in the Block or in the entire camp of 15,000 or so people had talked at any length with Miss Sasagawara (everyone happening to speak of her called her that, although her first name, Mari, was simple enough and rather pretty) after her first and only visit to use Mrs. Murakami's sewing machine, I never heard of it. Nor did she ever willingly use the shower room, just off the latrine, when anyone else was there. Once, when I was up past midnight writing letters and went for my shower, I came upon her under the full needling force of a steamy spray, but she turned her back to me and did not answer my surprised hello. I hoped my body would be as smooth and spare and well-turned when I was thirty-nine. Another time Elsie and I passed in front of the Sasagawara apartment, which was really only a cubicle because the once-empty barracks had soon been partitioned off into six units for families of two, and we saw her there on the wooden steps, sitting with her wide, wide skirt spread splendidly about her. She was intent on peeling a grapefruit, which her father had probably brought to her from the mess hall that morning, and Elsie called out, "Hello there!" Miss Sasagawara looked up and stared, without recognition. We were almost out of earshot when I heard her call, "Do I know you?" and I could have almost sworn that she sounded hopeful, if not downright wistful, but Elsie, already miffed at having expended friendliness so unprofitably, seemed not to have heard, and that was that.

Well, if Miss Sasagawara was not one to speak to, she was certainly one to speak of, and she came up quite often as topic for the endless conversations which helped along the monotonous days. My mother said she had met the late Mrs. Sasagawara once, many years before the war, and to hear her tell it, a sweeter, kindlier woman there never was. "I suppose," said my mother, "that I'll never meet anyone like her again; she was a lady in every sense of the word." Then she reminded me that I had seen the Rev. Sasagawara before. Didn't I remember him as one of the three bhikshus who had read the sutras at Grandfather's funeral?

I could not say that I did. I barely remembered Grandfather, my mother's father. The only thing that came back with clarity was my nausea at the wake and the funeral, the first and only ones I had ever had occasion to attend, because it had been reproduced several times since — each time, in fact, that I had crossed again the actual scent or suspicion of burning incense. Dimly I recalled the inside of the Buddhist temple in Los Angeles, an immense, murky auditorium whose high and huge platform had held, centered in the background, a great golden shrine touched with black and white. Below this platform, Grandfather, veiled by gauze, had slept in a long grey box which just fitted him. There had been flowers, oh, such flowers, everywhere. And right in front of Grandfather's box had been the incense stand, upon which squatted two small bowls, one with a cluster of straw-thin sticks sending up white tendrils of smoke, the other containing a heap of coarse, grey powder. Each mourner in turn had gone up to the stand, bowing once, his palms touching in prayer before he reached it; had bent in prayer over the stand; had taken then a pinch of incense from the bowl of crumbs and, bowing over it reverently, cast it into the other, the active bowl; had bowed, the hands praying again; had retreated a few steps and bowed one last time, the hands still joined, before returning to his seat. (I knew the ceremony well from having been severely coached in it on the evening of the wake.) There had been tears and tears and here and there a sudden sob.

And all this while, three men in black robes had been on the platform, one standing in front of the shining altar, the others sitting on either side, and the entire trio incessantly chanting a strange, mellifluous language in unison. From time to time there had reverberated through the enormous room, above the singsong, above the weeping, above the fragrance, the sharp, startling whang of the gong.

So, one of those men had been Miss Sasagawara's father .... This information brought him closer to me, and I listened with interest later when it was told that he kept here in his apartment a small shrine, much more intricately constructed than that kept by the usual Buddhist household, before which, at regular hours of the day, he offered incense and chanted, tinkling (in lieu of the gong) a small bell. What did Miss Sasagawara do at these prayer periods, I wondered; did she participate, did she let it go in one ear and out the other, or did she abruptly go out on the steps, perhaps to eat a grapefruit?

Elsie and I tired one day of working in the mess hall. And this desire for greener fields came almost together with the Administration annoucement that henceforth the wages of residents doing truly vital labor, such as in the hospital or on the garbage trucks that went from mess hall to mess hall, would be upped to nineteen dollars a month instead of the common sixteen.

"Oh, I've always wanted to be a nurse!" Elsie confided, as the Block manager sat down to his breakfast after reading out the day's bulletin in English and Japanese.

"What's stopped you?" I asked.

"Mom," Elsie said. "She thinks it's dirty work. And she's afraid I'll catch something. But I'll remind her of the extra three dollars."

"It's never appealed to me much, either," I confessed. "Why don't we go over to garbage? It's the same pay."

Elsie would not even consider it. "Very funny. Well, you don't have to be a nurse's aide, Kiku. The hospital's short all kinds of help. Dental assistants, receptionists....Let's go apply after we finish this here."

So, willy-nilly, while Elsie plunged gleefully into the pleasure of wearing a trim blue-and-white striped seersucker, into the duties of taking temperatures and carrying bedpans, and into the fringe of medical jargon (she spoke very casually now of catheters, enemas, primiparas, multiparas), I became a relief receptionist at the hospital's front desk, taking my hours as they were assigned. And it was on one of my midnight-to-morning shifts that I spoke to Miss Sasagawara for the first time.

The cooler in the corridor window was still whirring away (for that desert heat in summer had a way of lingering intact through the night to merge with the warmth of the morning sun), but she entered bundled in an extraordinarily long black coat, her face made petulant, not unprettily, by lines of pain.

"I think I've got appendicitis," she said breathlessly, without preliminary.

"May I have your name and address?" I asked, unscrewing my pen.

Annoyance seemed to outbalance agony for a moment, but she answered soon enough, in a cold rush, "Mari Sasagawara, Thirty-three-seven C."

It was necessary also to learn her symptoms, and I wrote down that she had chills and a dull aching at the back of her head, as well as these excruciating flashes in her lower right abdomen.

"I'll have to go wake up the doctor. Here's a blanket, why don't you lie down over there on the bench until he comes?" I suggested.

She did not answer, so I tossed the Army blanket on the bench, and when I returned from the doctors' dormitory, after having tapped and tapped on the door of young Dr. Moritomo, who was on night duty, she was still standing where I had left her, immobile and holding onto the wooden railing shielding the desk.

"Dr. Moritomo's coming right away," I said. "Why don't you sit down at least?"

Miss Sasagawara said, "Yes," but did not move.

"Did you walk all the way?" I asked incredulously, for Block 33 was a good mile off, across the canal.

She nodded, as if that were not important, also as if to thank me kindly to mind my own business.

Dr. Moritomo (technically, the title was premature; evacuation had caught him with a few months to go on his degree), wearing a maroon bathrobe, shuffled in sleepily and asked her to come into the emergency room for an examination. A short while later, he guided her past my desk into the laboratory, saying he was going to take her blood count.

When they came out, she went over to the electric fountain for a drink of water, and Dr. Moritomo said reflectively, "Her count's all right. Not appendicitis. We should keep her for observation, but the general ward is pretty full, isn't it? Hm, well, I'll give her something to take. Will you tell one of the boys to take her home?"

This I did, but when I came back from arousing George, one of the ambulance boys, Miss Sasagawara was gone, and Dr. Moritomo was coming out of the laboratory where he had gone to push out the lights. "Here's George, but that girl must have walked home," I reported helplessly.

"She's in no condition to do that. George, better catch up with her and take her home," Dr. Moritomo ordered.

Shrugging, George strode down the hall; the doctor shuffled back to bed; and soon there was the shattering sound of one of the old Army ambulances backing out of the hospital drive.

George returned in no time at all to say that Miss Sasagawara had refused to get on the ambulance.

"She wouldn't even listen to me. She just kept walking and I drove alongside and told her it was Dr. Moritomo's orders, but she wouldn't even listen to me."

"She wouldn't?"

"I hope Doc didn't expect me to drag her into the ambulance."

"Oh, well," I said, "I guess she'll get home all right. She walked all the way up here."

"Cripes, what a dame!" George complained, shaking his head as he started back to the ambulance room. "I never heard of such a thing. She wouldn't even listen to me."

Miss Sasagawara came back to the hospital about a month later. Elsie was the one who rushed up to the desk where I was on day duty to whisper, "Miss Sasagawara just tried to escape from the hospital!"

"Escape? What do you mean, escape?" I said.

"Well, she came in last night, and they didn't know what was wrong with her, so they kept her for observation. And this morning, just now, she ran out of the ward in just a hospital nightgown and the orderlies chased after her and caught her and brought her back. Oh, she was just fighting them. But once they got her back to bed, she calmed down right away, and Miss Morris asked her what was the big idea, you know, and do you know what she said? She said she didn't want any more of those doctors pawing her. *Pawing* her, imagine!"

After an instant's struggle with self-mockery, my curiosity led me down the entrance corridor after Elsie into the longer, wider corridor admitting to the general ward. The whole hospital staff appeared to have gathered in the room to get a look at Miss Sasagawara, and the other patients, or those of them that could, were sitting up attentively in their high, white, and narrow beds. Miss Sasagawara had the corner bed to the left as we entered and, covered only by a brief hospital apron, she was sitting on the edge with her legs dangling over the side. With her head slightly bent, she was staring at a certain place on the floor, and I knew she must be aware of that concentrated gaze, of trembling old Dr. Kawamoto (he had retired several years before the war, but he had been drafted here), of Miss Morris, the head nurse, of Miss Bowman, the nurse in charge of the general ward during the day, of the other patients, of the nurse's aides, of the orderlies, and of everyone else who tripped in and out abashedly on some pretext or other in order to pass by her bed. I knew this by her smile, for as she continued to look at that same piece of the floor, she continued, unexpectedly, to seem wryly amused with the entire proceedings. I peered at her wonderingly through the triangular peephole created by someone's hand on hip, while Dr. Kawamoto, Miss Morris, and Miss Bowman tried to persuade her to lie down and relax. She was as smilingly immune to tactful suggestions as she was to tactless gawking.

There was no future to watching such a war of nerves as this; and besides, I was supposed to be at the front desk, so I hurried back in time to greet a frantic young mother and father, the latter carrying their small son who had had a hemorrhage this morning after a tonsillectomy yesterday in the out-patient clinic.

A couple of weeks later on the late shift I found George, the ambulance driver, in high spirits. This time he had been the one selected to drive a patient to Phoenix, where special cases were occasionally sent under escort, and he was looking forward to the moment when, for a few hours, the escort would permit him to go shopping around the city and perhaps take in a new movie. He showed me the list of things his friends had asked him to bring back for them, and we laughed together over the request of one plumpish nurse's aide for the biggest, richest chocolate cake he could find.

"You ought to have seen Mabel's eyes while she was describing the kind of cake she wanted," he said. "Man, she looked like she was eating it already!"

Just then one of the other drivers, Bobo Kunitomi, came up and nudged George, and they withdrew a few steps from my desk.

"Oh, I ain't particularly interested in that," I heard George saying.

There was some murmuring from Bobo, of which I caught the words, "Well, hell, you might as well, just as long as you're getting to go out there."

George shrugged, then nodded, and Bobo came over to the desk and asked for pencil and paper. "This is a good place...." he said, handing George what he had written.

Was it my imagination, or did George emerge from his chat with Bobo a little ruddier than usual? "Well, I guess I better go get ready," he said, taking leave. "Oh, anything you want, Kiku? Just say the word."

"Thanks, not this time," I said. "Well, enjoy yourself."

"Don't worry," he said. "I will!"

He had started down the hall when I remembered to ask, "Who are you taking, anyway?"

George turned around. "Miss Sa-sa-ga-wa-ra," he said, accenting every syllable. "Remember that dame? The one who wouldn't let me take her home?"

"Yes," I said. "What's the matter with her?"

George, saying not a word, pointed at his head and made several circles in the air with his first finger.

"Really?" I asked.

Still mum, George nodded in emphasis and pity before he turned to go.

How long was she away? It must have been several months, and when, towards late autumn, she returned at last from the sanitarium in Phoenix, everyone in Block 33 was amazed at the change. She said hello and how are you as often and easily as the next person, although many of those she greeted were surprised and suspicious, remembering the earlier rebuffs. There were some who never did get used to Miss Sasagawara as a friendly being.

One evening when I was going toward the latrine for my shower, my youngest sister, ten-year-old Michi, almost collided with me and said excitedly, "You going for your shower now, Kiku?"

"You want to fight about it?" I said, making fists.

"Don't go now, don't go now! Miss Sasagawara's in there," she whispered wickedly.

"Well," I demanded. "What's wrong with that, honey?"

"She's scary. Us kids were in there and she came in and we finished, so we got out, and she said, 'Don't be afraid of me. I won't hurt you.' Gee, we weren't even afraid of her, but when she said that, gee!"

"Oh, go home and go to bed," I said.

Miss Sasagawara was indeed in the shower and she welcomed me with a smile. "Aren't you the girl who plays the violin?"

I giggled and explained. Elsie and I, after hearing Menuhin on the radio, had in a fit of madness sent to Sears and Roebuck for beginners' violins that cost five dollars each. We had received free instruction booklets, too, but unable to make heads or tails from them, we contented ourselves with occasionally taking the violins out of their paper bags and sawing every which way away.

Miss Sasagawara laughed aloud—a lovely sound. "Well, you're just about as good as I am. I sent for a Spanish guitar. I studied it about a year once, but that was so long ago I don't remember the first thing and I'm having to start all over again. We'd make a fine orchestra."

That was the only time we really exchanged words and some weeks later I understood she had organized a dancing class from among the younger girls in the Block. My sister Michi, becoming one of her pupils, got very attached to her and spoke of her frequently at home. So I knew that Miss Sasagawara and her father had decorated their apartment to look oh, so pretty, that Miss Sasagawara had a whole big suitcase full of dancing costumes, and that Miss Sasagawara had just lots and lots of books to read.

The fruits of Miss Sasagawara's patient labor were put on show at the Block Christmas party, the second such observance in camp. Again, it was a gay, if odd, celebration. The mess hall was hung with red and green crepe paper streamers and the greyish mistletoe that grew abundantly on the ancient mesquite surrounding the camp. There were even electric decorations on the token Christmas tree. The oldest occupant of the bachelors' dormitory gave a tremulous monologue in an exaggerated Hiroshima dialect; one of the young boys wore a bow-tie and whispered a popular song while the girls shrieked and pretended to be growing faint; my mother sang an old Japanese song; four of the girls wore similar blue dresses and harmonized on a sweet tune; a little girl in a grass skirt and superfluous brassiere did a hula; and the chief cook came out with an ample saucepan and, assisted by the waitresses, performed the familiar *dojo-sukui*, the comic dance about a man who is merely trying to scoop up a few loaches from an uncooperative lake. Then Miss Sasagawara shooed her eight little girls, including Michi, in front, and while they formed a stiff pattern and waited, self-conscious in the rustly crepe paper dresses they had made themselves, she set up a portable phonograph on the floor and vigorously turned the crank.

Something was past its prime, either the machine or the record or the needle, for what came out was a feeble rasp but distantly related to the Mozart minuet it was supposed to be. After a bit I recognized the melody; I had learned it as a child to the words,

> When dames wore hoops and powdered hair,
> And very strict was e-ti-quette,
> When men were brave and ladies fair,
> They danced the min-u-et....

And the little girls, who might have curtsied and stepped gracefully about under Miss Sasagawara's eyes alone, were all elbows and knees as they felt the Block's one-hundred-fifty or more pairs of eyes on them. Although there was sustained applause after their number, what we were benevolently approving was the great effort, for the achievement had been undeniably small. Then Santa came with a pillow for a stomach, his hands each dragging a bulging burlap bag. Church people outside had kindly sent these gifts, Santa announced, and every recipient must write and thank the person whose name he would find on an enclosed slip. So saying, he called by name each Block child under twelve and ceremoniously presented each eleemosynary package, and a couple of the youngest children screamed in fright at this new experience of a red and white man with a booming voice.

At the last, Santa called, "Miss Mari Sasagawara!" and when she came forward in surprise, he explained to the gathering that she was being rewarded for her help with the Block's younger generation. Everyone clapped and Miss Sasagawara, smiling graciously, opened her package then and there. She held up her gift, a peach-colored bath towel, so that it could be fully seen, and everyone clapped again.

Suddenly I put this desert scene behind me. The notice I had long awaited, of permission to relocate to Philadelphia to attend college, finally came, and there was a prodigious amount of packing to do, leave papers to sign, and goodbyes to say. And once the wearying, sooty train trip was over, I found myself in an intoxicating new world of daily classes, afternoon teas, and evening concerts, from which I dutifully emerged now and then to answer the letters from home. When the beautiful semester was over, I returned to Arizona, to that glowing heat, to the camp, to the family; for although the war was still on, it had been decided to close down the camps, and I had been asked to go back and spread the good word about higher education among the young people who might be dispersed in this way.

Elsie was still working in the hospital, although she had applied for entrance into the cadet nurse corps and was expecting acceptance any day, and the long conversations we held were mostly about the good old days, the good old days when we had worked in the mess hall together, the good old days when we had worked in the hospital together.

"What ever became of Miss Sasagawara?" I asked one day, seeing the Rev. Sasagawara go abstractedly by. "Did she relocate somewhere?"

"I didn't write you about her, did I?" Elsie said meaningfully. "Yes, she's relocated all right. Haven't seen her around, have you?"

"Where did she go?

Elsie answered offhandedly. "California."

"California?" I exclaimed. "We can't go back to California. What's she doing in California?"

So Elsie told me: Miss Sasagawara had been sent back there to a state institution, oh, not so very long after I had left for school. She had begun slipping back into her aloof ways almost immediately after Christmas, giving up the dancing class and not speaking to people. Then Elsie had heard a couple of very strange, yes, very strange things about her. One thing had been told by young Mrs. Sasaki, that next-door neighbor of the Sasagawaras.

Mrs. Sasaki said she had once come upon Miss Sasagawara sitting, as was her habit, on the porch. Mrs. Sasaki had been shocked to the core to see that the face of this thirty-nine-year-old woman (or was she forty now?) wore a beatific expression as she watched the activity going on in the doorway of her neighbors across the way, the Yoshinagas. This activity had been the joking and loud laughter of Joe and Frank, the young Yoshinaga boys, and three or four of their friends. Mrs. Sasaki would have let the matter go, were it not for the fact that Miss Sasagawara was so absorbed a spectator of this horseplay that her head was bent to one side and she actually had one finger in her mouth as she gazed, in the manner of a shy child confronted with a marvel. "What's the matter with you, watching the boys like that?" Mrs. Sasaki had cried. "You're old enough to be their mother!" Startled, Miss Sasagawara had jumped up and dashed back into her apartment. And when Mrs. Sasaki had gone into hers, adjoining the Sasagawaras', she had been terrified to hear Miss Sasagawara begin to bang on the wooden walls with something heavy like a hammer. The banging, which sounded as though Miss Sasagawara were using all her strength on each blow, had continued wildly for at least five minutes. Then all had been still.

The other thing had been told by Joe Yoshinaga who lived across the way from Miss Sasagawara. Joe and his brother slept on two Army cots pushed together on one side of the room, while their parents had a similar arrangement on the other side. Joe had standing by his bed an apple crate for a shelf, and he was in the habit of reading his sports and western magazines in bed and throwing them on top of the crate before he went to sleep. But one morning he had noticed his magazines all neatly stacked inside the crate, when he was sure he had carelessly thrown some on top the night before, as usual. This happened several times, and he finally asked his family whether one of them had been putting his magazines away after he fell asleep. They had said no and laughed, telling him he must be getting absent-minded. But the mystery had been solved late one night, when Joe gradually awoke in his cot with the feeling that he was being watched. Warily he had opened one eye slightly and had been thoroughly awakened and chilled in the bargain by what he saw. For what he saw was Miss Sasagawara sitting there on his apple crate, her long hair all undone and flowing about her. She was dressed in a white nightgown and her hands were clasped on her lap. And all she was doing was sitting there watching him, Joe Yoshinaga. He could not help it, he had sat up and screamed. His mother, a light sleeper, came running to see what had happened, just as Miss Sasagawara was running out the door, the door they had always left unlatched or even wide open in summer. In the morning Mrs. Yoshinaga had gone straight to the Rev. Sasagawara and asked him to do something about his daughter. The Rev. Sasagawara, sympathizing with her indignation in his benign but vague manner, had said he would have a talk with Mari.

And, concluded Elsie, Miss Sasagawara had gone away not long after. I was impressed, although Elsie's sources were not what I would ordinarily pay much attention to, Mrs. Sasaki, that plump and giggling young woman who always felt called upon to explain that she was childless by choice, and Joe Yoshinaga, who had a knack of blowing up, in his drawling voice, any incident in which he personally played even a small part (I could imagine the field day he had had with this one). Elsie puzzled aloud over the cause of Miss Sasagawara's derangement and I, who had so newly had some contact with the recorded explorations into the virgin territory of the human mind, sagely explained that Miss Sasagawara had no doubt looked upon Joe Yoshinaga as the image of either the lost lover or the lost son. But my words made me uneasy by their glibness, and I began to wonder seriously about Miss Sasagawara for the first time.

Then there was this last word from Miss Sasagawara herself, making her strange legend as complete as I, at any rate, would probably ever know it. This came some time after I had gone back to Philadelphia and the family had joined me there, when I was neck deep in research for my final paper. I happened one day to be looking through the last issue of a small poetry magazine that had suspended publication midway through the war. I felt a thrill of recognition at the name, Mari Sasagawara, signed to a long poem, introduced as "...the first published poem of a Japanese-American woman who is, at present, an evacuee from the West Coast making her home in a War Relocation center in Arizona."

It was a *tour de force*, erratically brilliant and, through the first readings, tantalizingly obscure. It appeared to be about a man whose lifelong aim had been to achieve Nirvana, that saintly state of moral purity and universal wisdom. This man had in his way certain handicaps, all stemming from his having acquired, when young and unaware, a family for which he must provide. The day came at last, however, when his wife died and other circumstances made it unnecessary for him to earn a competitive living. These circumstances were considered by those about him as sheer imprisonment, but he had felt free for the first time in his long life. It became possible for him to extinguish within himself all unworthy desire and consequently all evil, to concentrate on that serene, eight-fold path of highest understanding, highest mindedness, highest speech, highest action, highest livelihood, highest recollectedness, highest endeavor, and highest meditation.

This man was certainly noble, the poet wrote, this man was beyond censure. The world was doubtless enriched by his presence. But say that someone else, someone sensitive, someone admiring, someone who had not achieved this sublime condition and who did not wish to, were somehow called to companion such a man. Was it not likely that the saint, blissfully bent on cleansing from his already radiant soul the last imperceptible blemishes (for, being perfect, would he not humbly suspect his own flawlessness?) would be deaf and blind to the human passions rising, subsiding, and again rising, perhaps in anguished silence, within the selfsame room? The poet could not speak for others, of course; she could only speak for herself. But she would describe this man's devotion as a sort of madness, the monstrous sort which, pure of itself, might possibly bring troublous, scented scenes to recur in the other's sleep.

(1950)

Wilshire Bus

ilshire Boulevard begins somewhere near the heart of downtown Los Angeles and, except for a few digressions scarcely worth mentioning, goes straight out to the edge of the Pacific Ocean. It is a wide boulevard and traffic on it is fairly fast. For the most part, it is bordered on either side with examples of the recent stark architecture which favors a great deal of glass. As the boulevard approaches the sea, however, the landscape becomes a bit more pastoral, so that the university and the soldiers' home there give the appearance of being huge country estates.

Esther Kuroiwa got to know this stretch of territory quite well while her husband Buro was in one of the hospitals at the soldiers' home. They had been married less than a year when his back, injured in the war, began troubling him again, and he was forced to take three months of treatments at Sawtelle before he was able to go back to work. During this time, Esther was permitted to visit him twice a week and she usually took the yellow bus out on Wednesdays because she did not know the first thing about driving and because her friends were not able to take her except on Sundays. She always enjoyed the long bus ride very much because her seat companions usually turned out to be amiable, and if they did not, she took vicarious pleasure in gazing out at the almost unmitigated elegance along the fabulous street.

It was on one of these Wednesday trips that Esther committed a grave sin of omission which caused her later to burst into tears and which caused her acute discomfort for a long time afterwards whenever something reminded her of it.

The man came on the bus quite early and Esther noticed him briefly as he entered because he said gaily to the driver, "You robber. All you guys do is take money from me every day, just for giving me a short lift!"

Handsome in a red-faced way, greying, medium of height, and dressed in a dark grey sport suit with a yellow-and-black flowered shirt, he said this in a nice, resonant, carrying voice which got the response of a scattering of titters from the bus. Esther, somewhat amused and classifying him as a somatotonic, promptly forgot about him. And since she was sitting alone in the first regular seat, facing the back of the driver and the two front benches facing each other, she returned to looking out the window.

At the next stop, a considerable mass of people piled on and the last two climbing up were an elderly Oriental man and his wife. Both were neatly and somberly clothed and the woman, who wore her hair in a bun and carried a bunch of yellow and dark red chrysanthemums, came to sit with Esther. Esther turned her head to smile a greeting (well, here we are, Orientals together on a bus), but the woman was watching, with some concern, her husband who was asking directions of the driver.

His faint English was inflected in such a way as to make Esther decide he was probably Chinese, and she noted that he had to repeat his question several times before the driver could answer it. Then he came to sit in the seat across the aisle from his wife. It was about then that a man's voice, which Esther recognized soon as belonging to the somatotonic, began a loud monologue in the seat just behind her. It was not really a monologue, since he seemed to be addressing his seat companion, but this person was not heard to give a single answer. The man's subject was a figure in the local sporting world who had a nice fortune invested in several of the shining buildings the bus was just passing.

"He's as tight-fisted as they make them, as tight-fisted as they come," the man said. "Why, he wouldn't give you the sweat of his..." He paused here to rephrase his metaphor, "...wouldn't give you the sweat off his palm!"

And he continued in this vein, discussing the private life of the famous man so frankly that Esther knew he must be quite drunk. But she listened with interest, wondering how much of this diatribe was true, because the public legend about the famous man was emphatic about his charity. Suddenly, the woman with the chrysanthemums jerked around to get a look at the speaker and Esther felt her giving him a quick but thorough examination before she turned back around.

"So you don't like it?" the man inquired, and it was a moment before Esther realized that he was now directing his attenion to her seat neighbor.

"Well, if you don't like it," he continued, "why don't you get off this bus, why don't you go back where you came from? Why don't you go back to China?"

Then, his voice growing jovial, as though he were certain of the support of the bus in this at least, he embroidered on this theme with a new eloquence, "Why don't you go back to China, where you can be coolies working in your bare feet out in the rice fields? You can let your pigtails grow and grow in China. Alla samee, mama, no tickee no shirtee. Ha, pretty good, no tickee no shirtee!"

He chortled with delight and seemed to be looking around the bus for approval. Then some memory caused him to launch on a new idea "Or why don't you go back to Trinidad? They got Chinks running the whole she-bang in Trinidad. Every place you go in Trinidad..."

As he talked on, Esther, pretending to look out the window, felt the tenseness in the body of the woman beside her. The only movement from her was the trembling of the chrysanthemums with the motion of the bus. Without turning her head, Esther was also aware that a man, a mild-looking man with thinning hair and glasses, on one of the front benches was smiling at the woman and shaking his head mournfully in sympathy, but she doubted whether the woman saw.

Esther herself, while believing herself properly annoyed with the speaker and sorry for the old couple, felt quite detached. She found herself wondering whether the man meant her in his exclusion order or whether she was identifiably Japanese. Of course, he was not sober enough to be interested in such fine distinctions, but it did matter, she decided, because she was Japanese, not Chinese, and therefore in the present case immune. Then she was startled to realize that what she was actually doing was gloating over the fact that the drunken man had specified the Chinese as the unwanted.

Briefly, there bobbled on her memory the face of an elderly Oriental man whom she had once seen from a streetcar on her way home from work. (This was not long after she had returned to Los Angeles from the concentration camp in Arkansas and been lucky enough to get a clerical job with the Community Chest.) The old man was on a concrete island at Seventh and Broadway, waiting for his streetcar. She had looked down on him benignly as a fellow Oriental, from her seat by the window, then been suddenly thrown for a loop by the legend on a large lapel button on his jacket. I AM KOREAN, said the button.

Heat suddenly rising to her throat, she had felt angry, then desolate and betrayed. True, reason had returned to ask whether she might not, under the circumstances, have worn such a button herself. She had heard rumors of I AM CHINESE buttons. So it was true then; why not I AM KOREAN buttons, too? Wryly, she wished for an I AM JAPANESE button, just to be able to call the man's attention to it, "Look at me!" But perhaps the man didn't even read English, perhaps he had been actually threatened, perhaps it was not his doing—his solicitous children perhaps had urged him to wear the badge.

Trying now to make up for her moral shabbiness, she turned towards the little woman and smiled at her across the chrysanthemums, shaking her head a little to get across her message (don't pay any attention to that stupid old drunk, he doesn't know what he's saying, let's take things like this in our stride). But the woman, in turn looking at her, presented a face so impassive yet cold, and eyes so expressionless yet hostile, that Esther's overture fell quite flat.

Okay, okay, if that's the way you feel about it, she thought to herself. Then the bus made another stop and she heard the man proclaim ringingly, "So clear out, all of you, and remember to take every last one of your slant-eyed pickaninnies with you!" This was his final advice as he stepped down from the middle door. The bus remained at the stop long enough for Esther to watch the man cross the street with a slightly exploring step. Then, as it started up again, the bespectacled man in front stood up to go and made a clumsy speech to the Chinese couple and possibly to Esther. "I want you to know," he said, "that we aren't all like that man. We don't all feel the way he does. We believe in an America that is a melting pot of all sorts of people. I'm originally Scotch and French myself." With that, he came over and shook the hand of the Chinese man.

"And you, young lady," he said to the girl behind Esther, "you deserve a Purple Heart or something for having to put up with that sitting beside you."

Then he, too, got off.

The rest of the ride was uneventful and Esther stared out the window with eyes that did not see. Getting off at last at the soldiers' home, she was aware of the Chinese couple getting off after her, but she avoided looking at them. Then, while she was walking towards Buro's hospital very quickly, there arose in her mind some words she had once read and let stick in her craw: People say, do not regard what he says, now he is in liquor. Perhaps it is the only time he ought to be regarded.

These words repeated themselves until her saving detachment was gone every bit and she was filled once again in her life with the infuriatingly helpless, insidiously sickening sensation of there being in the world nothing solid she could put her finger on, nothing solid she could come to grips with, nothing solid she could sink her teeth into, nothing solid.

When she reached Buro's room and caught sight of his welcoming face, she ran to his bed and broke into sobs that she could not control.

Buro was amazed because it was hardly her first visit and she had never shown such weakness before, but solving the mystery handily, he patted her head, looked around smugly at his roommates, and asked tenderly, "What's the matter? You've been missing me a whole lot, huh?" And she, finally drying her eyes, sniffed and nodded and bravely smiled and answered him with the question, yes, weren't women silly?

(1950)

The Brown House

I n California that year the strawberries were marvelous. As large as teacups, they were so juicy and sweet that Mrs. Hattori, making her annual batch of jam, found she could cut down on the sugar considerably. "I suppose this is supposed to be the compensation," she said to her husband, whom she always politely called Mr. Hattori.

"Some compensation!" Mr. Hattori answered.

At that time they were still on the best of terms. It was only later, when the season ended as it had begun, with the market price for strawberries so low nobody bothered to pick number twos, that they began quarreling for the first time in their life together. What provoked the first quarrel and all the rest was that Mr. Hattori, seeing no future in strawberries, began casting around for a way to make some quick cash. Word somehow came to him that there was in a neighboring town a certain house where fortunes were made overnight, and he hurried there at the first opportunity.

It happened that Mrs. Hattori and all the little Hattoris, five of them, all boys and born about a year apart, were with him when he paid his first visit to the house. When he told them to wait in the car, saying he had a little business to transact inside and would return in a trice, he truly meant what he said. He intended only to give the place a brief inspection in order to familiarize himself with it. This was at two o'clock in the afternoon, however, and when he finally made his way back to the car, the day was already so dim that he had to grope around a bit for the door handle.

The house was a large but simple clapboard, recently painted brown and relieved with white window frames. It sat under several enormous eucalyptus trees in the foreground of a few acres of asparagus. To the rear of the house was a ramshackle barn whose spacious blue roof advertised in great yellow letters a ubiquitous brand of physic. Mrs. Hattori, peering toward the house with growing impatience, could not understand what was keeping her husband. She watched other cars either drive into the yard or park along the highway and she saw all sorts of people—white, yellow, brown, and black—enter the house. Seeing very few people leave, she got the idea that her husband was attending a meeting or a party.

So she was more curious than furious that first time when Mr. Hattori got around to returning to her and the children. To her rapid questions Mr. Hattori replied slowly, pensively: it was a gambling den run by a Chinese family under cover of asparagus, he said, and he had been winning at first, but his luck had suddenly turned, and that was why he had taken so long—he had been trying to win back his original stake at least.

"How much did you lose?" Mrs. Hattori asked dully.

"Twenty-five dollars," Mr. Hattori said.

"Twenty-five dollars!" exclaimed Mrs. Hattori. "Oh, Mr. Hattori, what have you done?"

At this, as though at a prearranged signal, the baby in her arms began wailing, and the four boys in the back seat began complaining of hunger. Mr. Hattori gritted his teeth and drove on. He told himself that this being assailed on all sides by bawling, whimpering, and murderous glances was no less than he deserved. Never again, he said to himself; he had learned his lesson.

Nevertheless, his car, with his wife and children in it, was parked near the brown house again the following week. This was because he had dreamed a repulsive dream in which a fat white snake had uncoiled and slithered about and everyone knows that a white-snake dream is a sure omen of good luck in games of chance. Even Mrs. Hattori knew this. Besides, she felt a little guilty about having nagged him so bitterly about the twenty-five dollars. So Mr. Hattori entered the brown house again on condition that he would return in a half hour, surely enough time to test the white snake. When he failed to return after an hour, Mrs. Hattori sent Joe, the oldest boy, to the front door to inquire after his father. A Chinese man came to open the door of the grille, looked at Joe, said, "Sorry, no kids in here," and clacked it to.

When Joe reported back to his mother, she sent him back again and this time a Chinese woman looked out and said, "What you want, boy?" When he asked for his father, she asked him to wait, then returned with him to the car, carrying a plate of Chinese cookies. Joe, munching one thick biscuit as he led her to the car, found its flavor and texture very strange; it was unlike either its American or Japanese counterpart so that he could not decide whether he liked it or not.

Although the woman was about Mrs. Hattori's age, she immediately called the latter "mama," assuring her that Mr. Hattori would be coming soon, very soon. Mrs. Hattori, mortified, gave excessive thanks for the cookies which she would just as soon have thrown in the woman's face. Mrs. Wu, for so she introduced herself, left them after wagging her head in amazement that Mrs. Hattori, so young, should have so many children and telling her frankly, "No wonder you so skinny, mama."

"Skinny, ha!" Mrs. Hattori said to the boys. "Well, perhaps. But I'd rather be skinny than fat."

Joe, looking at the comfortable figure of Mrs. Wu going up the steps of the brown house, agreed.

Again it was dark when Mr. Hattori came back to the car, but Mrs. Hattori did not say a word. Mr. Hattori made a feeble joke about the unreliability of snakes, but his wife made no attempt to smile. About halfway home she said abruptly, "Please stop the machine, Mr. Hattori. I don't want to ride another inch with you."

"Now, mother..." Mr. Hattori said. "I've learned my lesson. I swear this is the last time."

"Please stop the machine, Mr. Hattori," his wife repeated.

Of course the car kept going, so Mrs. Hattori, hugging the baby to herself with one arm, opened the door with her free hand and made as if to hop out of the moving car.

The car stopped with a lurch and Mr. Hattori, aghast, said, "Do you want to kill yourself?"

"That's a very good idea," Mrs. Hattori answered, one leg out of the door.

"Now, mother..." Mr. Hattori said. "I'm sorry; I was wrong to stay so long. I promise on my word of honor never to go near that house again. Come, let's go home now and get some supper."

"Supper!" said Mrs. Hattori. "Do you have any money for groceries?"

"I have enough for groceries," Mr. Hattori confessed.

Mrs. Hattori pulled her leg back in and pulled the door shut. "You see!" she cried triumphantly. "You see!"

The next time, Mrs. Wu brought out besides the cookies a paper sackful of Chinese firecrackers for the boys. "This is America," Mrs. Wu said to Mrs. Hattori. "China and Japan have war, all right, but (she shrugged) it's not our fault. You understand?"

Mrs. Hattori nodded, but she did not say anything because she did not feel her English up to the occasion.

"Never mind about the firecrackers or the war," she wanted to say.

"Just inform Mr. Hattori that his family awaits without."

Suddenly Mrs. Wu, who out of the corner of her eye had been examining another car parked up the street, whispered, "Cops!" and ran back into the house as fast as she could carry her amplitude. Then the windows and doors of the brown house began to spew out all kinds of people—white, yellow, brown, and black—who either got into cars and drove frantically away or ran across the street to dive into the field of tall dry weeds. Before Mrs. Hattori and the boys knew what was happening, a Negro man opened the back door of their car and jumped in to crouch at the boys' feet.

The boys, who had never seen such a dark person at close range before, burst into terrified screams, and Mrs. Hattori began yelling too, telling the man to get out, get out. The panting man clasped his hands together and beseeched Mrs. Hattori, "Just let me hide in here until the police go away! I'm asking you to save me from jail!"

Mrs. Hattori made a quick decision. "All right," she said in her tortured English. "Go down, hide!" Then, in Japanese, she assured her sons that this man meant them no harm and ordered them to cease crying, to sit down, to behave, lest she be tempted to give them something to cry about. The policemen had been inside the house about fifteen minutes when Mr. Hattori came out. He had been thoroughly frightened, but now he managed to appear jaunty as he told his wife how he had cleverly thrust all incriminating evidence into a nearby vase of flowers and thus escaped arrest. "They searched me and told me I could go," he said. "A lot of others weren't so lucky. One lady fainted."

They were almost a mile from the brown house before the man in back said, "Thanks a million. You can let me off here."

Mr. Hattori was so surprised that the car screeched when it stopped. Mrs. Hattori hastily explained, and the man, pausing on his way out, searched for words to emphasize his gratitude. He had always been, he said, a friend of the Japanese people; he knew no race so cleanly, so well-mannered, so downright nice. As he slammed the door shut, he put his hand on the arm of Mr. Hattori, who was still dumfounded, and promised never to forget this act of kindness.

"What we got to remember," the man said, "is that we all got to die sometime. You might be a king in silk shirts or riding a white horse, but we all got to die sometime."

Mr. Hattori, starting up the car again, looked at his wife in reproach. "A *kurombo!*" he said. And again, " A *kurombo!*" He pretended to be victim to a shudder.

"You had no compunctions about that, Mr. Hattori," she reminded him, "when you were inside that house."

"That's different," Mr. Hattori said.

"How so?" Mrs. Hattori inquired.

The quarrel continued through supper at home, touching on a large variety of subjects. It ended in the presence of the children with Mr. Hattori beating his wife so severely that he had to take her to the doctor to have a few ribs taped. Both in their depths were dazed and shaken that things should have come to such a pass.

A few weeks after the raid the brown house opened for business as usual, and Mr. Hattori took to going there alone. He no longer waited for weekends but found all sorts of errands to go on during the week which took him in the direction of the asparagus farm. There were nights when he did not bother to come home at all.

On one such night Mrs. Hattori confided to Joe, because he was the eldest, "Sometimes I lie awake at night and wish for death to overtake me in my sleep. That would be the easiest way." In response Joe wept, principally because he felt tears were expected of him. Mrs. Hattori, deeply moved by his evident commiseration, begged his pardon for burdening his childhood with adult sorrows. Joe was in the first grade that year, and in his sleep he dreamed mostly about school. In one dream that recurred he found himself walking in nakedness and in terrible shame among his closest schoolmates.

At last Mrs. Hattori could bear it no longer and went away. She took the baby, Sam, and the boy born before him, Ed (for the record, the other two were named Bill and Ogden), to one of her sisters living in a town about thirty miles distant. Mr. Hattori was shocked and immediately went after her, but her sister refused to let him in the house. "Monster!" this sister said to him from the other side of the door.

Defeated, Mr. Hattori returned home to reform. He worked passionately out in the fields from morning to night, he kept the house spick-and-span, he fed the remaining boys the best food he could buy, and he went out of his way to keep several miles clear of the brown house. This went on for five days, and on the sixth day, one of the Hattoris' nephews, the son of the vindictive lady with whom Mrs. Hattori was taking refuge, came to bring Mr. Hattori a message. The nephew, who was about seventeen at the time, had started smoking cigarettes when he was thirteen. He liked to wear his amorphous hat on the back of his head, exposing a coiffure neatly parted in the middle which looked less like hair than like a painted wig, so unstintingly applied was the pomade which held it together. He kept his hands in his pockets, straddled the ground, and let his cigarette dangle to one side of his mouth as he said to Mr. Hattori, "Your wife's taken a powder."

The world actually turned black for an instant for Mr. Hattori as he searched giddily in his mind for another possible interpretation of this ghastly announcement. "Poison?" he queried, a tremor in his knees.

The nephew cackled with restraint. "Nope, you dope," he said. "That means she's leaving your bed and board."

"Talk in Japanese," Mr. Hattori ordered, "and quit trying to be so smart."

Abashed, the nephew took his hands out of his pockets and assisted his meager Japanese with nervous gestures. Mrs. Hattori, he managed to convey, had decided to leave Mr. Hattori permanently and had sent him to get Joe and Bill and Ogden.

"Tell her to go jump in the lake," Mr. Hattori said in English, and in Japanese, "Tell her if she wants the boys, to come back and make a home for them. That's the only way she can ever have them."

Mrs. Hattori came back with Sam and Ed that same night, not only because she had found she was unable to exist without her other sons but because the nephew had glimpsed certain things which indicated that her husband had seen the light. Life for the family became very sweet then because it had lately been so very bitter, and Mr. Hattori went nowhere near the brown house for almost a whole month. When he did resume his visits there, he spaced them frugally and remembered (although this cost him cruel effort) to stay no longer than an hour each time.

One evening Mr. Hattori came home like a madman. He sprinted up the front porch, broke into the house with a bang, and began whirling around the parlor like a human top. Mrs. Hattori dropped her mending and the boys their toys to stare at this phenomenon.

"Yippee," said Mr. Hattori," banzai, yippee, banzai." Thereupon, he fell dizzily to the floor.

"What is it, Mr. Hattori; are you drunk?" Mrs. Hattori asked, coming to help him up.

"Better than that, mother," Mr. Hattori said, pushing her back to her chair. It was then they noticed that he was holding a brown paper bag in one hand. And from this bag, with the exaggerated ceremony of a magician pulling rabbits from a hat, he began to draw out stack after stack of green bills. These he deposited deliberately, one by one, on Mrs. Hattori's tense lap until the sack was empty and she was buried under a pile of money.

"Explain..." Mrs. Hattori gasped.

"I won it! In the lottery! Two thousand dollars! We're rich!" Mr. Hattori explained.

There was a hard silence in the room as everyone looked at the treasure on Mrs. Hattori's lap. Mr. Hattori gazed raptly, the boys blinked in bewilderment, and Mrs. Hattori's eyes bulged a little. Suddenly, without warning, Mrs. Hattori leaped up and vigorously brushed off the front of her clothing, letting the stacks fall where they might. For a moment she clamped her lips together fiercely and glared at her husband. But there was no wisp of steam that curled out from her nostrils and disappeared toward the ceiling; this was just a fleeting illusion that Mr. Hattori had. Then, "You have no conception, Mr. Hattori!" she hissed. "You have absolutely no conception!"

Mr. Hattori was resolute in refusing to burn the money, and Mrs. Hattori eventually adjusted herself to his keeping it. Thus, they increased their property by a new car, a new rug, and their first washing machine. Since these purchases were all made on the convenient installment plan and the two thousand dollars somehow melted away before they were aware of it, the car and the washing machine were claimed by a collection agency after a few months. The rug remained, however, as it was a fairly cheap one and had already eroded away in spots to show the bare weave beneath. By that time it had become an old habit for Mrs. Hattori and the boys to wait outside the brown house in their original car and for Joe to be commissioned periodically to go to the front door to ask for his father. Joe and his brothers did not mind the long experience too much because they had acquired a taste for Chinese cookies. Nor, really, did Mrs. Hattori, who was pregnant again. After a fashion, she became quite attached to Mrs. Wu who, on her part, decided she had never before encountered a woman with such bleak eyes.

(1951)

Yoneko's Earthquake

Yoneko Hosoume became a free-thinker on the night of March 10, 1933, only a few months after her first actual recognition of God. Ten years old at the time, of course she had heard rumors about God all along, long before Marpo came. Her cousins who lived in the city were all Christians, living as they did right next door to a Baptist church exclusively for Japanese people. These city cousins, of whom there were several, had been baptized en masse and were very proud of their condition. Yoneko was impressed when she heard of this and thereafter was given to referring to them as "my cousins, the Christians" She, too, yearned at times after Christianity, but she realized the absurdity of her whim, seeing that there was no Baptist church for Japanese in the rural community she lived in. Such a church would have been impractical, moreover, since Yoneko, her father, her mother, and her little brother Seigo were the only Japanese thereabouts. They were the only ones, too, whose agriculture was so diverse as to include blackberries, cabbages, rhubarb, potatoes, cucumbers, onions, and canteloupes. The rest of the countryside there was like one vast orange grove.

Yoneko had entered her cousins' church once, but she could not recall the sacred occasion without mortification. It had been one day when the cousins had taken her and Seigo along with them to Sunday school. The church was a narrow wooden building, mysterious-looking because of its unusual bluish-gray paint and its steeple, but the basement schoolroom inside had been disappointingly ordinary, with desks, a blackboard, and erasers. They had all sung "Let Us Gather at the River" in Japanese. This goes:

> Mamonaku kanata no
> Nagare no soba de
> Tanoshiku ai-masho
> Mata tomodachi to
>
> Mamonaku ai-masho
> Kirei-na, kirei-na kawa de

Tanoshiku ai-masho
Mata tomodachi to.

Yoneko had not known the words at all, but always clever in such situations, she had opened her mouth and grimaced nonchalantly to the rhythm. What with everyone else singing at the top of his lungs, no one had noticed that she was not making a peep. Then everyone had sat down again and the man had suggested, "Let us pray." Her cousins and the rest had promptly curled their arms on the desks to make nests for their heads, and Yoneko had done the same. But not Seigo. Because when the room had become so still that one was aware of the breathing, the creaking, and the chittering in the trees outside, Seigo, sitting with her, had suddenly flung his arm around her neck and said with concern, "Sis, what are you crying for? Don't cry." Even the man had laughed and Yoneko had been terribly ashamed that Seigo should thus disclose them to be interlopers. She had pinched him fiercely and he had begun to cry, so she had had to drag him outside, which was a fortunate move, because he had immediately wet his pants. But he had been only three then, so it was not very fair to expect dignity of him.

So it remained for Marpo to bring the word of God to Yoneko — Marpo with the face like brown leather, the thin mustache like Edmund Lowe's, and the rare, breathtaking smile like white gold. Marpo, who was twenty-seven years old, was a Filipino and his last name was lovely, something like Humming Wing, but no one ever ascertained the spelling of it. He ate principally rice, just as though he were Japanese, but he never sat down to the Hosoume table, because he lived in the bunkhouse out by the barn and cooked on his own kerosene stove. Once Yoneko read somewhere that Filipinos trapped wild dogs, starved them for a time, then, feeding them mountains of rice, killed them at the peak of their bloatedness, thus insuring themselves meat ready to roast, stuffing and all, without further ado. This, the book said, was considered a delicacy. Unable to hide her disgust and her fascination, Yoneko went straightway to Marpo and asked, "Marpo, is it true that you eat dogs?", and he, flashing that smile, answered, "Don't be funny, honey!" This caused her no end of amusement, because it was a poem, and she completely forgot about the wild dogs.

Well, there seemed to be nothing Marpo could not do. Mr. Hosoume said Marpo was the best hired man he had ever had, and he said this often, because it was an irrefutable fact among Japanese in general that Filipinos in general were an indolent lot. Mr. Hosoume ascribed Marpo's industry to his having grown up in Hawaii, where there is known to be considerable Japanese influence. Marpo had gone to a missionary school there and he owned a Bible given him by one of his teachers. This had black leather covers that gave as easily as cloth, golden edges, and a slim purple ribbon for a marker. He always kept it on the little table by his bunk, which was not a bed with springs but a low, three-plank shelf with a mattress only. On the first page of the book, which was stiff and black, his teacher had written in large swirls of white ink, "As we draw near to God, He will draw near to us."

What, for instance, could Marpo do? Why, it would take an entire, leisurely evening to go into his accomplishments adequately, because there was not only Marpo the Christian and Marpo the best hired man, but Marpo the athlete, Marpo the musician (both instrumental and vocal), Marpo the artist, and Marpo the radio technician:

(1) As an athlete, Marpo owned a special pair of black shoes, equipped with sharp nails on the soles, which he kept in shape with the regular application of neatsfoot oil. Putting these on, he would dash down the dirt road to the highway, a distance of perhaps half a mile, and back again. When he first came to work for the Hosoumes, he undertook this sprint every evening before he went to get his supper, but as time went on he referred to these shoes less and less and in the end, when he left, he had not touched them for months. He also owned a muscle-builder sent him by Charles Atlas which, despite his unassuming size, he could stretch the length of his outspread arms; his teeth gritted then and his whole body became temporarily victim to a jerky vibration. (2) As an artist, Marpo painted larger-than-life water colors of his favorite movie stars, all of whom were women and all of whom were blonde, like Ann Harding and Jean Harlow, and tacked them up on his walls. He also made for Yoneko a folding contraption of wood holding two pencils, one with lead and one without, with which she, too, could obtain double-sized likenesses of any picture she wished. It was a fragile instrument, however, and Seigo splintered it to pieces one day when Yoneko was away at school. He claimed he was only trying to copy Boob McNutt from the funny paper when it failed. (3) As a musician, Marpo owned a violin for which he had paid over one hundred dollars. He kept this in a case whose lining was red velvet, first wrapping it gently in a brilliant red silk scarf. This scarf, which weighed nothing, he tucked under his chin when he played, gathering it up delicately by the center and flicking it once to unfurl it — a gesture Yoneko prized. In addition to this, Marpo was a singer, with a soft tenor which came out in professional quavers and rolled r's when he applied a slight pressure to his Adam's apple with

thumb and forefinger. His violin and vocal repertoire consisted of the same numbers, mostly hymns and Irish folk airs. He was especially addicted to "The Rose of Tralee" and the "Londonderry Air." (4) Finally, as a radio technician who had spent two previous winters at a specialists' school in the city, Marpo had put together a bulky table-size radio which brought in equal proportions of static and entertainment. He never got around to building a cabinet to house it and its innards of metal and glass remained public throughout its lifetime. This was just as well, for not a week passed without Marpo's deciding to solder one bit or another. Yoneko and Seigo became a part of the great listening audience with such fidelity that Mr. Hosoume began remarking the fact that they dwelt more with Marpo than with their own parents. He eventually took a serious view of the matter and bought the naked radio from Marpo, who thereupon put away his radio manuals and his soldering iron in the bottom of his steamer trunk and divided more time among his other interests.

However, Marpo's versatility was not revealed, as it is here, in a lump. Yoneko uncovered it fragment by fragment every day, by dint of unabashed questions, explorations among his possessions, and even silent observation, although this last was rare. In fact, she and Seigo visited with Marpo at least once a day and both of them regularly came away amazed with their findings. The most surprising thing was that Marpo was, after all this, a rather shy young man meek to the point of speechlessness in the presence of Mr. and Mrs. Hosoume. With Yoneko and Seigo, he was somewhat more self-confident and at ease.

It is not remembered now just how Yoneko and Marpo came to open their protracted discussion on religion. It is sufficient here to note that Yoneko was an ideal apostle, adoring Jesus, desiring Heaven and fearing Hell. Once Marpo had enlightened her on these basics, Yoneko never questioned their truth. The questions she put up to him, therefore, sought neither proof of her exegeses nor balm for her doubts, but simply additional color to round out her mental images. For example, who did Marpo suppose was God's favorite movie star? Or, what sound did Jesus' laughter have (it must be like music, she added, nodding sagely, answering herself to her own satisfaction), and did Marpo suppose that God's sense of humor would have appreciated the delicious chant she had learned from friends at school today:

> There ain't no bugs on us,
> There ain't no bugs on us,
> There may be bugs on the rest of you mugs,

But there ain't no bugs on us?
Or did Marpo believe Jesus to have been exempt from stinging eyes when he shampooed that long, naturally wavy hair of his?

To shake such faith, there would have been required a most monstrous upheaval of some sort, and it might be said that this is just what happened. For early on the evening of March 10, 1933, a little after five o'clock this was, as Mrs. Hosoume was getting supper, as Marpo was finishing up in the fields alone because Mr. Hosoume had gone to order some chicken fertilizer, and as Yoneko and Seigo were listening to Skippy, a tremendous roar came out of nowhere and the Hosoume house began shuddering violently as though some giant had seized it in his two hands and was giving it a good shaking. Mrs. Hosoume, who remembered similar, although milder experiences from her childhood in Japan, screamed, *"Jishin, jishin!"* before she ran and grabbed Yoneko and Seigo each by a hand and dragged them outside with her. She took them as far as the middle of the rhubarb patch near the house, and there they all crouched, pressed together, watching the world about them rock and sway. In a few minutes, Marpo, stumbling in from the fields, joined them, saying, "Earthquake, earthquake!" and he gathered them all in his arms, as much to protect them as to support himself.

Mr. Hosoume came home later that evening in a stranger's car, with another stranger driving the family Reo. Pallid, trembling, his eyes wildly staring, he could have been mistaken for a drunkard, except that he was famous as a teetotaler. It seemed that he had been on the way home when the first jolt came, that the old green Reo had been kissed by a broken live wire dangling from a suddenly leaning pole. Mr. Hosoume, knowing that the end had come by electrocution, had begun to writhe and kick and this had been his salvation. His hands had flown from the wheel, the car had swerved into a ditch, freeing itself from the sputtering wire. Later it was found that he was left permanently inhibited about driving automobiles and permanently incapable of considering electricity with calmness. He spent the larger part of his later life weakly, wandering about the house or fields and lying down frequently to rest because of splitting headaches and sudden dizzy spells.

So it was Marpo who went back into the house as Yoneko screamed, "No, Marpo, no!" and brought out the Hosoumes' kerosene stove, the food, the blankets, while Mr. Hosoume huddled on the ground near his family.

The earth trembled for days afterwards. The Hosoumes and Marpo Humming Wing lived during that time on a natural patch of Bermuda grass between the house and the rhubarb patch, remembering to take three meals a day and retire at night. Marpo ventured inside the house many times despite Yonkeo's protests and reported the damage slight: a few dishes had been broken; a gallon jug of mayonnaise had fallen from the top pantry shelf and splattered the kitchen floor with yellow blobs and pieces of glass.

Yoneko was in constant terror during this experience. Immediately on learning what all the commotion was about, she began praying to God to end this violence. She entreated God, flattered Him, wheedled Him, commanded Him, but He did not listen to her at all—inexorably, the earth went on rumbling. After three solid hours of silent, desperate prayer, without any results whatsoever, Yoneko began to suspect that God was either powerless, callous, downright cruel, or nonexistent. In the murky night, under a strange moon wearing a pale ring of light, she decided upon the last as the most plausible theory. "Ha," was one of the things she said tremulously to Marpo, when she was not begging him to stay out of the house, "you and your God!"

The others soon oriented themselves to the catastrophe with philosophy, saying how fortunate they were to live in the country where the peril was less than in the city and going so far as to regard the period as a sort of vacation from work, with their enforced alfresco existence a sort of camping trip. They tried to bring Yoneko to partake of this pleasant outlook, but she, shivering with each new quiver, looked on them as dreamers who refused to see things as they really were. Indeed, Yoneko's reaction was so notable that the Hosoume household thereafter spoke of the event as "Yoneko's earthquake."

After the earth subsided and the mayonnaise was mopped off the kitchen floor, life returned to normal, except that Mr. Hosoume stayed at home most of the time. Sometimes if he had a relatively painless day, he would have supper on the stove when Mrs. Hosoume came in from the fields. Mrs. Hosoume and Marpo did all the field labor now, except on certain overwhelming days when several Mexicans were hired to assist them. Marpo did most of the driving, too, and it was now he and Mrs. Hosoume who went into town on the weekly trip for groceries. In fact Marpo became indispensable and both Mr. and Mrs. Hosoume often told each other how grateful they were for Marpo.

When summer vacation began and Yoneko stayed at home, too, she found the new arrangement rather inconvenient. Her father's presence cramped her style: for instance, once when her friends came over and it was decided to make fudge, he would not permit them, saying fudge used too much sugar and that sugar was not a plaything; once when they were playing paper dolls, he came along and stuck his finger up his nose and pretended he was going to rub some snot off onto the dolls. Things like that. So on some days, she was very much annoyed with her father.

Therefore when her mother came home breathless from the fields one day and pushed a ring at her, a gold-colored ring with a tiny glasslike stone in it, saying, "Look, Yoneko, I'm going to give you this ring. If your father asks where you got it, say you found it on the street." Yoneko was perplexed but delighted both by the unexpected gift and the chance to have some secret revenge on her father, and she said, certainly, she was willing to comply with her mother's request. Her mother went back to the fields then and Yoneko put the pretty ring on her middle finger, taking up the loose space with a bit of newspaper. It was similar to the rings found occasionally in boxes of Crackerjack, except that it appeared a bit more substantial.

Mr. Hosoume never asked about the ring; in fact, he never noticed she was wearing one. Yoneko thought he was about to, once, but he only reproved her for the flamingo nail polish she was wearing, which she had applied from a vial brought over by Yvonne Fournier, the French girl two orange groves away. "You look like a Filipino," Mr. Hosoume said sternly, for it was another irrefutable fact among Japanese in general that Filipinos in general were a gaudy lot. Mrs. Hosoume immediately came to her defense, saying that in Japan, if she remembered correctly, young girls did the same thing. In fact she remembered having gone to elaborate lengths to tint her fingernails: she used to gather, she said, the petals of the red *tsubobana* or the purple *kogane* (which grows on the underside of stones), grind them well, mix them with some alum powder, then cook the mixture and leave it to stand overnight in an envelope of either persimmon or taro leaves (both very strong leaves). The second night, just before going to bed, she used to obtain threads by ripping a palm leaf (because real thread was dear) and tightly bind the paste to her fingernails under shields of persimmon or taro leaves. She would be helpless for the night, the fingertips bound so well that they were alternately numb or aching; but she would grit her teeth and tell herself that the discomfort indicated the success of the operation. In the morning, finally releasing her fingers, she would find the nails shining with a translucent red-orange color.

Yoneko was fascinated, because she usually thought of her parents as having been adults all their lives. She thought that her mother must have been a beautiful child, with or without bright fingernails, because, though surely past thirty, she was even yet a beautiful person. When she herself was younger, she remembered she had at times been so struck with her mother's appearance that she had dropped to her knees and mutely clasped her mother's legs in her arms. She had left off this habit as she learned to control her emotions, because at such times her mother had usually walked away, saying, "My, what a clinging child you are. You've got to learn to be a little more independent." She also remembered she had once heard someone comparing her mother to "a dewy, half-opened rosebud."

Mr. Hosoume, however, was irritated. "That's no excuse for Yoneko to begin using paint on her fingernails," he said. "She's only ten."

"Her Japanese age is eleven, and we weren't much older," Mrs. Hosoume said.

"Look," Mr. Hosoume said, "if you're going to contradict every piece of advice I give the children, they'll end up disobeying us both and doing what they very well please. Just because I'm ill just now is no reason for them to start being disrespectful."

"When have I ever contradicted you before?" Mrs. Hosoume said.

"Countless times," Mr. Hosoume said.

"Name one instance," Mrs. Hosoume said.

Certainly there had been times, but Mr. Hosoume could not happen to mention the one requested instance on the spot and he became quite angry. "That's quite enough of your insolence," he said. Since he was speaking in Japanese, his exact accusation was that she was *nama-iki,* which is a shade more revolting than being merely insolent.

"*Nama-iki, nama-iki?*" said Mrs. Hosoume. "How dare you? I'll not have anyone calling me *nama-iki!*"

At that, Mr. Hosoume went up to where his wife was ironing and slapped her smartly on the face. It was the first time he had ever laid hands on her. Mrs. Hosoume was immobile for an instant, but she resumed her ironing as though nothing had happened, although she glanced over at Marpo, who happened to be in the room reading a newspaper. Yoneko and Seigo forgot they were listening to the radio and stared at their parents, thunderstruck.

"Hit me again," said Mrs. Hosoume quietly, as she ironed. "Hit me all you wish."

Mr. Hosoume was apparently about to, but Marpo stepped up and put his hand on Mr. Hosoume's shoulder. "The children are here," said Marpo, "the children."

"Mind your own business," said Mr. Hosoume in broken English. "Get out of here!"

Marpo left, and that was about all. Mrs. Hosoume went on ironing, Yoneko and Seigo turned back to the radio, and Mr. Hosoume muttered that Marpo was beginning to forget his place. Now that he thought of it, he said, Marpo had been increasingly impudent towards him since his illness. He said just because he was temporarily an invalid was no reason for Marpo to start being disrespectful. He added that Marpo had better watch his step or that he might find himself jobless one of these fine days.

And something of the sort must have happened. Marpo was here one day and gone the next, without even saying good-bye to Yoneko and Seigo. That was also the day the Hosoume family went to the city on a weekday afternoon, which was most unusual. Mr. Hosoume, who now avoided driving as much as possible, handled the cumbersome Reo as though it were a nervous stallion, sitting on the edge of the seat and hugging the steering wheel. He drove very fast and about halfway to the city struck a beautiful collie which had dashed out barking from someone's yard. The car jerked with the impact, but Mr. Hosoume drove right on and Yoneko, wanting suddenly to vomit, looked back and saw the collie lying very still at the side of the road.

When they arrived at the Japanese hospital, which was their destination, Mr. Hosoume cautioned Yoneko and Seigo to be exemplary children and wait patiently in the car. It seemed hours before he and Mrs. Hosoume returned, she walking with very small, slow steps and he assisting her. When Mrs. Hosoume got in the car, she leaned back and closed her eyes. Yoneko inquired as to the source of her distress, for she was obviously in pain, but she only answered that she was feeling a little under the weather and that the doctor had administered some necessarily astringent treatment. At that Mr. Hosoume turned around and advised Yoneko and Seigo that they must tell no one of coming to the city on a weekday afternoon, absolutely no one, and Yoneko and Seigo readily assented. On the way home they passed the place of the encounter with the collie, and Yoneko looked up and down the stretch of road but the dog was nowhere to be seen.

Not long after that the Hosoumes got a new hired hand, an old Japanese man who wore his gray hair in a military cut and who, unlike Marpo, had no particular interests outside working, eating, sleeping, and playing an occasional game of *goh* with Mr. Hosoume. Before he came Yoneko and Seigo played sometimes in the empty bunkhouse and recalled Marpo's various charms together. Privately, Yoneko was wounded more than she would admit even to herself that Marpo should have subjected her to such an abrupt desertion. Whenever her indignation became too great to endure gracefully, she would console herself by telling Seigo that, after all, Marpo was a mere Filipino, an eater of wild dogs.

Seigo never knew about the disappointing new hired man, because he suddenly died in the night. He and Yoneko had spent the hot morning in the nearest orange grove, she driving him to distraction by repeating certain words he could not bear to hear: she had called him Serge, a name she had read somewhere, instead of Seigo; and she had chanted off the name of the tires they were rolling around like hoops as Goodrich Silver-TO-town, Goodrich Silver-TO-town, instead of Goodrich Silvertown. This had enraged him, and he had chased her around the trees most of the morning. Finally she had taunted him from several trees away by singing "You're a Yellow-streaked Coward," which was one of several small songs she had composed. Seigo had suddenly grinned and shouted, "Sure!" and walked off leaving her, as he intended, with a sense of emptiness. In the afternoon they had perspired and followed the potato-digging machine and the Mexican workers—both hired for the day—around the field, delighting in unearthing marble-sized, smooth-skinned potatoes that both the machine and the men had missed. Then in the middle of the night Seigo began crying, complaining of a stomach ache. Mrs. Hosoume felt his head and sent her husband for the doctor, who smiled and said Seigo would be fine in the morning. He said it was doubtless the combination of green oranges, raw potatoes, and the July heat. But as soon as the doctor left, Seigo fell into a coma and a drop of red blood stood out on his underlip, where he had evidently bit it. Mr. Hosoume again fetched the doctor, who was this time very grave and wagged his head, saying several times, "It looks very bad." So Seigo died at the age of five.

Mrs. Hosoume was inconsolable and had swollen eyes in the morning for weeks afterwards. She now insisted on visiting the city relatives each Sunday, so that she could attend church services with them. One Sunday she stood up and accepted Christ. It was through accompanying her mother to many of these services that Yoneko finally learned the Japanese words to "Let Us Gather at the River." Mrs. Hosoume also did not seem interested in discussing anything but God and Seigo. She was especially fond of reminding visitors how adorable Seigo had been as an infant, how she had been unable to refrain from dressing him as a little girl and fixing his hair in bangs until he was two. Mr. Hosoume was very gentle with her and when Yoneko accidentally caused her to giggle once, he nodded and said, "Yes, that's right, Yoneko, we must make your mother laugh and forget about Seigo." Yoneko herself did not think about Seigo at all. Whenever the thought of Seigo crossed her mind, she instantly began composing a new song, and this worked very well.

One evening, when the new hired man had been with them awhile, Yoneko was helping her mother with the dishes when she found herself being examined with such peculiarly intent eyes that, with a start of guilt, she began searching in her mind for a possible crime she had lately committed. But Mrs. Hosoume only said, "Never kill a person, Yoneko, because if you do, God will take from you someone you love."

"Oh, that," said Yoneko quickly, "I don't believe in that, I don't believe in God." And her words tumbling pell-mell over one another, she went on eagerly to explain a few of her reasons why. If she neglected to mention the test she had given God during the earthquake, it was probably because she was a little upset. She had believed for a moment that her mother was going to ask about the ring (which, alas, she had lost already, somewhere in the flumes along the canteloupe patch).

(1951)

Morning Rain

I t was a little past nine.

Sadako, seated across the kitchen table from her father, watched him eat his eggs. He had always eaten them in this particular way, he would probably never change. First, he finished at his leisure everything but the eggs—the two pieces of toast, the tomato juice, the coffee—then, with two expert flips of his fork he tossed the two fried eggs, whole, into his mouth, chewed once or twice, then swallowed, and breakfast was over for him. Well, it could be worse, Sadako thought. She remembered a man in a story who demanded two fried eggs for breakfast every morning, one egg with a deep orange yolk and one egg with a light yellow yolk. Even her husband liked his eggs one way and not another; he could not abide fried eggs with a crusty bottom—the underside, as she had learned from bitter experience, *had* to be tender. (She liked crisp bottoms herself.) At least, her father didn't quibble about the manner of eggs served him.

"Well, what are your plans for today, *Oto-san?*" she asked. She asked it pretty well, too; she only had to resort to English for "plans."

Mr. Endo gave the question a lot of thought. He gave everything a lot of thought, or he appeared to, but he never said much. Sadako had time to start washing his dishes before his answer came. She had eaten much earlier with her husband, before he left for work, and those dishes were already done. The baby, right on schedule, was already taking her morning nap. Today, because it was raining, she would have to improvise a wash line inside for the diapers. And there would be no forenoon stroll for the baby. Well, it was just as well. It was always such a job getting the Taylor Tot down the steep outside stairs of the garage apartment.

"*Sa*, I think I'll visit with the Iwanagas this afternoon. I didn't see them the last time. Then there's a movie I want to see at the Fuji-kwan. Don't expect me for supper. I'll eat something down in Nihon-machi."

"Okay." Sadako was rather relieved. Supper times were always uneasy when her father was visiting from San Francisco, where he worked as a gardener for a well-to-do family (it was the same job he had held before the war). She tried her best to keep a pleasant digestible conversation going, but she always ended up tensely, delivering an overly ebullient monologue. Harry, tongue-tied when it came to Japanese, limited himself to asking her to pass the salt and pepper. And her father had never been one for iridescent chit-chat. Oh, once in a while, Harry tried, he really tried, but he always petered out in helpless English. Once or twice, too, her father had tried a bit of English. But the fact was that these two principal men in her life were, as far as communicating with each other was concerned (and that was what living was, was it not, communicating with each other?), incompatible.

"Is there anything you want from down there?" Mr. Endo asked, setting fire to his first cigarette of the day.

"Well, if it's not too much trouble, I think some *manju* would be nice."

"Okay." Mr. Endo smiled at himself for saying so, and Sadako smiled into the dishwater. Each remembered privately, how freely and blithely Mrs. Endo had used the term when she was alive.

"You'd better take my umbrella. This rain doesn't look as though it'll let up soon."

"Is it raining?" Mr. Endo asked, mildly surprised.

"Certainly, it's raining." Sadako turned from the cupboard, where she was stacking dishes. "After all, it's November already. It's about time we had some rain, Los Angeles or no Los Angeles."

Then, sharply, she looked at her father, her mouth agape. "Is it raining? You mean you can't hear that rain?"

Mr. Endo shook his head, no.

They stared at each other for a moment, father and daughter, he not really seeing her and she as though seeing him for the first time in her life.

Then, while Sadako continued to stare at him, Mr. Endo, stepping suddenly to the misted kitchen window, cleared an egg-sized space on it with the heel of his hand and peered out. Sure enough, there was water dribbling steadily from the eaves, and the slender, bare limbs of the thorned stone pear tree down below in the yard stood out black and wetly shining in the whitish air. He closed his eyes, knowing a second's vertigo as he strained with all his might and even then could not hear the sound of that considerable rain, which, all this time, must have been noisly strumming the roof.

"You like the green ones, don't you, the green ones with *kinako*?"

Sadako nodded with unnecessary vigor. She watched him put on his overcoat and then brought him the umbrella. As he was going out the door, she realized she had not said a word to him since she asked him whether he could hear the rain.

"Oh, yes," she said, "get a lot of the green ones, the green ones with *kinako*!" It was only when the baby cried out a second later that she became aware that she had been shouting at the top of her lungs.

(1952)

Epithalamium

For Yuki Tsumagari, the Japanese girl from San Francisco, it was the next-to-the-last day at the Zualet Community on Staten Island. Tomorrow, Madame Marie would drive her to the village station and she would embark on the three-thousand mile journey by bus which would take her back to her mother and father on Saturn Street, to her married younger brother and his wife (with the two little girls who looked just like Japanese dolls), to her friend Atsuko who had been her soul mate since they had first met during the war at the Utah concentration camp called Topaz.

Also, although she did not know it, today was her wedding day. Yet, she should have suspected something unusual. She had awakened in the morning with Hopkins running through her mind:

> The world is charged with the grandeur of God.
> It will flame out, like shining from shook foil;
> It gathers to a greatness, like the ooze of oil
> Crushed...

As bookish as she had been all her life, she had never come to consciousness before with poetry singing in her head. Perhaps this was to be the first and last time. In any case, the lines had sustained her all that strange day long; walking the wooded mile down Meadowvale Lane to meet Marco at the village trolley station (he had phoned and threatened, still drunk, to go away forever if she did not marry him that very day); riding with him on the trolley to St. George; standing before the city clerk in that little room with the podium, the American flag, and the potted palm, where a fellow civil servant had hastily been called in as a witness; promising to love, honor, and obey this inebriated man.

Afterwards, Marco was quite miffed because Yuki had refused to go to his hotel room with him. He went by himself to check out and return the key and must have found a bottle in his room because he came back to the rear stairway, where she had been waiting, drunker than ever. They rode the trolley only as far back as Princess Bay station, and because he was in no condition to take back to the Community, they remained there at the covered wooden waiting bench. He passed out with his head on her lap, and as she sometimes gazed down at that once perfect (many women had sought him), now battered face, flushed and swollen with drink, she thought, "This is my husband." For better or for worse, for richer for poorer, in sickness and in health, till death do us part.

The months since March, when he had first confessed his love, had been alternately lovely and sordid and terrible and sweet. She had got more than she bargained for, certainly. Once they had walked up Meadowvale Lane in the spring rain and stopped every few minutes to cling and kiss, careless of their sodden clothes and the few cars that slowly passed. There was scarcely a nook or cranny of the Community that they had not defiled, as well as the wooded stretch of beach belonging to a nearby monastery and seminary, and various parts of the woods. Against her will? Hardly (she had made no outcry; she could have firmly refused to go for those walks), but she had urgently sensed that it was against God's will, as though some supernatural agent had been sent to deter them from their immorality; each moment stolen for love had been unmistakably tainted.

On the beach belonging to the monastery, where Yuki had been so enchanted on Holy Wednesday and Thursday nights by the sweet, pure voices of the young seminarians as they took turns singing the psalms of the Tenebrae; where she had, amazed, felt the trickle of tears down her cheeks during a couple of the responsories when the black-gowned young men had clustered together (met together as though they might have been in some football huddle) and boomed out:

> ...Latro de cruce clamabat, dicens: Memento mei, Domine, dum veneris in regnum tuum. (The thief from the cross cried out: "Lord, remember me when Thou comest into Thy kingdom.")
> ...Quomodo conversa es in amaritudinem, ut me crucifigeres, et Barabbam dimitteres? (How art thou turned to bitterness, that thou shouldst crucify me, and release Barabbas?)

—it was there that she had learned for herself (pushed down with insistence onto the rocky ground amidst the trees) about man's desire. She had not known that it would be so painful the first time, or so quick. She thought, I am being killed! And she remembered that as a small child, it had taken the full strength of both her grandfather and father to hold her over the Japanese wooden tub of the bathroom for her mother to wash her hair, as she kicked and struggled and screamed, *"Shini-yoru! Shini-yoru!* I'm dying! I'm dying!"

Later (they had not been able to look at each other for awhile), as they sat on the huge damp rocks at low tide, some instinct, so positive that she had blushed for shame, informed her that they had been watched, in shocked silence, by some young seminarian who had come to pray by the ocean in solitude.

It was the same elsewhere. On another stretch of beach, semi-hidden by a semi-circle of rocks, they had either been nearly discovered or discovered by a couple of kids racing their horses up and down the edge of the water. In the woods, those enormous black mosquitoes (Staten Islanders claim that they come over in squadrons every summer from the marshes of New Jersey across the bay), had bitten every inch of her thighs. Near the creek, where she had been so delighted to find earlier that spring (it had been St. Joseph's Day) those first curious shells, striated maroon and pale green, of skunk cabbage, the back of her dress had been streaked with mud. And always there had been the anxiety of being suddenly come upon, of scandalizing the whole Community, and most of all, of giving grief to saintly, gentle Madame Marie.

Thus, she had become a physical, moral, and spiritual ruin. She had secretly endured a miscarriage towards the middle of July, and hadn't been of much help to the Community since then, with general pains in the womb and kidney regions. She had bled for twenty days, and for a few days, she had barely been able to walk. She had hid in her room then, emerging only for meals. How relieved she was to remember that this was the only hard and fast Rule of the Zualet Community, that one show up for the three meals of the day.

Madame Marie, in her wisdom, had early suspected that something was amiss. "Are you having trouble with your period?" she stopped to ask one day when Yuki was making a halfhearted effort to straighten out the Clothes Room. The Clothes Room always needed straightening out— members of the Community were forever trying on this or that item of clothing contributed by its benefactors, and nothing was put back in order. "No", Yuki had lied. She had held up a large brassiere and tried to make a joke of it. "I've never needed one of these," she said. "Once I bought a couple, the smallest I could find, and they just kept hiking up on me and making me uncomfortable." Madame Marie had smiled. "Delusions of grandeur!" she commented. And the inquisition was over.

But the time Yuki had remained in her room for several days, Madame Marie had called her into her own cozy and book-lined room for a conference. Not a conference, exactly. She had glimpsed Marco and Yuki together in Yuki's room, too physically close to each other for mere conversation, and she had decided to tell Yuki a few of the love stories of the Zualet Community during its twenty years of existence.

Many alcoholics had come to the Community to recuperate, she said; a few had stayed on to help in the Work. And several of them had fallen in love with the idealistic young and not-so-young women who, like Yuki, had been drawn there ostensibly by God but probably more because of their own ambiguous reasons, to assist Madame Marie. One young woman had insisted on marrying one who also had the unfortunate compulsion of unbuttoning his fly in public. She had had several children by him before they had separated, and now she bitterly blamed the Community for the outcome. Another young woman had married one who had stopped drinking for two years. On their wedding night, he began drinking again and had not stopped since. That was seven children ago, and she still remained with him, although he had beaten her regularly and although she had had to work all these years as a waitress to support the family. "If I don't love him, who will?" Madame Marie quoted her as saying, and Yuki had been moved to tears. In contrast, there was the wise virgin who, immediately upon realizing that she was coming to regard an alcoholic with unseemly tenderness, had decided to leave the Zualet Community. Now she was leading a happy and useful life with a group of Catholic laywomen.

Madame Marie was trying to dissuade her from marrying Marco, Yuki knew. "But if I give him up, won't that be suffering, too?" she couldn't help asking. Suddenly, Madame Marie shook her head and looked away. "You'll never know how I suffered," she said, "You'll never know…" Then Yuki remembered Madame Marie's published autobiography, the book that had changed her whole life and brought her all the way across the country, in which she had told of the origins of the Zualet Community, of her meeting with René Zualet, the Basque scholar-farmer (now dead), who had eventually talked her into establishing this Catholic lay community where all would live together in Christian love and voluntary poverty, working on the land and studying together, accepting all who came because they had nowhere else to go—the alcoholics, the laicized priests, the mentally disturbed, the physically handicapped, the unwed mothers, the rejected Trappists, the senile, the offscouring of the world—as Ambassadors of Christ. As a young woman, Madame Marie (then Marie Chavy, a carefree Greenwich Village refugee from a convent school) had lived with a man whom she loved very much.

One day, while she was sitting alone on a bench in Central Park, eating a lunch of crackers and cheese, a pigeon (a dove sent from God?) had alighted on her shoulder, and she had experienced, over and above her earthly contentment, an illumination which had convinced her that man had been placed here upon this spinning globe to love and honor the Father, the Son, and the Holy Ghost. Her lover, a confirmed agnostic, had refused to marry her in the Church. So she had no choice but to leave him. And her autobiography had admitted that it had been many, many anguished nights before she had stopped yearning for the consolation of his arms.

So Yuki continued to bleed and confine herself to her room. Madame Marie sent in irrepressible Brigid McGinty, who, with her extravagant Brooklyn-Irish judgments of other members of the Community, could always make Yuki laugh, to cheer her up, but Yuki only succeeded in depressing Brigid McGinty. How could she possibly tell her? And she prayed and prayed, how she prayed, remembering how a woman had been healed of a discharge of years, merely by touching, in complete faith, the hem of Christ's robe. The bleeding stopped on August 5, on the Feast of Our Lady of Snows, which Madame Marie had appointed Yuki's feast day when she had learned that Yuki was the Japanese word for snow. Yuki presumptuously and gratefully accepted this miracle as a feast day gift from God.

She was able then to resume baking bread for the Community, eight loaves a day, but whether because Grace had totally deserted her (bread must be kneaded and baked with *caritas,* or it just won't come out right) or because Madame Marie or somebody had decided to try the heavier whole wheat flour from a nearby organic farm, Yuki removed from the oven batch after batch of wheaten bricks which could have been used for the new chapel Madame Marie had her heart set on building. Once she had been able to bring forth such loaves that someone had remarked, "Say, this is better than cake!"

And Marco became jealous of Chic, a new member of the Community, fresh from serving a term for forgery, who had enthusiastically taken over the cooking. His imagination and his remembrances of his own irregular life as a seaman had created a lively side romance, and his accusations had left Yuki miserable and helpless.

But some of the early weeks had been beautiful, before anyone had suspected that there was the least attachment between this tall Italian seaman from Worcester, Mass., this Marco Cimarusti, who had come to the Community to recover after a bender, and this plain-faced Japanese girl who had been such a serious and devout member of the Community for two years. He was completely sober then, for almost a month, and there were stolen kisses in the morning, the joy of making piles of whole wheat toast for the breakfast table together, and the bittersweet of trying to say goodnight at curfew, loath to leave one another.

One day, when Marco was well and ready to leave the Community, he had gone out to the Battery to see if he could get a seasonal job as engineer on the *S.S. Hudson Belle,* one of the summer excursion boats which twice daily carries tourists and vacationers from such points as the Battery, Yonkers, Jersey City, Elizabeth, and Bayonne, to crowded Rockaway Beach and back, and which even schedules special moonlight dances and showboat cruises on certain nights. Madame Marie had given Yuki leave to go over to the Battery to wait with him till the boat got back in. His seaman friend Manuel, a Negro from Baltimore, who was a steward on the liner *America,* was with him, too, and the trio had sat there on a bench and talked about the warm weather. Meanwhile, a car crashed into a pole nearby and the police discovered it was driven by a couple of men from Seamen's House who had kidnapped a woman tourist, stolen her car, and kept her captive drunk in the rear seat. And in the playground, a little girl was hurt on the concrete, so the police were tending to that, too. Yuki was rather dazed by everything. She and Marco went over to get some coffee and doughnuts across the street, and they came back to sit there in the hot sun on a Battery Park bench, sipping from paper cups and watching the pigeons, waiting for the *S.S. Hudson Belle* to come in, waiting for the *Robert E. Lee.* Manuel was at the scene of the auto accident. When the boat came in, they gladly took Marco on; he waved goodbye from the gangplank, and Yuki noticed that he sure could have used a haircut.

Then Manuel and Yuki talked a bit. "I've knowed that man for five years," said Manuel. "He's my best friend, I guess. But the way he is, when he's drinking, you can't trust him with a quarter to go across the street and come back with a loaf of bread."

Well, to get back to Yuki's wedding day—several trolleys went by and curious passengers stared at this small Oriental girl wearing a blue-printed cotton dirndl and embroidered nylon blouse (the clothes that a generous visitor to the Community had taken off her back and given to Yuki, just because she had commented on how pretty they looked, had been her wedding dress), cradling on her lap the head of this mould of man, big-boned and hardy-handsome.

O bright unhappiness. O shining sorrow. Why this man? Yuki could not understand why she loved him. Because he represented all the courage, moral and physical, which she had always felt she lacked (she was afraid of elevators; she had never had the nerve to learn how to drive a car)? Because in spite of all he had been through (wounded three times in the recent war, he wore a good-sized crater just below his left rib), he retained an enormous vitality? "It's the physical attraction," Madame Marie had said. "He has a gift for work that not many are given. See how he spades the ground out there, with such ease, such grace. Oh, he is wonderfully made!"

Yuki remembered the bull sessions back in San Francisco. After Topaz, as soon as California had permitted the return of the Japanese, her father had resumed his former occupation as a gardener, and she had become chief cook and bottle-washer for a small Japanese daily which printed one page of English and three pages of Japanese. She was allowed a weekly column in which she was free to write as she pleased; this had attracted a bunch of somewhat younger companions who all dreamed of one day writing the Great Nisei Novel, and they had all talked of everything under the sun, mostly trying to analyze one another. Sometimes Yuki had been the one under the floodlight of their probing, and sometimes she had been made very uncomfortable, mostly because she was unmarried at 31 and did not appear particularly anxious to perpetuate an alliance with any male.

"What are you, anyway, a Lesbian? " someone had finally asked.

Yuki laughed. "No, I'd like to get married someday."

"Well, what kind of guy does it have to be? You sure must be particular."

"I read a poem by e.e. cummings once," said Yuki.

...lady through whose profound and fragile lips the sweet small clumsy feet of April came into the ragged meadow of my soul.

If someone would say such a thing to me, I'd melt. That would be the end of my spinsterhood!"

"Do you know something? You're nothing but a shopgirl at heart. 'Lady through whose profound and fragile lips...' Sheer corn!"

(Then was this the why of her total response to Marco—because she sensed that if he had been a poet, he would have confirmed those gratifying lines? But there was no need for poetry; the mere thought of Marco was enough to make her bowels as molten wax. Not that he was exactly the inarticulate man, when it came to recounting his sailing and drinking adventures. But then neither did Marco comprehend why he had chosen her, after so many other women, some of them breathtakingly beautiful, had indicated their willingness to marry him at a moment's notice. As one member of the Community had observed, Marco was the type of man who should have been driving a Cadillac convertible, that expensive wristwatch glinting in the sunlight as he impatiently drummed his left hand on the outside of the door, waiting for the light to change—with yes, some golden-haired goddess by his side. Yet, looking into Yuki's plain brown face, he would say in puzzlement, "I can't understand it. It's like you've got a rope tied around my neck that won't let go." Or, "If I had a million dollars, I'd just sit here all day long and just look at you!")

Yuki had shrugged. "You're a snob. What's so wrong about being a shopgirl? Don't they come under human beings?"

But it was not only these friends that wondered about Yuki. Her mother had sighed over her. "*Komaru-ne...*what a worry you are. What's wrong with Michio-san? He's such a fine boy. He would make a good husband. College education and everything, and a good job as a draftsman for the City." And she would point up the model of her young brother Taro, a moderately successful insurance salesman, who had early married a suitable and sweet girl and had already presented her with two splendid grandchildren.

"Mama, don't worry about me. It's just that I feel in my heart that there are some things I have to do first, before I start having children and settling down."

Her father would side with her. "Leave her alone, Mama. She's happy, she's healthy. What more do you want?"

Usually, each time her mother got onto the subject, Yuki could not help smiling. It always reminded her of the lyric of the mother's fretting in a novel called *The Time of Man:* "Where's the fellows that ought to be a-comen?...A big brown girl, nigh to eighteen, and no fellows a-comen!" A couple of times, the echo in her mind of this singsong plaint, "Where's the fellows that out to be a-comen?" had made her burst out giggling, and her mother, who saw not a whit of levity concerning the matter at hand, had looked very much pained.

One day, however, Yuki had been feeling out of sorts when her mother began on this perpetual theme.

"Maybe I'm a *katawa*, Mama," she had answered tartly. "Nothing but a freak."

Her mother had fiercely denied such a possibility. "You're not a *katawa*! How can you say such a thing? The midwife said you were one of the most perfectly formed babies she'd ever seen!"

Poor Mama. Now what would her mother say? She had been distressed enough when Yuki had announced that she was going to New York, and on such a bewildering mission. She had been absolutely dismayed when Yuki had later written to say that she had begun taking Catholic instruction. But Yuki had for some reason never got around to being baptized. For one thing, to reject Buddhism entirely and to accept the Catholic theory that, as heathens, the most that good Buddhists could hope for was not the Heaven where God, dazzling in all His glory, would be met face-to-face, but merely a Natural Heaven called Limbo, where only a profane serenity awaited—this would be equivalent to rejecting her mother and father, and Yuki could not bring herself to cause this irreparable cleavage. For the time being, she consoled herself that she was in her heart a Catholic, through what Fr. McGillicuddy had described as the "baptism of desire."

Sooner or later, her mother would have to learn that her daughter had married an alcoholic, and a *hakujin* (white) alcoholic, at that. Suddenly, Yuki could not see ahead at all, because she did not care to contemplate either the suffering she would have to inflict or that she herself would doubtless have to undergo. She was leaving the Community tomorrow on the advice of Madame Marie, who wanted her to consult her family before coming to any decision about Marco. She would, of course, be unable to confess today's marriage to Madame Marie (I will write later and explain, she promised herself). Marco will join me in another week or so after he accumulates enough bus fare. After another drinking bout, he had been ousted from the engine room and was now, black bow tie and all, a waiter on the *Hudson Belle*.

Finally, Marco came to enough so that the newlyweds could catch the trolley to their own stop. He promptly bought a bottle at the village liquor store, and they had to take the taxi back to the Community.

On the way, with Marco slumped heavily against her, Yuki kept remembering Hopkins. Perhaps she wanted to believe that this was a sign from God (*it is a wicked and unfaithful generation that asks for a sign*) that this was the way He meant it to be:

> The world is charged with the grandeur of God.
> It will flame out, like shining from shook foil;
> It gathers to a greatness, like the ooze of oil
> Crushed...

> *...And though the last lights of the black West went*
> *Oh, morning, at the brown brink eastward, springs —*
> *Because the Holy Ghost over the bent*
> *World broods with warm breast and with ah! bright wings.*

Anyway, she could not think of an epithalamium that she would more prefer, Hopkins permitting. Incidentally, this morning at Mass, Fr. McGillicuddy had worn red vestments. It was the Feast Day of the Beheading of St. John the Baptist, and in this connection there always came to her mind that very last, that devastating line of Flaubert's *Herodias*, about Iaokanan's severed head: "As it was very heavy, they carried it alternately." The missal had also noted that it was the commemoration of St. Sabina, a Roman widow who had been converted by a maidservant, beheaded under the Emperor Hadrian, and secretly buried. A church had been built on the site of her home on the Aventine in 425. Considered a gem of basilical architecture, it was used as the station on Ash Wednesday. However, the missal had added, it was not certain whether such a woman had existed at all.

(1960)

Las Vegas Charley

There are very few Japanese residing in Las Vegas proper, that glittering city which represents, probably, the ultimate rebellion against the Puritan origins of this singular country. A few Japanese families farm on the outskirts, but I can't imagine what they grow there in that arid land where, as far as the eye can see from a Greyhound bus (and a Scenicruiser it was, at that), there are only sand, bare mountains, sagebrush, and more sand. Sometimes the families come into town for shopping; sometimes they come for a feast of Chinese food, because the Japanese regard Chinese cuisine as the height of gourmandism, to be partaken of on special occasions, as after a wedding or a funeral.

But there are a handful of Japanese who live in the city itself, and they do so because they cannot tear themselves away. They are victims of Las Vegas fever, that practically incurable disease. And while they usually make their living as waiters or dishwashers, their principal occupation, day after hopeful day, is to try their luck at feeding those insatiable mechanical monsters which swallow up large coins as though they were mere Necco wafers, or at blotting out on those small rectangular slips of paper imprinted with Chinese characters the few black words which may justify their whole existence.

The old Japanese whom everyone knew as Charley (he did not mind being called that—it was as good a name as any and certainly easier to pronounce than Kazuyuki Matsumoto) was a dishwasher in a Chinese restaurant. His employer, a most prosperous man named Dick Chew, owned several cafes in the city, staffed by white waitresses and by relatives he had somehow arranged—his money was a sharp pair of scissors that snipped rapidly through tangles of red tape—to bring over from China. Mr. Chew dwelt with his wife and children in a fabulous stucco house which was a showplace (even the mayor had come to the housewarming). He left most of the business in the hands of relatives and went on many vacations. One year he had even gone as far as England, to see London and the charms of the English countryside.

As for Charley, he worked ten hours a night in five-hour shifts. He slept a few hours during the day in a dormitory with the Chinese kitchen employees; the rest of his free time was spent in places called the Boulder Club, the California Club, the Pioneer Club, or some such name meant to evoke the derring-do of the Old West. He belonged to the local culinary union, so his wages were quite satisfactory. His needs were few; sometimes he bought a new shirt or a set of underwear. But it never failed: at the end of each month he was quite penniless.

Not that life was bleak for Charley, not at all. Each day was exciting, fraught with the promise of sudden wealth. Why, one Japanese man who claimed to be eighty-five years old had won $25,000 on a keno ticket! And he had been there only a day or two on a short holiday from Los Angeles. The Oriental octogenarian's beaming face (Charley decided the man had lied about his age; he looked to be more his own age — 62 or so) had been pictured on the front page of the *Las Vegas Sun,* and Charley had saved the whole newspaper to take out and study now and then in envy and hope.

And all the waitresses were nice to Charley, not only because Charley was a conscientious dishwasher (better than those sloppy Chinese, they confided), but because he was usually good for the loan of a few dollars when their luck had been bad. The bartender was also very good to him. When he came off shift at six o'clock in the morning, tired to the bone, there was always waiting for him a free jigger or two of whiskey, which would ease his body and warm his spirit, reminding him sometimes of the small glass of *sake* he had been wont to sip with an appetizer of pickled greens just before supper, after a day's toil out in the fields. (But it seemed as though it had been another man and not himself, who had once had a farm in Santa Maria, California, and a young wife to share his work and his bed.)

Then there had been the somewhat fearful time when the Army had conducted those atom bomb tests in the Nevada desert. Everyone had talked about it. The whole town had been shaken by intermittent earthquakes, each accompanied by a weird flash of light that hovered over the whole town for a ghastly instant. It was during this time that Charley had been disconcerted by a tipsy soldier, who, after their first encounter, had searched out Charley time and again. Although Charley's command of pidgin English was not sufficient to take in every meaning of the soldier's message, he had understood that the man was most unhappy over having been chosen to push the button that had dropped the atomic bomb over Hiroshima.

Indeed, once, tears streaming down his cheeks, the soldier had grabbed Charley by the shoulders and apologized for the heinous thing he had done to Charley's people. Then he had turned back to his drink, pounded the counter with one tight fist, and muttered, "But it was them or us, you understand, it was them or us!"

Charley had not said a word then. What was there to say? He could have said he was not from Hiroshima but from Kumamoto, that province whose natives are described as among the most amiable in all Japan unless aroused, and then they are considered the most dangerous. He could have said that the people of Kumamoto-ken had always regarded the people of Hiroshima-ken as being rather too parsimonious. But his English was not up to imparting such small talk and he doubted, too, that information of this kind would have been of much interest to such a deeply troubled man.

So Charley was doubly relieved when the Army finally went away. The soldier had revived a couple of memories which Charley had pushed far back in his mind. There had been that time, just after the war, when he had been a janitor in Los Angeles' Little Tokyo and he had been walking down the sidewalk just minding his own business. This white man had come out of nowhere, suddenly shoved Charley against a wall, and placed an open penknife against his stomach. "Are you Japanese or Chinese?" the man had demanded, and Charley had seen then that the man, middle-aged, red-faced, had been drinking. Charley had not said a word. What was there to say at such a startling time? "If you're Chinese, that's okay, but if you're Japanese...!" The man had moved the point of the penknife a little closer to Charley's stomach. Charley had remained silent, tense against the brick wall of the building. Then, after a few moments, possibly because he obtained no satisfaction, no argument, the man had closed his penknife and gone unsteadily on his way.

There had been a similar incident not long after, but Charley had talked his way out of that one. Charley had just gotten off the streetcar when he bumped into a Mexican man about his own age. This man, who had also reeked of liquor, had grabbed his arm tightly and cursed him. "My boy, my Angel, he die in the war! You Japs keel him! Only nineteen years old and you Japs keel him! I'm going to keel you!" But somehow a Mexican had not been as intimidating as a white man; hadn't he hired Mexicans once upon a time, been their boss each summer when he and his wife had needed help with the harvesting of vegetables?

"Mexicans, Japanese, long time good friends," Charley had answered. "My boy die in the war, too. In Italy. I no hate Germans. No use."

Wonderingly, the Mexican had released his grip on Charley's arm.
"Oh, yeah?" he had asked, tilting his head.

The magic word had come to Charley's tongue. *"Verdad,"* he had
said. *"Verdad."*

So this man, too, had turned away and gone, staggering a bit from
side to side.

It was not long after that that Charley, dismissed from his janitorial
duties for spending too much time in the pool hall down in the basement,
had been sent by the Japanese employment agency to Las Vegas, where
dishwashers were in great demand.

It was like Paradise: the heavy silver dollars that were as common as
pennies; the daily anticipation of getting rich overnight; the rejoicing
when a fellow worker had a streak of luck and shared his good fortune
with one and all, buying presents all around (the suitcase under Charley's
bed became full of expensive neckties which were never used), and
treating everyone to the drink of his choice.

It was a far cry from Tomochi-machi, that small village of his birth in
the thirtieth year of the reign of the Emperor Meiji. The place had been
known in those days as Hara-machi, meaning wilderness, and it had
been a lonely backwoods in a sector called Aza-Kashiwagawa or
Oakstream. Above his father's tiny house had risen the peaks of Azame-
yama and Karamata-dake; beyond that mountains higher still. Below was
Midori-kawa, Emerald Lake, where abounded the troutlike fish called
ayu. The mountains about were thick with trees, the larger of them pine
and redwood, and he had as a small boy been regularly sent to bring
down bundles of wood.

He still wore a deep purple scar on his leg from those days and there
was a bitterness he could not help when he remembered why. A nail had
lodged deep in his leg, too deep to remove; the leg had swollen to a
frightening size and finally the nail had burst out with the pus. He could
not forget that when he was in agony from the pain and unable to walk,
his mother (that good, quiet woman) had asked, "Will you bring down
one more load of wood from the mountain?"

He had attended school for two or three years, but he was not much
for studying so he had hired out as a baby sitter, going about his chores
with some damp baby strapped to his back. Older, he had worked on
farms.

When he was twenty, he had ridden the *basha*, the horsedrawn car-
riage, to the town of Kumamoto, from thence taken the train to Nagasaki
where he had boarded the Shunryo-Maru as a steerage passenger bound

for America, that far land where, it was said, people had green hair and red eyes and where the streets were paved with gold.

In Santa Maria friends who had preceded him there from his village had helped him lease a small farm (Japanese were not allowed to buy property, they told him — it was part of something called a Gentleman's Agreement between Japan and the United States). A couple of years later, his picture bride, Haru, had joined him and she had been a joy as refreshing as the meaning of her name (Spring), hard-working, docile, eager to attend to his least wants. Within the first year she had presented him with a boy-child, whom they had named Isamu, because he was the first.

What New Year celebrations they had held in this new land! Preparations had begun about Christmastime with relatives and friends gathering for the day-long making of rice cakes. Pounds and pounds of a special glutinous rice, soaked overnight in earthen vats, would be steamed in square wooden boxes, two or three piled one atop the other, over an outside fire. The men would all tie handkerchiefs or towels about their heads to absorb the sweat, then commence to clean out the huge wooden mortar, the tree trunk with a basin carved out at the top. One box of the steaming rice would be dumped into the basin; then the rhythmic pounding of the rice would begin, the men grunting exaggeratedly as they wielded the long-handled wooden mallets. Usually two men at a time would work on the rice, while one woman stood by with a pan of cold water. It was the woman's job to quickly dab water at the rice dough so it would not stick to the mortar or mallets, while the men did not once pause in their steady, alternate pounding.

The rest of the aproned women would be waiting at a long table spread with befloured newspapers and when the rice had become a soft lump of hot dough, it was thrown onto the table where each woman would wring off a handful to pat into shape before placing it on a floured wooden tray. Some of the cakes would be plain, some filled with a sweet mealy jam made of an interminable boiling together of tiny, maroon Indian beans and sugar. There were not only white cakes; there were pink ones, made so during the pounding with a touch of vegetable coloring; green ones, made so during the steaming with the addition of dried seaweed; and yellow ones, which were green ones dusted with orangeish bean flour.

But the main purpose of the work was to make the larger unsweetened cakes, which in tiers two or three high (one tier for each member of the family, topped with choice tangerines with the leafy stems left on) decorated the *hotoke-sama*, the miniature temple representing the Buddha which occupies a special corner in every Buddhist household. On New Year's morning the cakes, reverently placed, would be joined by miniature bowls of rice and miniature cups of *sake*.

Sometimes enough *mochi* was made to last almost throughout the whole year, either preserved in water periodically changed or cut into strips and dried. The sweet cakes would be eaten early, toasted on an asbestos pad over the tin winter stove (when done, the dark filling would burst out in a bubble); the soaked would be boiled and eaten plain with soy sauce or sugared bean flour, or made into dumplings with meat and vegetables. The dried flinty strips would be fried in deep oil until they became crisp, puffy confections which were sprinkled with sugar.

How rosy the men had grown during the cake-making, not only from their exertions but from frequently repairing to the house for a taste of fresh *mochi* and a sip of *sake*. There would be impromptu singing above the sound of the slapping mallets; women chasing men with threatening, floury hands; and continuous shouted jokes with earthy references more often than not.

Then, on New Year's Eve, Haru would prepare the last meal of the year, to be eaten just before midnight. This was *soba*, the very thin, grey, brown-flecked noodles served with *tororo*, the slippery brown sauce of grated raw taro yams. At the stroke of midnight, Kazuyuki Matsumoto (he was not Charley then) went outside with his shotgun and used up several shells to bid appropriate farewell to the passing year.

On New Year's morning, dressed in brand-new clothing, Kazuyuki and Haru would, following tradition, eat that first breakfast of the New Year: the thick soup of fresh *mochi* dumplings, vegetables, tender strips of dried cuttlefish. It was also necessary to take from tiny cups token sips of hot mulled *sake*, poured from a small porcelain decanter shaped like a rosebud vase.

Then it was open house everywhere for almost the whole week and it was an insult not to accept token sips of hot *sake* at each house visited. Sometimes Kazuyuki Matsumoto was so polite that when they somehow arrived home, in that old topless Ford, Haru had to unlace his shoes, undress him, and tuck him in bed.

And the ritual was the same with each friend seen for the first time in the year, each solemn, prescribed greeting accompanied by deep, deep bows:

"*Akema-shite omedeto gozai-masu.*" (The old year has ended and

the new begun — congratulations!)
"Sakunen wa iro-iro o-sewa ni nari-mashite, arigato gozai-masu."
(Thank you for the many favors of the past year.)
"Konnen mo onegai itashi-masu." (Again this year, I give myself
unto your care.)

What a mountain of food Haru had prepared on New Year's Eve,
cooking till almost morning: bamboo shoots, stalks of pale green bog
rhubarb, both taken from cans with Japanese labels; red and white fish
galantines, fish rolls with burdock root centers, both of these delicacies
purchased ready-made from the Japanese market; fried shrimp; fried
chicken; thin slices of raw fish; gelatinous red and white agar-agar cakes,
tasting faintly of peppermint; sweet Indian-bean cakes; dried herring roe
soaked in soy sauce; vinegared rice rolls covered with thin sheets of dried
seaweed and containing in the center thin strips of fried egg, canned eel,
long strings of dried gourd, mushrooms, carrots, and burdock root —
neatly sliced; triangles of fried bean curd filled with vinegared rice and
chopped vegetables; sliced lotus root stems, which when bitten would
stretch shimmering, cobwebby filaments from the piece in your mouth to
the remnant between your chopsticks. The centerpiece was usually a
huge red lobster, all appendages intact, or a red-gold sea bream, resting
on a bed of parsley on the largest and best platter in the house.

But that had been long, long ago. The young Japanese, the *Nisei*,
were so Americanized now. While most of them still liked to eat their
boiled rice, raw fish, and pickled vegetables, they usually spent New
Year's Eve in some nightclub. Charley knew this because many of them
came to Las Vegas from as far away as San Francisco and Los Angeles to
inaugurate the New Year.

Then, abruptly, Haru, giving birth to the second boy, had died. He
had been a huge baby, almost ten pounds, and the midwife said Haru,
teeth clenched, had held with all her might to the metal bed rods behind
her head; and at long last, when the infant gargantua had emerged, she
had asked, "Boy or girl?" The midwife had said, "It's a boy, a giant of a
boy!" And Haru, answering, "Good...," had closed her eyes and died.

Kazuyuki Matsumoto had sent his two small sons over to a cousin of
Haru's, but this woman with five older children of her own had eventually, embarrassedly, confessed that her husband was complaining that the
additional burden was too much, that the babies did not allow her enough
time in the fields. So Kazuyuki had taken his sons to Japan, to Tomochi-
machi, where his own mother had reluctantly accepted them.

Returning to California, Kazuyuki had stopped farming on his own and worked for friends for twenty cents an hour with room and board. Frugal, he sent most of his wages to Japan, where at the favorable rate of exchange his mother and father had been able to build a larger house and otherwise raise their standard of living as well as their prestige in the sector.

For several years Kazuyuki had kept to this unvaried but rewarding way of life. Friends had shaken their heads over his truly self-sacrificing ways; he was admired as an exceptional fellow.

But Kazuyuki, living in bunkhouses with the other seasonal workers who were usually bachelors, gradually came to love the game of *hana-fuda*, flower cards, which relaxed him of evenings, giving him a more immediate pleasure to look forward to than taking a hot bath and going to bed. So the money orders to Japan became fewer and farther between before they had finally stopped. By that time Kazuyuki had wandered the length of California, picking grapes in Fresno, peaches in Stockton, strawberries in Watsonville, flowers in San Fernando, cantaloupe in the Imperial Valley, always ending his day and filling his Saturdays off with the shuffling and dealing of flower cards.

His mother had written once in a while in her unpunctuated *katakana*, unacknowledged (he was not one for writing letters) messages which nevertheless moved him to the core, saying that his sons were fine and bright, but that both she and his father were getting older and that they would like to see him once more before they died. When was he coming to visit them? Finally, his father had died during the New Year holidays; they had found him drunk, lying helplessly there on the steep path home after visiting friends in the village below. Since this had become a common event, they had merely carried him home and put him to bed. But this, as it happened, was the sleep from which he never awoke.

Learning of this news, Kazuyuki had secretly wept. Like father, like son, the saying went, and it was true, it was true. He was as worthless, as *tsumara-nai*, as his father had in the end become.

The shock had the effect of reforming him; he gave up flower cards and within a couple of diligent years had saved enough money to send for his boys. The wages had risen to fifty cents per hour with room and board; the rate of exchange had become even more favorable, so his few hundred American dollars had amounted to a considerable pile of yen.

With his sons by his side to assist him, he leased again a small farm, this time in Orange County, but somehow things did not go well. They tried things like tomatoes and Italian squash. The vegetables flourished, but it seemed that since the man called Rusuberuto had been elected President of the United States, there had come into being a system called prorating in which one had to go into town and get coupons which limited the number of boxes one could pick and send to market. This was intended to keep the prices up, to help the farmer. The smaller the farm, the fewer the coupons it was allotted, so it was a struggle. They lived on tomato soup and sliced Italian squash fried in batter—this was quite tasty, with soy sauce—and, of course, boiled rice, although the cost of a hundred-pound sack of Blue Rose had become amazing. During the winter the fare was usually the thick yellow soup made by adding water to soy bean paste, and pickled vegetables.

At first, too, the relationship with his sons had been a source of distress. They had expected wondrous things of America, not this drudgery, this poverty. Alien, too, to their father, they had done his bidding as though he were some lord and master who expected them to wash his feet. This had annoyed him and he had treated them sternly, too sternly. And both of them had been resentful of the fact that their contemporaries here, the *Nisei,* looked down upon them as *Kibei,* for lacking English, as though there were rice hulls sticking to their hair.

As he had come to know them better, however, he saw that the two were as different as grey and white. Isamu, now nineteen, was quick to pick up colloquial English, eager to learn how to drive the old pick-up truck, fascinated with the American movies which now and then they were able to afford and his father perceived that he was ambitious, perhaps too ambitious, restless for the day when he could own a shining automobile and go on his way. Noriyuki, two years younger, was more like Haru, quiet, amiable, content to listen to the Japanese popular songs which he played over and over on the Victrola (he sang a nice baritone himself as he worked out in the fields). And he spoke nostalgically of his grandmother, the blue-green coolness of Midori-kawa, the green loveliness of the fields of rape and barley in the spring.

Then, after only a little more than a year together, had come the incredible war, and the trio, along with all the other Japanese on the West Coast, had been notified that they would be sent to concentration camps. How uneasy they had been in those days with government men coming in unannounced on three occasions to inspect the small wooden house for evidence of sabotage. In their panic they had burned all their

Japanese magazines and records, hidden the *hotoke-sama,* buried the *judo* outfits and the *happi* coats the boys had brought with them from Japan. They had had to turn in their little Kodak (it had never been retrieved), lest they be tempted to photograph American military installations and transmit them secretly to Japan.

But the Arizona concentration camp, once they became accustomed to the heat and dust and mud storms, was not too unbearable. In fact Noriyuki, with his repertoire of current Japanese songs, became quite popular with even the *Nisei* girls and he was in great demand for the amateur talent shows which helped illuminate that drab incarceration. Kazuyuki Matsumoto settled for a job as cook in one of the mess halls; Isamu immediately got a job driving one of the covered surplus Army trucks which brought supplies to these mess halls; and Noriyuki went to work with the men and women who were making adobe bricks for the school buildings which the government planned to build amidst the black tar-papered barracks.

One day a white officer, accompanied by a *Nisei* in uniform, came to recruit soldiers for the United States Army and Isamu was among the few who unhesitatingly volunteered. He was sent to Mississippi where an all-Japanese group from Hawaii and the mainland was being given basic training and his regular letters to his father and brother indicated that he was, despite some reservations, satisfied with his decision. Once he was able to come on a furlough and they saw that he was a new man, all (visible) trace of boy gone, with a certain burliness, a self-confidence that was willing to take on all comers. Then, after a silence, came small envelopes called V-Mail, which gave no indication of his whereabouts. Finally, he was able to tell them that he was in Italy and he sent them sepia postcards of the ancient ruins of Rome. Almost on the heels of this packet, the telegram had come informing them of the death in action of Pfc. Isamu Matsumoto; a later letter from his sergeant had filled in the details—it had occurred near a town called Grosseto; it had been an 88-millimeter shell; death had been (if it would comfort) instantaneous.

Kazuyuki Matsumoto continued to cook in the mess hall and Noriyuki went on making adobe bricks. After the school buildings were completed—they turned out quite nicely—Noriyuki decided to attend classes in them. As he was intelligent and it was mostly a matter of translating his solid Japanese schooling into English, he skipped rapidly from one grade to the next, and although he never lost the accent which marked him as a *Kibei,* he was graduated from the camp high school with honors.

By this time, Kazuyuki Matsumoto was on the road that would lead, inexorably, to Las Vegas. At first, in that all-Japanese milieu, he had taken courage and tried courting a *Nisei* spinster who worked as a waitress in the same mess hall. Once he had even dared to take her a gift of a bag of apples, bought at the camp canteen; but the woman already had her eye on a fellow waiter several years her junior. She refused the apples and proceeded to ensnare the younger man with a desperation which he was simply not equipped to combat. After this rejection Kazuyuki Matsumoto had returned to his passion for flower cards. What else was there to do? He had tried passing the time, as some of the other men did, by making polished canes of mesquite and ironwood, by carving and enameling little birds and fish to be used as brooches, but he was not truly cut out for such artistic therapy. Flower cards were what beguiled—that occasional unbeatable combination of the four cards: the pink cherry blossoms in full, festive bloom; the black pines with the stork standing in between; the white moon rising in a red sky over the black hill; and the red-and-black crest symbolizing the paulownia tree in flower.

Then had come the day of decision. The government announced that all Japanese wanting to return to Japan (with their American-born children) would be sent to another camp in northern California to await the sailings of the Swedish *Gripsholm*. The removal was also mandatory for all young men of draft age who did not wish to serve in the United States Army and chose to renounce their American citizenship. Kazuyuki Matsumoto, busy with the cooking and absorbed in flower cards, was not too surprised when Noriyuki decided in favor of Japan. At least there would not be another son dead in Europe; the boy would be a comfort to his grandmother in her old age. As for himself, he would be quite content to remain in this camp the rest of his life—free food, free housing, friends, flower cards; what more could life offer? It was true that he had partially lost his hearing in one ear from standing by those hot stoves on days of unbearable ·heat, but that was a small complaint. The camp hospital had provided free treatment, free medicines, free cotton balls to stuff in his bad ear. Kazuyuki Matsumoto was far from agreeing with one angry man who had one day, annoyed with a severe dust storm, shouted "America is going to pay for every bit of this suffering! Taking away my farm and sending me to this hell! Japan will win the war and then we'll see who puts who where!"

So Noriyuki was among those departing for Tule Lake, where, for a time, he thoroughly enjoyed the pro-Japanese atmosphere, the freedom of shouting a *banzai* or two whenever he felt like it. Then, despite himself, he kept remembering a *Nisei* girl in that Arizona camp he thought he had been glad to leave behind. She had wept a little when he left. He recalled the habit she had of saying something amusing and then sticking out her tongue to lick a corner of her lip. He began to dream of her almost nightly. Once, he wired together and enameled with delicate colors a fragile corsage, fashioned of those tiny white seashells which one could harvest by the basketful in that region. This he sent on to her with a tender message. One morning his dormitory mates teased him, saying he had cried out in his sleep, clear as a bell, "Alice, Alice, don't leave me!" In English, too, they said. So, one day, Noriyuki, as Isamu had before him, volunteered for service in the Army of the United States. He spent most of his hitch in Colorado as an instructor in the Japanese language and ended up as a technical sergeant. Alice joined him there and they were married in Denver one fine day in June.

Since the war had ended in the meantime, Noriyuki and Alice went to live in Los Angeles where most of their camp friends had already settled and Kazuyuki Matsumoto, already in Las Vegas, already Charley, received a monthly long-distance call from them, usually about six in the morning, because, as they said, they wanted to make sure he was still alive and kicking.

Noriyuki was doing well as an assistant in the office of a landscape architect; Alice had first a baby girl, then another. Each birth was announced to Charley by telephone and while he rejoiced, he was also made to feel worthless because he was financially unable to send even a token gift of felicitations.

But he would make up for it, he knew. One day his time would come and he would return in triumph to Los Angeles, laden with gifts for Noriyuki (a wristwatch, probably), for Alice (she might like an ornate necklace, such as he had seen some of these rich women wear), and an armload of toys for the babies.

But Charley began having trouble with his teeth and he decided to take a short leave of absence in order to obtain the services of a good Japanese dentist in Los Angeles. He had to stay with Noriyuki and his family, and they, with no room for a houseguest, allowed him the use of the couch in the front room which could be converted into a bed at night. Charley, paid at the end of each month, had brought some money with him, so at first the reunion went quite well. After his visits to the dentist, who decided to remove first all the upper teeth, then all the lower, and then to fit him with plates, he remembered to bring back a gift box of either the rice-cakes and bean confections of all shapes and colors known as *manju*, or of *o-sushi*, containing a miscellany of vinegared rice rolls and squares. He bought a musical jack-in-the-box for the older child and a multi-colored rubber ball for the baby. After a while the dentist asked for a hundred dollars as part payment and Charley gave it to him, although this was about all he had left, except for the return bus ticket to Las Vegas.

About the middle of his month in Los Angeles Charley felt unwelcome, but there was no help for it. The dentist was not through with him. He could hear from the sofa bed the almost nightly reproaches, sometimes accompanied with weeping, that Noriyuki had to listen to. Since his hearing was not too good, he could not make out all that Alice said, but it seemed there was the problem of his napping on the couch and thus preventing her from having friends over during the day, of his turning on the television (and so loud) just when she wanted the children to take their nap, and just how long did that father of his intend to stay? Forever?

Charley was crushed; it had never been his intention to hurt anyone, never once during his lifetime. The dentist, however, took his time; a month was up before he finally got around to inserting both plates and he still wanted Charley to return for three appointments in order to insure the proper fit. But Charley ignored him and returned to Las Vegas, post-haste, to free Noriyuki and Alice from their burden.

Some days before he left, Alice, who was not at heart unkind, but irritable from the daily care of two active youngsters and the requirement of having to prepare three separate meals (one for the babies, one for herself and husband, and a bland, soft diet for toothless Charley) had a heart-to-heart talk with her father-in-law. Noriyuki, patient, easygoing, had never mentioned the sorrows of his wife.

In halting Japanese, interspersed with the simplest English she could think of, Alice begged Charley to mend his ways.

"You're not getting any younger," she told him. "What of the future, when you're unable to work any longer? You're making a good salary; if you saved most of it, you wouldn't have to worry about who would take care of you in your old age. This *bakuchi* (gambling) is getting you nowhere. Why, you still owe the dentist two hundred dollars!"

Charley was ashamed. Every word she spoke was the truth. "You have been so good to me," he said, "when I have been so *tsumara-nai*. I know I have been a lot of trouble to you."

There and then they made a pact. Charley would send Alice at least a hundred dollars a month; she would put it in the bank for him. When he retired at sixty-five, he would be a man of substance. With his Social Security he could visit Japan and see his mother again before she died. He might even stay on in Japan; at the rate of exchange, which was now about three thousand yen for ten American dollars, he could lead a most comfortable, even luxurious life.

But once in Las Vegas again, Charley could not keep to the pact. His compulsion was more than he could deny; and Noriyuki, dunned by the dentist, felt obliged to pay the two hundred dollars which Charley owed. Alice was furious.

Then Charley's mother died, and Charley was filled with grief and guilt. Those letters pleading for one more visit from her only son, her only child, of whom she had been so proud; those letters which he had not once answered. But he would somehow atone. When he struck it rich, he would go to Japan and buy a fine headstone for the spot under which her urn was buried. He would buy chrysanthemums (she had loved chrysanthemums) by the dozens to decorate the monument. It would make a lovely sight, to make the villagers sit up and take notice.

Charley's new teeth, handsome as they were (the waitresses were admiring, saying they made him look ten years younger), were troublesome, too. Much too loose, they did not allow the consumption of solids. He had to subsist on rice smothered with gravy, soft-boiled eggs, soups. But at least he did not have to give up that morning pickup that the bartender still remembered him with. That whiskey was a marvel, warming his insides (especially welcome on chilly winter mornings), giving him a glow that made him surer than ever that one day he too would hit the jackpot of jackpots.

But Charley's health began to fail. His feet would swell and sometimes he had to lean against the sink for support in order to wash the endless platters, plates, dishes, saucers, cups, glasses, knives, forks, spoons, pots, and pans. Once, twice, he got so dizzy climbing the stairs to the dormitory that he almost blacked out and, hearing him cry out, his Chinese roommates had to carry him the rest of the way to his bed.

One day Mr. Chew, coming to inspect, looked at Charley and said with some concern, "What's the matter? You look bad." And Charley admitted that he had not been feeling up to snuff of late.

Mr. Chew then insisted that he go home to his son in Los Angeles for a short rest. That was what he probably needed.

By that time Charley was glad for the advice. He was so tired, so tired. One of the waitresses called Noriyuki on the telephone and asked him to come after his father. Charley was pretty sick, she said; he could probably use a good vacation.

So Noriyuki in his gleaming station wagon, which was only partly paid for, sped to Las Vegas to fetch his father. Charley slept on and off during most of the long trip back.

The young Japanese doctor in Los Angeles shook his head when Charley listed his symptoms. Charley thought it was his stomach; there was a sharp pain there sometimes right between the ribs.

The young Japanese doctor said to Noriyuki, "When an *Issei* starts complaining about his stomach, it's usually pretty serious." He meant there was the possibility of cancer. For some reason, possibly because of the eating of raw fish, Japanese are more prone to stomach cancer than other races.

But the pain in Charley's stomach turned out to be an ulcer. That was not too bad. As for the swollen feet, that was probably an indication of hepatitis, serious but curable in time. Then, in the process of studying the routine X-rays, the doctor came upon a dismaying discovery. There was definite evidence of advanced cirrhosis of the liver.

"Cirrhosis of the liver?" said Noriyuki. "Doesn't that come from drinking? My father gambled, but he didn't drink. He's no drunkard."

"Usually it comes from drinking. Your father says he did drink some whiskey every day. And if his loose plates kept him from eating a good diet, that could do it, that could do it."

So Charley went to stay at the Japanese Hospital, where the excess fluid in his abdomen could be drained periodically. He was put on a low-sodium diet and the dietitian was in a quandary. A salt-free diet for a man who could not eat solids; there was very little she could plan for him, hardly any variety.

Subsequent X-rays showed up some dark spots on the lungs. The young Japanese doctor shook his head again.

"It's hopeless," he said to Noriyuki. "That means cancer of the liver, spreading to the lungs. He doesn't have much time left."

Noriyuki told Alice, who, relieved that the culinary union had provided for insurance which would take care of the hospital bills, tried to console him. "Who can understand these things?" she said. "Look at your mother — dead at twenty-four, with so much to live for..."

Biting her lips, she stopped. She had said the wrong thing. Noriyuki, all his life under his surface serenity, had known guilt that his birth had been the cause of his mother's death.

Thus Charley died, leaving a son, a daughter-in-law, two grandchildren. Towards the end his mind had wandered, because the medication for the cirrhosis had drained him of potassium and the pills prescribed to make up the lack had not sufficed. There was a huge stack of sympathy cards from Las Vegas, from the kitchen employees, the waitresses, the cashier, the sweet, elderly lady-bookkeeper who had always helped Charley file his income tax statements, a cab driver, and a few others who had come to accept Charley as part of the Las Vegas scene. They even chipped in to wire him an enormous floral offering.

The young Japanese doctor would not take his fee (the union insurance had not provided for his services). "The worst mistake I made in my life was becoming a doctor," he confided to Noriyuki. "Life is hell, nothing but hell."

"But you help people when they need help the most," Noriyuki tried to tell him. "What could be more satisfying than that?"

"Yeah, and you see people die right in front of you and there isn't a damn thing you can do about it! Well, at least your father had a good time—he drank, he gambled, he smoked. I don't do any of those things; all I do is work, work, work. At least he enjoyed himself while he was alive."

And Noriyuki—who, without one sour word, had lived through a succession of conflicting emotions about his father—hate for rejecting him as a child; disgust and exasperation over that weak moral fiber; embarrassment when people asked what his father did for a living; and finally, something akin to compassion, when he came to understand that his father was not an evil man, but only an inadequate one with the most shining intentions, only one man among so many who lived from day to day as best as they could, limited, restricted, by the meager gifts Fate or God had doled out to them—could not quite agree.

(1961)

Life Among the Oil Fields
A Memoir

> "They rode through those five years in an open car with the sun on their foreheads and their hair flying. They waved to people they knew, but seldom stopped to ask a direction or check on the fuel, for every morning there was a gorgeous new horizon...They missed collisions by inches, wavered on the edge of precipices, and skidded across tracks to the sound of the warning bell."
>
> —F. Scott Fitzgerald

There has been some apprehension this year about the possibility of another depression such as overtook this country in the autumn of 1929. I was eight years old at the time and was unaware that there were people then who were leaping out of windows to their deaths. But our family was never distant from poverty, so we probably did not have that far to fall.

Over the years, however, I have managed to piece together this or that homely event with the corresponding dates—the Flaming Twenties, the Volstead Act, Al Capone, Black Thursday—and realize that there were signs of the great debacle around us all along.

My mother has given me four pennies to take to school. Two cents are for me to spend, but the other two cents are for candy for my little brother Johnny at home. At noon, a little Japanese girlfriend and I cross over to the little grocery near the school so that I can make my purchases. After due deliberation over the penny Abba-Zabbas, which are supposed to resemble the bones worn through their noses by the black figures on the checkered wrapper, the long white strips of paper pebbled with pastel buttons of graduated hue, the large white peppermint pills, the huge jaw-breakers with the strange acrid seed in the middle, the chicken bones covered with golden shredded coconut, the bland imitation bananas, the black licorice whips, I settle for two white wax animals filled with colored syrup, one for me and one for Johnny, and, always one for a bargain, eight little wrapped caramel and chocolate taffy squares, which come four for a penny. The man behind the counter, white-haired and kindly, gives me one wax candy and four chews, then hands the same to my little friend.

Before I can protest, my friend dashes off with the candy clutched tightly in her fist, the candy which I am supposed to take home to my brother. I sputter my inadequate English at the storekeeper and give furious chase to my friend, who knows what the deal is. But, running like the wind, she has already escaped. The rest of the school day I spend seething about this introduction to incredible treachery and worrying about what to tell my mother.

It does not occur to me to forego eating my share of the candy, to take to my little brother.

It was at the same school, Central school in Redondo Beach, that I once watched in wonderment as two thin tow-headed children, a boy and a girl, delved into one of the trash baskets filled with lunchtime litter. They came up with a banana skin which they gravely shared, taking turns scraping the white insides of the yellow peeling with their lower teeth.

But I don't know why I was attending Central school, when I had begun kindergarten at South school, since we were still living at the same house with the enormous piano and orchard. I do know that I went back to South school subsequently, where, at the beginning of the second grade, I encountered obstacles in being admitted to the proper classroom. On the first day of that school year, I was among the milling children lining up to march into the building. When I tried to line up with the second grade children, a teacher steered me over to the first grade column. I did not command enough English or nerve to argue, but meekly joined the first-graders and prepared to go through the first grade all over again.

After some weeks, though, I must have made enough noise about it at home, because my mother was upset. Since the same bus serviced both Central and South schools, unloading first at Central school, she counseled me to get off at Central school, there to see if the second grade wouldn't accept me. In trepidation I obeyed, but there, too, I was consigned to the first grade. I sat woefully at the rear of the room that day, like one suspended in limbo, while Central school tried to figure out how to handle this deluded Oriental shrimp with second-grade pretensions. As it turned out, probably because of my grassroots revolt, South school found out that I did indeed belong in the second grade. The bus driver came after me in his own car later that day and transported me to South school, where I was finally delivered to the second grade. I was so secretly delighted to be in my proper niche at last that I took steps to make myself known to the teacher. Taking my reader up to her, I asked how to read the word "squirrel" which I knew very well. I guess this was like pinching myself to make sure there was order in the world again, the seconds of the personal attention constituting her confirmation.

When I was still in the second grade, we moved to our last location in Redondo Beach, going a little distance south to a farm among the oil fields. We were not the only oil field residents. There was a brown clapboard house diagonally across the road, first occupied by an Italian family whose home garden included Thompson seedless grapes, then by a Mexican family. Next to a derrick at the far end of the next oil tract to the west lived an older gentleman in what I recall as more of a tent than a house. Once a few years later after we had moved inland, we stopped by to visit with him and found him tending a baby in a canvas swing set up outside his canvas-and-wood abode. It seemed to be a grandchild left in his care. He showed us the special canned milk he fed the baby. Each can came completely wrapped in plain cream-colored paper, so it seemed a more elegant product than the condensed Carnation milk we used.

There was a white family in the corner of a diagonal tract, where we played with the children. A Japanese family with two little ones farmed in the middle of a tract to the north and I remember one day watching the father smearing a poisoned red jam on little pieces of bread in order to kill the rats in his barn. Beyond, I remember visiting a blonde schoolmate named Alice whose older sister was named Audrey.

Our house, bathhouse, barn, stable, long bunkhouse, outhouse, water tower and kitchen garden were set down adjoining a derrick along the country road. Derricks then were not disguised by environmental designers to be the relatively unobtrusive, sometimes pastel-colored pumps that one comes across nowadays. Constructed of rough lumber, tar-smeared and weathered, they were ungainly prominences on the landscape. They reared skyward in narrow pyramids from corrugated tin huts and raised platforms whose planks accommodated large wooden horse heads nodding deliberately and incessantly to a regular rhythm. Each derrick had its rectangular sump hole, about the size of an olympic swimming pool. The reservoir of rich dark goop, kept in check by sturdy, built-up dirt walls, might be a few inches deep or nearing the top. Occasionally a derrick caught fire, but I remember only a couple of times when, off in the distance, we could see the black smoke rising in a column for days.

We must have lived day and night to the thumping pulse of black oil being sucked out from deep within the earth. Our ambiance must have been permeated with that pungency, which we must have inhaled at every breath. Yet the skies of our years there come back to me blue and limpid and filled with sunlight.

But winter there must have been, because there was the benison of hot *mochi* toasted on an asbestos pad atop the wood-burning tin stove, the hard white cake softening, bursting, oozing out dark globs of sweet Indian bean filling. Or Mama would take out from the water in the huge clay vat a few pieces of plain *mochi* which she would boil. The steaming, molten mass, dusted with sugared golden bean flour, would stretch from plate to mouth, and the connection would have to be gently broken with chopsticks.

It must have been chilly January, too, when my father, with horse and plow, dug up the ground. After the earth was raked and leveled, he would pull after him the gigantic pegged ruler which marked off the ground for planting, first one way and then across, so that seen from the sky the fields would have been etched with a giant graph.

Some of the preparation was done in the empty bunkhouse at night, the bulging, thin-slatted crates of strawberry plants arriving from somewhere to be opened up, each damp plant to be trimmed of old leaves and its clump of earthy roots to be neatly evened off with a knife.

Each plant was inserted into the soil where the lines on the ground intersected—first a scoop of dirt out, the plant in, followed by a slurp of water, the dirt and a quick tamping. Once in a while, before the strawberry runners started to grow, we could find tiny red berries to pop into our mouths.

Then with the horse again, my father would make long furrows between the plants. Others, including my mother, would go crawling down the rows with wooden paddles with which to mound the dirt up around the strawberry plants; then they would plug in the roots of the runners at suitable intervals. Regular irrigation would smooth the channels between the rows and, *viola*, there would be the strawberry fields, row upon row thick with green leaves and white blossoms and by early summer gleaming red berries.

Our fields stretched to the east end of that particular tract, to another road whose yonder side was a windbreak of fir trees, but there was an interruption in the center, a long corrugated tin building with a neat sand-and-gravel yard. Also sand and gravel was the compacted narrow road which sliced the tract in half lengthwise and which must have been for the convenience of the oil company. (We used our end of it as a driveway.) The building was visited from time to time by inspectors of some kind but was usually kept locked. I remember entering that building once, but its contents were mysterious and mechanical. I do not know how reliable my memory is in conjuring up a giant hangarful of gas pump-size gauges that stood at attention like robot troops.

My mother learned how to drive among the oil fields. The whole family, which by then would have included three brothers and me, went along in the open car while my father instructed her in the fine points of chauffeuring. Chugging around with her at the steering wheel was for me a harrowing experience, and I insisted on being let off when we arrived at an intersection near the house. I walked home by myself, relieved to be on terra firma. In later years my mother even drove trucks, but she never seemed to have learned how to get across an intersection after a stop without the vehicle undergoing a series of violent jerks and spasms that were terribly disconcerting. Besides, as one endured the eternity it took to traverse the intersection, one knew the whole world was laughing at the spectacle.

It was among the oil fields that we first subscribed to an English-language newspaper. I remember the thud of the newspaper arriving on Sunday morning. First out to the porch, I would open up the funny papers and spread them out right there, to be regaled by noveau-riche Maggie and Jiggs arguing over his fondness for corned beef and cabbage; Barney Google and the dismal, blanketed excuse for a horse named Spark Plug; Tillie the Toiler at the office with her short boyfriend Mac whose hair grew in front like a whiskbroom; the stylized sophisticates of Jefferson Machamer. There were several assortments of little boys who were always getting into mischief. Hans and Fritz, the Katzenjammer Kids, usually got away with murder but sometimes would get caught by the Captain or Mama and soundly spanked, to wail their pain as they felt their smarting behinds. The little rich boy Perry, in his Fauntleroy suit, associated with a rag-taggle gang. There was also a chunky little guy named Elmer with a baseball cap that he sometimes wore backwards. Was it Perry or Elmer who had a chum who was always saying, "Let's you and him fight!", who was always offering to hold coats so the fight could commence? The only comic strip I had reservations about was Little Nemo, a little kid who seemed to spend an inordinate amount of time wallowing in a welter of bedclothes, surrounded by a menagerie of ferocious animals from (I gathered) his nightmares.

We still used kerosene lamps then. One of my jobs was to remove the glass from the lamp and blow my breath into it, so that I could wipe off the soot inside with a wadded newspaper. I remember my mother saying how disillusioned she was to come to America and find such primitive conditions. In rural Japan, she said, her family had already had electricity running the rice-threshing machinery.

Our staples included 100-pound sacks of Smith rice; the large *katakana* running down the middle of the burlap sack said Su-mi-su. The sack must have cost less than five dollars because I seem to hear my mother exclaiming some years later about the price going up to five. We had five-gallon wooden tubs of Kikkoman soy sauce, wooden buckets of fermented soy bean paste, green tea in large metal boxes, lined with thick, heavy foil, with hinged lids. There were quart jars of red pickled plums and ginger root, Japanese cans of dark chopped pickles. The house was redolent with the fragrance of some vegetable or other — cabbage, Chinese cabbage, white Japanese radish — salted in a crock and weighed down with a heavy rock.

But we also bought bread from the Perfection Bakery truck that came house-to-house, fish and tofu and meat from the Italian fish man who would break off wieners from a long chain of them and give them to us as treats. In summer the iceman brought fifty-pound chunks of ice which he hefted to his leather clad shoulder with huge tongs, and we always rummaged around the back of the dripping truck to find a nice piece to chomp on.

We used butter but also white one-pound blocks of oleomargarine which we made butter-colored with a small packet of red powder, mixing and mixing so as not to leave orange streaks hiding inside. Coffee came in a red can dominated by a white-bearded gentleman in a white turban, long yellow gown sprinkled with flowers, tiny black slippers that curled up at the toe. Salt was always in a blue carton with the girl under the umbrella happily strewing her salt into the rain. The yellow container of scouring cleanser pictured a lady in a white poke bonnet chasing dirt with a stick.

Medicines were bought from a tall Korean gentleman who spoke fluent Japanese. He brought us ginseng in pale carroty roots and silvery pills. There was the dark dried gall of a bear for stomachaches; fever called for the tiniest pills of all, infinitesimal black shot that came in a wee black wooden urn in a teeny brocaded box.

The financial world might have been on the verge of collapse, but I was wealthy, well on my way to becoming a miser. In my little coin purse

They told us later (Johnny and I must have been at school) that they had siphoned gasoline from the car to clean the tar baby off.

Indeed, Jemo seems to have had the most traumatic of childhoods during our stay among the oil wells.

One evening my two brothers and I race home from the neighbors. We have about reached the far end of our stable when we hear a car coming up the road. We separate to opposite sides of the road and continue running, my brothers on the side nearest our property and I on the other. The car speeds by and all of a sudden, there is Jemo lying over there on the shoulder of the road.

He does not move. His eyes are closed. His still face is abraded by dirt and gravel. I run the fifty or so steps past the stable and tall barn. The house is set back from the road, from where I, terror-stricken, scream my anguished message, *"Jemo shinda, Jemo shinda!"*

My mother must be putting supper on the table, my father perhaps reading the Japanese paper while he waits. My unearthly shrieks summon the father of the friends we have been visiting. He comes running up the slope to the scene and is carrying Jemo's body towards our house when Mama and Papa finally dash out to the road in response to my cries.

As it turned out, no limbs were broken. He was only stunned, probably flipped aside by the car's front fender. But his concussion and contusions had to be attended to at the hospital in Torrance. When he came home, he was clothed in bandages, including one like a turban around his head and face. When we took him back for a checkup and Papa afterwards bought us a treat of vanilla ice cream and orange sherbet in paper cups, I had to spoon-feed him with the little balsa spoon as we rode home.

My folks thought the hit-and-run driver of the car ought to pay something towards the hospital costs. The *hakujin* neighbor who had come running up the hill was acquainted with the couple in the car, who lived way down the road in a two-story house. He must have seen the car go zooming by, as it frequently did, before the accident and had some kind of foreboding. Else how had he, farther away, reached the scene before my parents even?

My father and the neighbor conferred, and the neighbor offered to try and negotiate a settlement of some kind for us. He came back shaking his head; the couple had refused to accept any responsibility for Jemo's injuries. They said it was all Jemo's fault.

Mama and Papa were indignant. Mostly, it was because such cold-

ness of heart was not to be believed. The couple had not even the decen-
cy to come and inquire after Jemo's condition. Were we Japanese in a
category with animals then, to be run over and left beside the road to die?
My father contacted a Japanese lawyer in the city, who one day came out
to talk first with us and then with the couple. He, too, returned with bad
news: the couple absolutely denied any guilt.

But the scenario was not played out as simply as I have written it.
This is more of a collage patched together from the fragments of
overheard conversations, glimpses of the earnest expressions on the
faces of my father, our neighbor, the young lawyer in the dark suit, their
comings and goings, my own bewildered feelings.

So that must have been the end of the matter. I have no recollection
of the roadster whizzing by our place after that. The couple must have
chosen an alternate route out from the oil fields to the highway.

When I look back on that episode, the helpless anger of my father
and my mother is my inheritance. But my anger is more intricate than
theirs, warped by all that has transpired in between. For instance, I
sometimes see the arrogant couple from down the road as young and
beautiful, their speeding open roadster as definitely and stunningly red.
They roar by; their tinkling laughter, like a long silken scarf, is borne back
by the wind. I gaze after them from the side of the road, where I have
darted to dodge the swirling dust and spitting gravel. And I know that
their names are Scott and Zelda.

(1979)

The Eskimo Connection

I n the late winter of 1975 Emiko Toyama was really surprised when she got a letter from a young Eskimo. It seemed he'd come across a reprinted poem of hers that he'd read in an Asian American publication that was several years old and as a fellow Asian American had taken a chance and written her in care of the magazine.

The surprise was two-fold when Alden Ryan Walunga, for that was his name, identified himself as a prisoner-patient at a federal penitentiary in the midwest. A Yupik, he was only twenty-three years old, young enough to be one of her children. She wondered whether she should write back. What commonality was there between a probably embittered young man and an aging Nisei widow in Los Angeles with several children, three still at home, whose main avocation was not writing poetry but babysitting the grandchildren? He had enclosed with his letter a photocopied prison weekly containing an essay of his and he asked for a "critique."

More reason not to reply. The article was brief but remarkably confused. It was a passionate cry against the despoiling of his native land which somehow turned into a sermon repeating the Biblical prophecy that such an evil was only part of the wholesale corruption to precede the return of Christ, so it was like he didn't know whether to laugh or cry. And the language was imprecise, not enough to set her teeth on edge as sometimes happened, but almost.

Emiko had begun learning rather early to soft-pedal her critical instincts. As a young woman in camp, she had hung out sometimes with people who wrote and painted and she knew what vulnerable psyches resided in creative critters. And it wasn't just them, either. She had a relative who had stopped writing letters for years because, among other things, her husband and daughter had once laughed at her syntax. And Emiko herself had once been actually pummeled by a dear friend whose poem she had made light of. This friend had stopped writing poems for years. People ought to be more callous, she knew, they ought to be more determined. But, alas, most egos were covered with the thinnest of egg-shells.

And then to tamper with words written with feeling was to destroy the feeling, usually.

Nevertheless, against her own better judgment, she wrote a careful note telling Alden Ryan Walunga as tactfully as possible that the essay was eminently worth writing but that the message might be made stronger, clearer, with a revision of language here and there. She encouraged him with the observation that certainly, a strong voice was needed to speak up on behalf of the Eskimo.

He took it very gracefully, but he mentioned that he had studied two semesters at the University of Alaska and that his mother was wondering whether it was all right to send on his Air Force text of Robert Penn Warren's *Modern Rhetoric*. As the sporadic exchange of letters continued, she pieced together enough to learn that he was the third of seven children with two older sisters and four younger brothers, which he attributed to the Eskimo need for survival; that he was being treated for depression (he mentioned massive doses of thorazine); that he attended meetings of Alcoholics Anonymous there at the prison; that he had come to Christ with such fervor that he considered the study of His Word the main preoccupation of his life.

To this end, he had already paraphrased four Pauline epistles using Strong's *Exhaustive Concordance of the Bible* (with Greek dictionary) and he mentioned his greed for other resources like Josephus' historical works as well as the treatises on Biblical psychology and demonology. He wrote that he was frustrated by prison rules which allowed only one book at a time to be borrowed once a month from area libraries. In one letter he said his next borrowing would be a dictionary on the Bible, more "elaborate" than the one he already had.

He also read other things: Victor Hugo's *The Hunchback of Notre Dame*, Fyodor Dostoevsky's *The Brothers Karamazov*, N. Scott Momaday's *House Made of Dawn*, and he asked whether she had read any of Yukio Mishima whom he described as "a Japanese writer who famously and traditionally committed suicide with a sword." He also recommended Peter Freuchen's *Book of the Eskimo* and a Stanford University study of the Alaskan native, as being accurate depictions of his people.

Emiko tried to send him an Asian American literary magazine on one occasion and was taken aback when it was returned to her with a form letter stipulating that she must get permission from the prison chaplain before submitting such materials. So she sent the magazine to the chaplain's office and received a polite note saying that although an exception had been made and the magazine given to the prisoner, the chaplain's office was authorized to pass on religious materials only and other literature should be sent in care of the education department.

She felt something like a cold hand touch her when she received these official notices—that was what being in prison was, was it, the relinquishment of every liberty that those on the outside took for granted?

But Alden Ryan Walunga seemed to be an exuberant spirit even under these stifling conditions. The whole first page of his letter would be taken up with the salutation, thusly:

DEAR EMIKO!
                        EMIKO!
                                            EMIKO!

before the actual letter began on page two. Once, staring at the first page, she was amused to see that with the addition of one letter, she could write him back:

DEAR ESKIMO!
                        ESKIMO!
                                            ESKIMO!

but she decided it would be rather childish and desisted.

In one letter he wrote that a poem he had submitted a couple of years before to a New York magazine called *A.D.* had been accepted for publication. He had been called to the chaplain's office to be shown a $50 check, with the warning that all literary submissions had to first be officially approved. She wrote to congratulate him.

Then, for awhile, there was no word from Alden Ryan Walunga, but Emiko, trying as usual to cope with the needs of her brood, scarcely noticed. Her husband's insurance was adequate if she managed shrewdly, but it was always something—dentist, doctor, marijuana, living together without marriage, distressing report cards, flu, filling out unwieldy applications for college grants, keeping up with the seasonal needs of the yard, a new roof or water heater that had to be squeezed in somehow. Besides these routine cares, something else was in the air, something insidious and seemingly contagious: most of her friends, neighbors, and relatives seemed to be getting divorced, many of them after twenty-five years of marriage or more! If Mits had not died, would they too be undergoing such trauma?

So, when after some months Alden Ryan Walunga resumed corresponding with a somewhat apologetic note explaining that he had been through some kind of spiritual crisis involving "deception," implying a self-delusion, so that he was now back to square one, she answered him with, "So what else is new?" or words to that effect. Without going into detail, she mentioned the discombobulations taking place in her neck of the woods. He wrote back that such upheavals were to be expected, of course, since pandemonium had been prophesied, and he stressed the importance of holding fast to the Lord Jesus Christ.

Alden Ryan Walunga never mentioned the reason for his incarceration and Emiko never asked. If he did not wish to reveal the nature of his crime, she did not wish to know it, but in the back of her mind she decided that he was in prison for forgery. This was because years ago she had an apartment neighbor who had twice been in prison for forgery and he was among her pleasanter memories: he played Bach on the piano but he seemed to be one of the innocents of the world, living about a foot off the ground. She especially remembered him, with his bushy grey hair and horn-rimmed glasses, because of two occasions when he had asked her to remove a sliver from his hand. Both times, when she returned with a needle which she sterilized with the flame of a match, he had begun whimpering and cringing. The first time she had laughed out loud, thinking he was kidding, until she saw that his tears and cries were real. He had actually been terrified!

Besides, Emiko was not sure that prisons were the answer to crime. It was a known fact, was it not, that prisons, as most of them were now constituted, rarely rehabilitated? Not only was she against capital punishment, she was also against prisons, even though, pinned down in an argument, she admitted that there must be some system to temporarily segregate those who persisted in preying on others. She agreed with the wise man who had called for a society "in which it is easier to be good."

She remembered the horror of the year before, the mousetrapping and cooking alive of five young men and women who had gotten disillusioned with the establishment and taken matters into their own hands. She could not forget the extravagantly leaping fire which came across almost real on the peacock screen — so real that you could almost hear them screaming. And then to hear the mayor of the city afterwards proclaiming that it was only "morally right" to reimburse those in the neighborhood whose homes had been damaged. She had never been able to get his definition of morality out of her mind.

In February of 1976 there came a belated and elegant valentine card with the news that he was being transferred to McNeil Island Penitentiary via Terminal Island and Lompoc, and he wondered whether Emiko was anywhere in the environs of either stopping-off place. He thanked her for the snapshots of her family she had dug up and sent at his request. Bogged down by another family crisis, she wrote that she would not be able to go and meet him. But she felt guilty. "That which I should have done, I did not do," chanted a small voice in the back of her mind.

If Alden was disappointed, he did not mention it. His first letter from McNeil Island contained an appreciation of the place:

"It is beauty that I am after in my writing. There is lots of beauty in McNeil. Today I was a little depressed as I had allowed my mind to stray away from Jesus Christ and that attitude chain-reacted to a sin that reinforced the negative feelings. After supper I isolated myself in the sloping green lawn and layed down, closed eyes.

The sun made itself felt as the cumulus clouds departed. A gentle breeze swept across. Somewhere, where there was a small sandy beach, the surfs ran back and forth, lazily, back and forth sweeping. The air's odor reminded me of home quiescently and of my love, Ophelia. God was soothing me, telling me that I am His child and he forgives. I fell asleep, and relaxed. He massaged my soul. Alleluia!"

There were two publications there, he said, *Newsbuoy,* a weekly inmate paper, and *Smoke Talk,* "a quarterly for us American Indians." He had attended an American Indian Alcoholic Seminar and Transactional Analysis seminar given by the Pacific Institute. He had become a member of AA, he added, and was "enjoying the spiritual aspect of it":

"We had an AA banquet where I danced with the brave ladies recovering from the evil of that (heinous) drug. In the brotherhood of American Indians we will be having our pow wow this coming 26th. The sun rises for us and the bell tolls for us; what else can they do?"

Then life took one of those odd turns, so that Emiko felt that she was being given a second chance — maybe she and her correspondent were destined to meet after all. The only son of her childhood friend, Mary, was getting married to a girl in Seattle and Mary Fukuda insisted that Emiko go along with her and her husband. The matter was settled, she said, they were footing the bill for the plane and hotel. So Emiko wrote to

McNeil and asked Alden if she might be able to see him.

She found out that she would have to get permission first from his Case Manager, so she wrote for the proper form, filled it out, and sent it back. She had not received permission by the day of departure—they left the city gratefully in the midst of a heat wave—but she did not worry too much about it. Once in Seattle, she figured, it would be a simple matter to reach the proper authorities and explain her mission. Surely, since she had already asked to be put on Alden's visitors list, and since she was coming all the way from Los Angeles, permission would be forthcoming

Despite a soft drizzle, the early July wedding was grand, and Emiko was swept up in the before-and-after festivities for a time. The Fukudas were staying on for a few days to take in the sights and Emiko, it was agreed, would try to get over to Steilacoom from where she could take the prison boat over. The Fukuda's son had a friend working at McNeil, so she was referred to him for assistance. In like Flynn, she thought, with such help.

But for some reason, permission was denied. Was his crime so terrible then? Or was it merely some prison protocol that had to be observed? Emiko was crestfallen but she joined the Fukudas in their sight-seeing and managed to enjoy the rest of her stay in the Northwest. She phoned home only once to make sure all was peaceful there, and as she told the Fukudas, she got the impression that the kids didn't care if she ever got back. (Years later, she was to find out that her younger daughter, rebelling at last against her sister's authoritarianism, had dragged her all the way around the house by her long hair.)

When she arrived home, the waiting pile of mail contained the letter from the penitentiary informing her that she had been placed on Alden Ryan Walunga's visitors list. Thanks a lot, she thought, knowing she would probably never have occasion to go to Seattle again.

But she read the regulations out of curiosity. Steilacoom, the paper said, was thirteen miles southwest of Tacoma, and there was a free twenty-minute ride on the prison boat to McNeil Island. An inmate was permitted only four visits a month and female visitors were "requested to be careful of the attire they wear to the institution," with "skin-tight leotards and stretch pants, short miniskirts and lowcut dresses considered improper in the prison setting." Well, she would have to bear that in mind. No bikinis, either, she supposed.

No one was to alight from the boat until a bell rang to give permission. One could buy a $1.00 meal ticket for a box lunch (available all visiting days) to be eaten with the man being visited; vending machines and soft drinks were available in the visiting room. No food (such as cakes that might contain hacksaws or hashish brownies, Emiko interpolated) was allowed to be brought in by visitors, no article allowed to be exchanged. Pictures could be shown with permission from the Visiting Room Officer; hobby craft might be given to visitors in the visiting room with the prior approval of the Hobby Shop Officer.

A handshake and embraces were permitted before and after the visit only; "during the visit you may have no physical contact"; visits could be terminated at any time if the Visiting Room Officer detected any untoward behavior; inmates might take one sealed package of cigarettes if they wanted because they would not be allowed to carry any cigarettes from the visiting room.

Alden must have been inured to disappointment; he did not dwell on her failure to visit. He only wrote that he was happy to have her on his visitors list. Besides, he had applied for and received a Basic Educational Opportunity Grant, so he was looking forward to taking classes from Tacoma Community College in the fall. Also, armed with a course in Greek New Testament Grammar from Moody Bible Institute, he was continuing his attack on the Greek original in order to make his own translation of the Gospels.

He also sent her a short story he had written, titled "The Coffin of 1974."

Emiko found the story disturbing. It was afflicted with the same dichotomous anguish as that first essay of his that she had read:

> Snowbirds ran through the air, rapidly singing the Bering
> Sea Spring song in the thin and white air, landing upon the
> melting and softening snow, very wild, almost invisible as they
> blended with the snow and exposed gravel of earth, and then
> suddenly they would be driven by some unfelt wind to find
> another place to seek out stone fly meals, flies who had long
> hibernated and were trying to restore the littleness of their
> lives.
>
> Quietly the snowbirds were alerted as they sensed the
> approaching crunches on the tundra snow. Their heads
> became uneasy and loose, as if they were unscrewing them
> off. Their wings rose momentarily to flap but were doubtfully
> lowered back. They were getting confused. They were getting
> scared. Their ancestor snowbirds had transmitted them a
> traditional wariness against homo sapiens, especially against
> little Eskimo boys, fat parkas on with overflowing fur outlining

their faces, armed with slingshots.

The coffin, borne by "six dark people," was heavy because the deceased had gained 27 pounds in prison:

The sky was inky blue. The silent clouds hardly moved and seemed to refuse to move. The Bering Sea was belligerently nervous with three-foot size ripples in response to a current that was breaking up and enclosing the island with ice floes and icebergs. The breeze was tranquil and smelled of raw and recent butcher of brown walruses. The village houses appeared wet and were wooden and light brown, some with tarpaper and some with peeling and peeling white paint, and most with chimneys lazily exhaling silver smoke, but all with that glassy wet, relaxing and tired countenance. Most also had bloodied melting Bering Sea Spring snow, because the walrus spoil of the day.

The tiny black and white eyes of the little snowbirds united their focus to the approaching mystery but their little warm hearts had ceased their tachycardia. In fact, they were lining up in a file as if in response to a military and folk-hero who was honoring them a pass.

The mother was grieving for her oldest son. He was the one in the coffin. And if Emiko read the story correctly, it was the oldest son who, with a twenty-two Remington magnum rifle, had killed both his uncle (his mother's youngest brother) and a girl relative. The girl relative had also been raped.

There was a lot of blood in the story, both walrus and human. But there was, all of a sudden, a happy ending. The oldest son had not died, after all. He was reborn in Christ, a new man, washed clean of his sins! Alleluia!

Emiko was stunned by the story. Was this, then, Alden's story?

But she merely sent it back to him with the "corrections, suggestions, and remarks" for which he had asked, praising the poetry of the stark landscape with the snowbirds.

The last communication she got from Alden had a regular stamp on the envelope, unlike the previous envelopes with the printed prison frank. He wrote from the Seattle City Jail, where he had been transferred for his own protection after telling the authorities what he had seen of a homosexual rape at the prison. He did not much care for the Seattle City Jail with the constant sounds of traffic and sirens rising day and night from the street way down below. He expressed distaste for "the occupants of a neighboring cell, a bunch of black and white homosexuals" whose "demonic malaria becomes active in pretentious talk and behavior...the pitiful perverts are even called by their feminine nicknames by the officers."

But he reported gladsome news, too. He had been recommended for a transfer to Alaska! That was around September. Wallowing in the mire of modern family life, Emiko did not answer Alden until just before Christmas, when she wrote him a brief note in a greeting card. She had managed, meanwhile, to send him another Asian American literary magazine on the assumption that she would no longer have to go through all the red tape as before.

The card was returned by the jail, stamped Unclaimed. But the magazine may have reached its destination, for although it was never acknowledged, neither was it returned. Emiko liked to think that Alden still kept it somewhere among his prison mementos even though paroled. He was probably very busy spreading the Word of God there in that isolated settlement overlooking the Bering Sea.

Or, if not paroled, there would be frequent visits there in the Alaska prison from his mother, his sisters and brothers, from his beloved Ophelia, and Lord knows whom else. There would be piles of studying to do, lots of poems, stories and essays to write.

Either way, Emiko — holding fast to the Lord Jesus Christ and refusing to consider any other alternatives — imagined he was probably much too busy back there on his home ground to continue to be the pen pal of some old woman way down there in California.

(1983)

My Father Can Beat Muhammad Ali

That evening Henry Kusumoto had two cans of beer with dinner, his favorite chiles rellenos. Usually he had only one can, but he had had more than the usual hassles at the Crenshaw supermarket where he was in charge of produce, so he felt entitled. In the glow that followed, he listened amiably as the two boys Dirk and Curt (his wife Marge must have gotten the names out of the romance novels she devoured one after the other like peanuts), discussed the merits of current fighters like Larry Holmes and Marvin Hagler.

"Them guys couldn't hold a candle to Muhammad Ali in his prime," said Dirk, at fourteen the elder.

"Yeah, he was the greatest all right," agreed Curt.

Henry felt obliged to protest.

"Muhammad Ali, Muhammad Ali!" he said impatiently. "Ridiculous, the way he got away with dancing around every fight. Don't you remember how he beat the sumo wrestler by making all kinds of rules and regulations in his own favor? You call that the greatest? Man, I call that chicken."

"That was afterwards, Dad," Dirk reminded him. "He was already on his way out when he put on that show."

"Yeah, he shoulda quit when he was ahead," added Curt.

"He shoulda quit before he started," insisted Henry. "We had fighters in our time—Joe Louis, Gene Tunney, Rocky Marciano..."

"Well, that's ancient history," said Dirk. "We're talking *now*."

"Shoot, I coulda beat that fraud," claimed Henry.

Dirk and Curt hooted in unison.

"Dad, you're five feet six and Ali is over six feet," Dirk objected between hoots, while Curt pretended to be falling out of his chair.

"Five feet six-and-three-quarters! Anyway, height has nothing to do with it," Henry was starting to get annoyed. He didn't care to be reminded about his stature, which had been one of the sore points of his high school athletic career. (Always warming the football bench, when he knew he could have gone out there and won the game. "You've got the guts all right," the coach would say, but I need some size here." And that had been on the B team.)

"It's intelligence that counts," he continued. "That guy may be tall all right but he's no genius. All a shorter guy has to do is study his technique and concentrate on where he's vulnerable—he's got his weaknesses."

At this, both Dirk and Curt fell writhing to the floor in uncontrollable spasms.

Marge decided it was time to step in. "Okay, boys," she ordered. "Cut it out. Get back to the table."

They obeyed sheepishly and each began stabbing his fork at the remnants of Mexican rice and egg. They decided to change the subject.

"Hey, you know Carlos, he says he's gonna go in for javelin next year. He's been practicing and he found out he's pretty good at it." Dirk pointed his fork towards the middle of the table and imitated Carlos hurling the javelin.

"What's the record in that?" Curt asked.

"Oh, I dunno—over 300 feet, I think."

"Wow! Three hundred feet! That's a long ways, huh?"

"Three hundred feet is nothing," said Henry. "I could do that easy."

The boys couldn't help it. They hadn't really recovered from their first attack, so they fell on the floor again, gasping for breath.

"Dirk! Curt! Stop it, stop it!" Marge shouted. "Get back up here, or no dessert!"

But this time the two had gone beyond recall. "What, the *manju* Grandma brought? Yuck, no thanks!" managed Curt, still twitching on the floor.

And Henry, too, was beyond reach. Marge saw the familiar obstinacy in the set of his jaw. "I'll show you!" he said to the boys. "Come out in the backyard."

This was an unexpected turn of events, but the boys picked themselves up off the floor and followed their father through the kitchen out into the long backyard of their Gardena house.

It was almost summer and Marge, who helplessly let herself get caught in the undertow and followed the boys, smelled the jacaranda that had fallen to the ground. It was an over-rich perfume that did not please her. "Have to remember to rake that up tomorrow, " she promised herself. But it was an inconvenience she was willing to put up with. Every May, the jacaranda coming into full bloom stopped her in her tracks; the enormous pale purple cloud never failed to amaze and delight her.

It was that time of the year when the skies were usually overcast and the sun came out just in time to go down, so there was still a good hour of daylight. "Why can't we just sit out there and smell the flowers?" she thought. But no, Henry was scrounging around near the garden shed way out in back for something, while the boys stood about halfway down the path, waiting for his performance.

A slight breeze was beginning to usher out the afternoon heat. Marge, leaning against the kitchen door, watched Henry coming towards the boys with something in his hand. What was it? A bamboo pole?

It was a bamboo from the pile he'd stacked next to the shed when he had dug up the towering growth that had burgeoned towards the power lines and threatened to turn the yard into a jungle.

He came to the back steps near Marge and called the boys over.

"Watch this, guys," he said. "This yard is almost 300 feet from here to the back wall."

Snickering, the boys came and stood alongside Marge, while their father prepared to throw.

A step forward, a sharp grunt, and the lance sailed about 50 feet before it clattered to the walk.

"Ha, not even close!" chortled Curt.

"The wind was against me," said Henry. "I can do it this time."

He came back to the kitchen steps and tried again. Two steps this time, a fiercer grunt, and the javelin fell even sooner than the first.

"Well, they don't use bamboo, anyway," Henry said. "They use special materials for everything nowadays. When I was going to high school, a pole-vaulter did good if he got near 14 feet. Now they got fiberglass poles, a big thick foam cushion underneath to land on..."

The boys weren't even listening. Caterwauling now, mercilessly, they punched each other with great glee, and their mother could not stand another second.

"Shut up!" she told them, "Go to your room and do your homework! And keep that stereo down!"

They obeyed, leaving little sniggers in their wake, and Marge followed them in and began clearing the table. She scraped the plates and put everything in the dishwasher alongside the fewer dishes from the staggered breakfasts and her solitary lunch. She poured in the detergent and pushed the start button.

"How about some coffee?" she asked out the back door.

There was no answer, but she started the coffeemaker anyway, before she went to the living room to pick up her book. Both the dishes and coffee were long done before Henry decided at last to come in.

(1986)

Underground Lady

Igrocery shop for the week on Fridays now, but until a couple of years ago I regularly shopped on Saturdays. The reason for the switch is that my husband Ed has retired and one of his diversions on Saturdays is to climb to Mt. Wilson from the Pasadena foothills or at least partway to Henninger Flats, so he needs a combination breakfast-lunch packed, and he's gone most of the day. So now I clean house on Saturdays, relieved not to have him underfoot while I run the vacuum.

Anyway, I met the Underground Lady late one Saturday afternoon when I emerged from the supermarket with my cart and went over to the phones to call home for a ride. In those days, after calling home, I used to go over to the crumbling cement bench in front of the store to sit and wait, because sometimes Ed was watching TV and wanted to see how a movie came out before leaving the house. So I sometimes had time for a cigarette, a leafing-through of the Sunday book review section (I always bought the Sunday paper while I was at it), and sometimes I even finished the Sunday crossword puzzle.

That particular Saturday, however, I found I couldn't push my cart over to the bench because the way was blocked by a woman and her cart, which was overflowing with what looked like a quilt and other household goods.

So I shrugged inwardly and decided to wait near the phone, lighting up as usual. The woman, quite tall and dressed in too much clothing for a sunny December afternoon—a shapeless black hat, a long woolen scarf, a thick brown coat—turned to me and began talking about tobacco.

She said some lady had given her a pack of Benson and Hedges, which fact caused her to shudder, "I don't know why anybody smokes them. They're terrible." She said she knew she had a pack of Camels in her gear somewhere, but she gestured towards the cart helplessly, as if to say it would take her some doing to find it.

So I offered her one of mine and let her keep the matches. She told me she was homeless. Her Japanese neighbors, who hated her, had burned her house down.

I wondered why she was telling me, another Japanese, about it. Either she didn't return the hate or maybe she wanted to heap coals on my head, for standing there with my cartful of groceries.

"Are you sure?" I asked.

"They hate me," she said, totally convinced of the fact.

"What kind of Japanese are those?" I wondered aloud, to indicate that I was one of the Japanese that didn't hate her, at least not until she could give me a good reason.

"Well," she said, "his name is Stanley Onodera. He works for the Harbor Department. What better way to infiltrate, eh, to signal the Japanese in World War II? Remember Pearl Harbor."

"How old a person is he?" I asked.

"Forty-five," she said.

"So he must have been five at the most during World War II," I said.

"That doesn't matter," she said, dismissing logic with a wave of her hand. But she did decide to try another tack.

"They had three Akita dogs and two died," she said, "and the remaining one is afraid of his own shadow."

For a fleeting second, I wondered how the dogs had met their death. We'd had a couple in our neighborhood, both beautiful, spirited animals; one, directly across the street, had been named Taisho.

But she changed the subject again. "The man has about $25,000 worth of motorcycles and cars.

"Now he's sick," she continued, "High blood pressure, and he's going deaf and he's got other things wrong with him. And his wife, she's getting fat!"

"Well, if they burned down your house," I said, "I guess they deserve it."

"Oh, I get along with them," she said. She put her hands together prayerfully and bowed respectfully. "That's the way they want me to be. Like a Japanese—quiet."

Also, she said, she had once knocked on their door to borrow a flashlight when her lights went out. And Stanley Onodera had lent her a flashlight, "stolen from the Harbor Department, don't you know."

When she went to return it, he had told her to keep it.

"It's a magnificent flashlight, Starlight, six batteries. It can throw a beam way over there." She pointed over to the intersection beyond the supermarket parking lot. "Powerful!"

So she got along with her Japanese neighbors, she said, again putting her hands together and bowing. "I'm quiet and polite, just like a

Japanese."

She said she grew her own vegetables on her lot. And she was building her own house. She didn't need much, maybe one room ten by ten, enough for a bed, a kitchen, a bathroom, that was all. Her house that had burned down had been 350 square feet—too large. Now she was building a house sufficient for her needs, that was all she required.

"Good for you, if you can get away with it," I said.

"Oh, I can," she said confidentially. And she bent towards me and intoned, "Underground!"

So I got the impression she went back to her lot, on a hill behind another supermarket, at night, and slept down in the cellar or basement of her burned house.

She then confided that she had worked in Washington during World War II, before being transferred to San Francisco. She had worked for the Office of Counter Intelligence.

"OSS?" I asked.

"No, no, CIC," she said.

"Oh," I said.

Her current income was something over three hundred dollars, which didn't go too far.

I wondered if it was disability. She didn't look old enough to be on Social Security. She was a good-looking woman under the assorted clothing and smudge. In fact, cleaned up, coiffed and appropriately gowned, she might have cut a statuesque and elegant figure in some Washington ballroom or at some long dinner table with notables on either side of her. But then she could have been a filing clerk.

She then told me her age—62—and this gave me a turn because I was a year older then. She didn't appear to be the least grey of hair or lined of face. She could have passed for someone much younger.

All of a sudden, I felt apologetic about all my groceries. So I said I tried to make them last all week, but my son had been screaming that morning because there was no bread or milk.

"Throw him out," she said.

Excellent advice, but I didn't tell her that after he'd found something to eat, Butchie had told me the dream he'd had before he woke up. He said that some kids in his class (he was a special education aide at a local high school) had called him outside, "Look, look, Mr. Hori! Look at the rainbow!" They could evidently see it plain as day, but search the sky as he might, he couldn't see the rainbow.

But it was hardly the kind of anecdote you tell a stranger.

About that time Ed arrived and he took the cart to wheel to the car. He glanced at my new friend and she looked back at him. It took awhile to load the bags into the hatchback and when I took the empty cart back to the front of the store, I saw the lady crossing the street with her shopping cart.

On the way home I told Ed of my encounter, and he said he'd seen the woman before. She had been at another supermarket down the street under the shelter of the front arcade during the last rain, early in the morning when he went to buy the paper before going on to Griffith Park for his daily jog.

Before he could get out of the car, she had rapped at the window and asked for a light. So when he handed her a matchbook, she had said she couldn't light it because of the rain. She handed him her cigarette inside the car and asked him to light it.

Which he did, but she didn't budge from the window. She evidently wanted to talk. So he had to roll up the window to get her away from it. When he got out to get the paper, she was right behind him. So he offered her the paper (when he goes jogging, he only takes one quarter for the paper), but she said she already had one. Then she said maybe she could sell it, so he gave it to her.

He went on to the park to jog, he said, but he wiped his mouth just in case the cigarette was germy or something. The episode had left him feeling uneasy.

So when we got home and I was putting all the junk away, we conjectured about the woman, and Butchie, overhearing a snatch, exclaimed, "Why do you call her that?"

I had used the term "bag lady." So I explained that was the term in current use for the homeless women you saw everywhere and especially downtown who carried all their possessions with them, usually in plastic shopping bags or even trash bags, wherever they went.

"Why?" I said. "Have you seen her?"

"No, but the guys have talked about her."

So, apparently, she had been around for awhile. Had she recognized Ed from the rainy day encounter? Or did she make a habit of having men light her cigarette? Maybe, using this ploy, she had gotten somebody else more compassionate or less wary to treat her to breakfast? Other possibilities occurred to me.

I sometimes think of her, especially on rainy nights. By now I hope the house of her desiring is all finished and furnished. I imagine her cozy house, one-room, much like the sod houses of the pioneers of the northern plains, with her bed, her stove, her fridge, and her bathing facilities connected to the existing sewer. I see her snug in bed under her quilt, maybe even reading by the light of the magnificent flashlight with the six batteries.

(1986)

A Day in Little Tokyo

I t was a lovely Saturday morning towards the end of May. There would be no rain in Southern California from now until November, if the pattern of previous years held. Soon the harvest of strawberries and tomatoes would begin in earnest, to continue throughout the summer.

Mrs. Kushida knew the two older children had felt neglected and confined since the birth of the baby in February, and probably her husband was champing at the bit as well, so she suggested that they all spend a day at the beach. She would stay home with the baby and catch up on her sewing. She had a treadle Singer, as did all her friends, and she made most of the family's clothes—*nemaki,* shirts, dresses, her own long work gloves and white bonnets.

Chisato, going on fourteen, and her younger brother Shuzo were all for it. At the mention of ocean, Chisato could already see the endless blue, smell the salt air, hear the music of the merry-go-round, and feel the warm sand between her toes and the chill tickle of water around her ankles. Regular school five days a week, Japanese school on Saturdays, homework, helping out in the fields where they could—a day off, playing hooky from Japanese school, was an unusual treat. And the ocean was Chisato's very favorite thing in the whole world. Shuzo started talking about the good hot dogs, with mustard and relish and ketchup.

Mr. Kushida, however, didn't feel the pull of the seashore as strongly. "How about going to see the wrestlers?" he asked them. "They're here from Japan for the big tournament."

"No, no! Beach!" chorused Chisato and Shuzo.

Mrs. Kushida tried to be diplomatic. "The ocean will always be there," she said. "The wrestlers are only here for one time."

"You're the one that said beach, Mama!" Chisato reminded her.

"I forgot about the wrestlers. There was a story in the newspaper the other day about the tournament. Maybe you could have *China-meshi* first."

The bribery didn't work on Chisato. "We've already got our bathing suits on underneath!" Chisato protested, muttering to Shuzo, "Making us go to all this trouble..."

Shuzo, more pliable, said, "*China-meshi* sounds good. I love that *chashu* and almond duck!"

"That's all you think about—food! You're going to be a fat tub of lard, Shooz, if you don't watch out!"

"I really want to go to the beach, too," he said, remembering the hot dogs. "But Papa wants to go see the sumo wrestlers."

"Beach, beach, beach!" said Chisato.

Their father was already in the blue Hudson sedan, waiting for them, so they got in, Shuzo in front and Chisato alone in the back. Their mother, carrying the baby, came half-running across the dirt yard to bring them all sweaters.

But the car, after it had bumped up and down the dirt road from the house to the highway, didn't make the right turn that led west to Santa Monica. It turned left, towards the highway that went north to Los Angeles.

Chisato felt betrayed. She gave Shuzo a furtive poke in the back. He turned around and grinned, knowing that either destination promised beautiful food.

Chisato was so angry that she hardly saw anything out the car window. The green meadow where they went mushroom-hunting after rain, the orange groves, the dairies, the pepper trees dripping onto the street, the eucalyptus windbreaks, the several hamlets, all were passing blurs made invisible by her fury. She knew when they reached and passed the enormous and mysterious walled estate or factory there on Telegraph Road which looked like something Egyptian maybe. She did not, this time, wonder what was inside that ornate entrance; all it meant today was that Little Tokyo, phooey, was not far away.

Somewhere after that Mr. Kushida stopped to buy each of them Eskimo pies from the Good Humor truck parked near an intersection. These were actually little round pies, with a thin chocolate-covered crust over vanilla ice cream. Shuzo enjoyed his as they resumed their inexorable trip towards the city, but Chisato nibbled at hers with such grudging slowness that the chocolate melted on her fingers and she got a blotch of it on the front of her white middy dress, in a rather embarrassing place.

This made her more disconsolate than ever, so when Mr. Kushida found a place to squeeze the car in on Central Avenue, down from the Nishi Hongwanji, she decided to stay in the car for the rest of her life. "Come on, Chisato," said Mr. Kushida, but she only pouted and refused to even look at his proffered hand.

"Come on, Cheese," echoed Shuzo, but he retreated when she shot him a look expressing her attitude toward collaborators.

She watched the two malevolently as they walked towards East First, after her father had given up. "Well, we won't be long. We're late, but maybe we can catch the end of it."

Abandoned, Chisato fumed for awhile, then got out of the car and walked slowly in the opposite direction towards Jackson Street, then came back towards the temple and stood on its steps. This was where she had once gone to a wedding, but there was little sign of festivity today. Maybe there was something going on inside, but she could see nothing from where she stood except some murky depths. Now and then someone went past her to go in or leave. She looked across the street at the old brick backsides of businesses and their corrugated metal delivery doors — nothing interesting there — and walked back to the car.

She remembered once being on the block when the street was entirely crammed with people standing and watching and applauding a program of dances on a long stage, draped with ideogrammed curtains, set up against the business buildings. For some reason she recalled the woman standing in front of her who appeared to be about her mother's age and who had startled her by speaking in fluent English to her child (or whomever). She had envied the child dancers with their faces painted dead white, their blackened eyebrows and bright red bee-stung lips. They seemed a world apart in their brilliant silken kimonos, in their gliding movements to the plucked music and wailing song, in their convoluted black wigs a-dangle with chains of cherry blossoms. Then she had glimpsed a girl changing in the wings and noticed that she wore underwear with rubber buttons, the kind that fit onto metal hooks. Did all city kids wear such underwear? Or maybe all the kids who took *odori* lessons? The privileged ones. Like the Meglin Kiddies who performed between intermissions at the movies and at parades. She had watched them, too, with envy, and then she had been bemused to see the quite soiled bottoms of the satin ballet slippers.

The car was hot and Chisato began to perspire — no way to remove her bathing suit — so she got out and leaned against the side of the door. She remembered a family friend who lived in the very middle of the whole block, smack dab in the center, enclosed by the back walls and fences of the businesses on four streets. Her family had visited this friend now and then, in her small wooden frame house, with its large vegetable garden in front of the house and an outhouse in a corner of the garden.

But she couldn't go there—the woman, who was about her mother's age, was a Nisei but she seemed to speak mainly Japanese. Chisato didn't quite grasp the connection—the parents of the woman had come from the same village in Japan as her parents? And what would the woman do if Chisato appeared on her doorstep? Laugh at her, no doubt. She was a pretty woman who laughed a great deal. She was always at the yearly village picnics which were held at places like White's Point or Elysian Park. Chisato remembered her once regaling her folks with the account of this absolutely naked *(mappadaka)* man who had come leaping over the fence from the back of that hotel over there, gasping, *"Tasukete* — save me!" It seemed the husband of his lady friend was after his hide. "That's the fastest I've seen anybody run in my whole life!" the woman had exclaimed, as she joined in the gale of laughter.

Chisato's thoughts were interrupted by a pair of white men who stopped in front of her.

"Hello, little lady," said the taller of the two.

"Hello," she mumbled, suddenly shy, acutely aware of the chocolate stain, a large irregular brown flower in the lap region.

They were both in suits but did not appear to be really clean. The shorter one had a leg missing. He used wooden crutches, and one pant leg was folded up and tied with cord above where the knee should have been. Had he been in the World War?

Murakami-san had been in the World War. He had been one of the hired men last year, but he hadn't stayed long. A roly-poly kind of man with thinning hair, he had been a hard worker and very good-natured. A few weeks into strawberry time, however, he had been unable to work. When someone talked to him, he would smile and laugh, in great good humor, but all he would do was loll around here and there. Once he took out a snapshot of himself which showed him smiling happily as he lay on a lawn in front of a white house. He said the picture had been taken in Connecticut. Mr. Kushida had taken him back to the boarding house in the city and brought back another man who bowed a lot.

Chisato knew the men had stopped to talk to her because she was cute. Short for her age and wearing long shiny black braids, she would now and then overhear someone saying to a companion, "Isn't she cute?" as they glanced at her in passing.

And that's what Mr. Fitzpatrick called her in class, "Cute little dimpled Cheese," once he learned that her friends called her Cheese. That was because he was always berating her for not keeping up with the other violinists. Her friend Mutsuko, who also played violin, had started crying once when rebuked, so from then on Mr. Fitzpatrick tried to temper his exasperation by humorously adding something about "cute little dimpled Cheese," whenever he took exception to Chisato's ideas of musicianship. Except that she never would have cried. She only made faces back at him when he wasn't looking.

Especially after that smarty-pants in the class, Albert Mandell, had stage whispered, "Is that like Swiss cheese?" And those around him had guffawed mightily.

She had even toyed with the idea of changing her name. Chisato was so ugly. Gloria, after Gloria Stuart. Or Madge, after Madge Evans. Or maybe Florine, like Florine McKinney. She even tried writing them down: Gloria Kushida, Madge Kushida, Florine Kushida. But somehow she never got up the nerve to actually make the switch.

"Here, honey," said the taller man. He handed her some coins and, not knowing what else to do, she took them.

After they had ambled on, she opened her hand and counted the pennies. Enough for a newspaper, she couldn't help thinking.

A brief debate with herself, then she carefully draped the blue sweater on her left arm to hide the spot on her dress before she started up East First. She strolled past the fish market whose smells reminded her that she should have been at the beach, past a new and elegant cafe called Far East (what was it like in there behind all that shining glass? — her family usually ate upstairs at Nikko Low and San Kow Low); past the book shop with its one hundred different Japanese magazines displayed colorfully in front, most of them with a comely female face on the cover; past Asahi Dry Goods with the shoes and clothes in the windows; and here was the small drug and jewelry shop owned by another fellow villager. This gentleman would load his pharmaceuticals and cosmetics, cameras and watches into his car and make the rounds of rustic customers. Once he had taken out a golf club and ball from his car and showed her mother and father what he enjoyed doing on his days off. Then there was the sushi restaurant with its artful arrangements of delectable morsels in the window, the confectionery window brimful of boxes of decorated rice cakes and bags of rice crackers (she didn't even have enough for a little box of *ame* candy).

And here on the corner was the jewelry and optometric shop where her mother came for glasses.

All the parking spaces on First Street were filled, but there weren't as many people on the sidewalk as there usually were on a Saturday. The produce terminal downtown was closed on Sunday, so Saturday was the day the farm families would take off, many to flock to Little Tokyo from as far away as Orange County. Maybe everybody was at the sumo matches. She didn't know exactly where they were taking place, but deep from somewhere inside the bowels of Little Tokyo came the muffled sound of applause, yelling and cheering from time to time.

She had to go a block or so beyond, towards the awesome white spire of City Hall, to find a newspaper stand, but when she finally retraced her steps and got back in the car with the newspaper, she felt a sense of loss. She tried to read the funnies, but nothing seemed to be very funny. She looked at the pictures of Marion Davies and Jeannette Mac-Donald in the movie section, but when she tried to read about them she had to keep going back to read the same sentence over and over. Nothing seemed to sink in. The radio schedule reminded her that she could have stayed home and listened to the weekly fairy tale from New York City, with kids like Billy and Florence Halop and Albert Alley always perfect in every story. This made her pause for a muted rendition of the Cream of Wheat song, which she knew by heart. She rolled up the newspaper and used it as a baton to keep her rhythm:

> Cream of Wheat is so good to eat
> that we have it every day.
> Cream of Wheat is so good to eat
> that it makes us shout, "Hurray!"
> It's good for growing babies,
> And grown-ups too, to eat.
> For all the family's breakfast,
> You can't beat Cream of Wheat!
> Ta-dah....

But as soon as she finished singing, she felt kind of sick at the stomach again, as though she had done something horribly wrong. She shouldn't have taken the money from the two men, she thought—she was the one who should have given them money, if she'd had any.

Dusk was just beginning when her father and brother came back. Mr. Kushida was in a hurry and Shuzo was scurrying to keep up with him. They didn't seem to notice that she had a newspaper.

"We're late," Mr. Kushida said. "It lasted longer than I expected. We'd better get back home. Mama is probably worrying."

"What about the *China-meshi?*" asked Shuzo, plaintively.

"It's too late now. We'd better go home and eat."

It was Shuzo's turn to protest. "I'm hungry!"

"You're always hungry." Mr. Kushida observed mildly, as he started up the car.

"Yeah, Fatso," said Chisato. She wasn't hungry at all, with this ache at the pit of her stomach.

"I'm not fat!" Shuzo really wasn't, but she had gotten used to calling him that because he ate anything and everything, even cooked *daikon* and *gobo,* which she herself couldn't abide.

"Fatso, Fatso, Shooz is a Fatso!" chanted Chisato.

"Cheese, Cheese, big fat Cheese!" he retorted.

They continued this exchange with scant variation as Mr. Kushida, driving faster than was his wont, wended his way past the pungent White King soap factory and up the First Street bridge.

So it came as a big shock that, several blocks later, they found themselves trembling on the sidewalk, the Hudson propped against a leaning city lamppost, a crowd gathering around them and a police car arriving on the scene.

Shuzo had an enormous lump on his forehead where he had banged up against the windshield. Mr. Kushida didn't appear to be hurt, nor Chisato. But Chisato's knees were like jelly, quivering and threatening to give way.

"Who screamed?" asked a bystander. "Boy, it sounded like someone going over a cliff!"

Chisato didn't remember screaming, but who else could it have been.

"It was the other driver's fault," Mr. Kushida was saying. He was saying it in Japanese, however, so it was as though he were explaining it to himself.

Mr. Kushida tried to explain in English to the police that there had been a car coming from the opposite direction which had suddenly decided to make a turn into the cross street. He had speeded up and swerved to avoid a crash and landed up against the lamp post.

Whether anyone understood or believed him or not (he was later to get a $99 bill from the city for the lamp post), the crowd eventually dispersed and the police ascertained that the car was still operable. The front bumper was pretty badly dented, however. Meanwhile, Shuzo was taken away by one policeman in the police car and later returned. His injuries had been checked and found not too serious, or so Chisato gathered.

It was already night when they finally got home, Mr. Kushida shaken and driving with utmost caution a vehicle which seemed to have added several new rattles and squeaks to its repertoire. Chisato and Shuzo both sat in the back, put on their sweaters and did not utter a peep the rest of the way home.

Chisato peered at the protuberance on Shuzo's forehead. It reminded her of the man in the comedy they'd seen the last time they'd gone to Moneta to see a Japanese movie. It wasn't a Charlie Chaplin comedy this time, but about a lady and her husband going camping. The lady seemed to be doing all the work, unloading everything from the car and pounding the tent stakes with a mallet. She walked jerkily around the tent and came around to the front, where she saw her husband already sitting down to enjoy the view. She brought the mallet down on the man's head, whoomp, and a huge balloon sprouted from the top of his head.

Mrs. Kushida had been terribly worried about them, because what decent person stays at the beach after dark? She gave a cry when she saw Shuzo's head; her worst fears had been confirmed.

After Mr. Kushida had calmed her down and given his version of the accident, he added remorsefully, "It's all my fault. *Ii-bachi*. We should have gone to the beach."

It should have been a moment of triumph for Chisato. But she, still weak in the knees and still aware of that strange sensation in her stomach, knew it was not that simple. She knew it was because she had taken the pennies from the man with one leg.

(1986)

Reading and Writing

The irony in our Mutt-and-Jeff relationship has bemused me from time to time. Hallie's forefathers had probably come not long after the Mayflower bunch and their descendants had pioneered in Tennessee. Perhaps they took to the hills during the Civil War. I, Kazuko, was the daughter of Japanese immigrants.

While neither of us could lay claim to belonging here, English was generally accepted as the country's language, and by virtue of a longer family history here, Hallie should have been able to use English backwards, forwards, upside down and sideways.

But here I was, causing her moments of anguish not only by mentioning my passion for Scrabble and addiction to word puzzles, but by assuming she could read and write—advising her to take a bus when she couldn't make out street names; urging her to take a nursing course when she couldn't begin to read, much less fill out, an application for the class.

It was partly her own fault, of course. How was I to know? She was pretty clever about it. And she never once came out and admitted she was illiterate. It took me years to catch on, and by then it was much too late.

I have to admit I was kind of turned off when Hallie and I first met. We met over the telephone because Hallie's husband was on my husband Akira's annual last minute Christmas card list, and, having only a phone number for Biff Schaeffer, I was calling it to find out the address.

Hallie answered, and I figure it took at least an hour to get her and Biff's address, because she gave me not only her location in Rosemead but a leisurely survey of her life to date. I guess it's because I'm Japanese—I listened to her patiently, without once begging to be excused because I had a houseful of little kids to referee.

So in that first phone exchange, I found out that this marriage to Biff was her third and his second. She had first married at 14 and had a daughter who was now 15. The guy had really loved her, but he'd had this habit of beating up on her every time he got drunk. Then she had married this old guy with three kids. She found out all he had wanted was somebody to cook and wash and milk the cows. That was all right, but she couldn't take the mean way the man and his kids had treated her daughter Angela. So she had taken Angela and come out by bus to San Pedro, where her married older sister was living.

I had some trouble at first getting used to her near-Southern drawl, but I clearly grasped the importance she attached to Angela's education. Angela was in high school now, in the 10th grade. "Don't you think I've done my duty?" Hallie asked. "In a couple of years, she'll be graduating high school."

After that, our friendship continued mostly by phone. Our conversations were long and rambling, but when she said, "Oh, let's you and me go get drunk—on a cup of coffee!" I knew she was saying goodbye.

Our husbands visited one another often because of their mutual interest in electronics. They had met at work and found out they were both tinkering at home with radios and TV sets, as well as using citizens' band. Relatives, neighbors and co-workers were continually bringing both of them failed electric gadgets to bring back to life, so they not only exchanged ideas and helped each other on particularly puzzling problems, but empathized with each other about people always bringing them really botched-up TVs which they had obviously tried to revive themselves.

The day came when Hallie and I met in person and I was pleasantly surprised. Here was this gorgeous, statuesque creature with auburn hair, about five ten, tiny feet, big bosom. She was wearing a simple sleeveless dress, white sprinkled with tiny green sprigs, so I got this impression of a fresh breeze blowing into my house.

Not exactly what you'd expect to be married to Biff. Biff was only in his forties then, but he didn't have much hair left and he shuffled around as though he was weary to the bone, so he seemed older.

Hallie prided herself on having saved Biff from a premature death. They'd been apartment neighbors in San Pedro, where she supported herself and Angela by slapping up hamburgers, coffee, hot dogs and Coke at a small stand nearby.

Biff, also newly divorced, had been pretty weird, going out only to work and spending all his free time in his room, absorbed in his assortment of electrical doodads, soldering this to that, fiddling with wires, tubes, condensers. He barely took time out to eat, but he'd come out to the stand occasionally for a cup of coffee and a hot dog. Hallie had taken to joshing him about his eating habits and, by golly, he'd started coming to the stand with something like regularity, and before you knew it she was inviting him to her place for a piece of quick skillet cake or chicken and dumplings or real pancakes, made from scratch. It turned out he was from Tennessee too, although his folks had been immigrants from Germany.

After they got married, they moved to a housing project in Los Angeles. Most of their neighbors were Black and the Schaeffers got along well with everyone because Hallie was always noticing who needed this or who could use that and made a point of supplying what she could. "I always like to help people," she said. "That's the way I am."

So we also became beneficiaries of her charity. It was she who got our girls their first bras, nylons and lipsticks, long before I even connected such items to their welfare. She also brought them embroidery sets to work on, with hoops, colored skeins of thread and iron-on patterns.

But she knew how to scrimp, too, as most of us children of the Depression do, so by the time we became friends, she and Biff had bought a cozy little white house in Rosemead, with a big backyard shaded by an enormous avocado tree which kept them plentifully supplied in season. This was where they lived the dozen or so years that we knew them as a couple.

The property had a huge double garage out back, where Biff bit by bit outfitted a workshop with an amazing variety of tools and machinery. "He's got about every kind of tool there is," Akira reported. "He doesn't even use most of them."

Then Biff began reverting to his old ways, spending an inordinate amount of time back there, so Hallie was fit to be tied. One day she took an axe and broke the lock on the double garage door, and he seemed to get the message, at least for a while.

He remodeled the closet space in their bedroom into a large walk-in closet with sliding doors. That done, Hallie was able to fulfill her dream of a lavender bedroom. She bought the king-sized bed she'd seen advertised on TV, with free linens. Something happened to the bed the first week. It appeared to collapse towards the middle, so there was something of a hassle getting it repaired.

Then Hallie got Biff to build counters and cupboards all the way around the kitchen, so she had plenty of storage and work space. When all the remodeling was done, we dropped in to see the bedroom and kitchen.

Biff had done a terrific job.

But what caught my eye in the kitchen was a neat rainbow assortment of vials on one counter, a very intriguing touch. "What are those—cake decorations?" I asked.

"They're my medicines," Hallie said, proudly identifying each bottle and container. There were remedies for every possible ailment—tablets, capsules, sprays, liquids, vitamins. This one for headache, that one for fever, that there for lower back pain, for sore muscles and joints, for nasal congestion, for dieting, for stomach distress, for allergy. And there was even one for her nerves, which the doctor had prescribed.

I was properly impressed, but I couldn't help wondering what all those medications would do inside the body when they were mixed together. Wouldn't there be a collision of some kind, an inside explosion?

I guess the nerve pills came in handy, though, when Angela got pregnant during the summer and dropped out of school. Hallie was distressed, but she got the young couple to agree to marriage and she soon become a doting grandma. About a year later, she was grandmother to two, and she often took care of the little guys so Angela and Phil could go out to eat or take in a movie.

Somewhere along here Biff was hospitalized for a stomach ailment. It was around the Christmas season, and Hallie did the cards that year. It was when we got their card that I first got a glimpse of Hallie's secret. The handwriting on the envelope and card was evidently accomplished with much pain; that scrawl was the most tortured calligraphy I had ever seen.

My suspicion grew one afternoon when Hallie and Biff came over, Biff to repair to the workshop with Akira (or Ike, as he called him; and Hallie had been relieved to know that friends called me Kassie), while Hallie and I had coffee in front of the TV.

When a commercial came on about a spray disinfectant, Hallie nodded approvingly and remarked that she always used it. Later she indicated the same about a cooking spray. So was this how she had acquired her medications, that riot of color on her kitchen counter—on the advice of the TV?

Then there were funerals for them to attend, Hallie losing her mother and Biff losing his some months later. When the estates were settled, Hallie and Biff inherited several thousand dollars apiece. Biff got a new pickup and Hallie a color TV, which no one else was allowed to touch. I suspect now that Hallie wanted absolute control over the buttons because she would have difficulty locating the channels if someone else had messed with them.

But Hallie's main purchase was a cemetery plot for herself and Biff. This acquisition seemed to give her peace of mind, and she more than once expressed contentment with it. We were at her house once in front of her new TV when she pointed at the advertisement for her cemetery, a beautiful place embowered with roses. "That's where I'm going to be buried," she said happily.

She had inherited her mother's sofa and decided she would have it re-upholstered. She chose a velour spangled with large pink roses and large green leaves at an upholstery shop around the corner. While the work was in progress, she took to dropping by the shop and struck up a friendship with the owner, who did the work himself. Seeing him at the power sewing machine, she got the idea that she might like to do some upholstering herself. Maybe he could teach her to be an operator and she could help him out in the shop?

"Sure, sure," the fellow had agreed enthusiastically. He promised to teach her the ropes as soon as he had some time.

The bill for the upholstery work came to $700 or so, but she decided not to tell Biff about it. "He'd split a gut," she explained. I gathered the amount had flabbergasted her too, but she said stoutly, "It was worth it. I wanted to keep the sofa to remember my mama by." Besides, she was going to learn the trade, wasn't she?

Months went by before I remembered to ask her about the sewing lessons. "Oh, he says he hasn't got the time just now," she said, and what I heard in the tone of her voice was that she'd resigned herself to the fact that he never would.

Then she mentioned that there was one field she would have gone into if she'd had the chance: she really would have enjoyed being a nurse.

"It's not too late," I said. I told her about the programs in licensed vocational nursing or even regular nursing that most school districts had. I knew a couple of older women who had graduated such programs and both were now working in nearby hospitals.

"Biff don't let me drive," she said.

"Take the bus, Hallie!" I exhorted.

She made some kind of excuse, and I didn't pursue the matter. How cruel I was being I did not then know. Later it occurred to me that Biff wouldn't let her drive because she had no license. How could she when she couldn't read the written test?

But I guess she suspected by then that I was catching on. She spoke of going to a family get-together and she began making preparations from months before. She brought over the catalogs from a Midwestern mail-order house that she liked, and she showed me the pictures of the lovely turquoise dress and sable-like fake fur that she had ordered.

"Angie wrote out the order for me," she said casually. "I'll show that sister of mine. Ruby's always saying I don't know how to dress."

She later reported jubilantly that the preparations had all been worthwhile. "Ruby says, 'You do know how to dress, Hallie!' " She modeled for us the outfit that had elicited this accolade. And she did look stunning.

But her triumph was followed by a persistent illness that mystified the doctor.

There was this annoying scaly rash up and down her arms that would not go away, and she was having difficulty breathing. She took to carrying a small whirring fan inside a pen-shaped container that she could quickly uncap and use in front of her face when her breathing got labored.

Next we heard she was in a distant hospital where hard-to-diagnosis diseases were the specialty. The place did come up with a diagnosis: scleroderma. And the probable cause, they said, was an excess dosage of the cortisone that had been prescribed for her arthritis. They also informed her that there was no known cure.

We only visited her a few times there in the hospital. While they were at it, they found a malignancy in one breast and removed it. When we visited her just after that, she was quite chipper and joked that the resulting scar resembled a giant eyebrow on her chest.

She also listed the preparations she had made for her departure. The plot had long been bought, so she had chosen an elegant coffin as well as the pastor to deliver the eulogy. She had specified that she be laid to rest in the turquoise dress.

I was torn between indignation and admiration. Why did she not fight? She had been a pretty spunky lady all along. Why was she giving in to this so easily? The doctors were educated, sure, but they didn't know everything. Then I couldn't help but wonder whether I could look death in the face so calmly. Nope, I was sure I would snivel and cringe in fear and trembling.

But did she really expect to die? Not very soon, because she also spoke of going back to her old stomping grounds in Tennessee in the fall, along about October, when the leaves were turning. She hadn't been back there since coming to California.

The last time I saw Hallie alive was at the hospital. She had been moved to another room and I had to search around the corridors a while before I found the right number. I peeked in and saw an elderly woman in the bed opposite the door. The woman looked at me. I looked over to the other bed, but it was empty. Even as I was looking at the empty bed, however, it struck me like a thunderclap that the old woman in the other bed, the old woman with white hair, was Hallie.

"Are you all alone in here?" I asked, pretending.

"All by my lonesome," she said. If she saw through me, she didn't let on.

We chatted of this and that, but I could see that talking was tiring her. It obviously cost her just to breathe.

But there was one spark of the old spunk. "Hah, they come in here and want to talk about God!" she exclaimed scornfully.

I remembered she had once mentioned being a longtime Jehovah's Witness. She had left their ranks when she decided to approve a blood transfusion for Biff, that time he was in the hospital. "I sure wasn't gonna let him die," she explained.

A day or so after our visit, Biff phoned to tell us Hallie was gone. She had died peacefully. He said Angela and Phil had just been to see her that afternoon.

Angela had a special reason for visiting. After several years of going to school at night, she had finally graduated and she had come to show her mother the high school diploma.

(1987)

PREFACE TO THE REVISED AND EXPANDED EDITION

Four selections have been added to this revised edition of *Seventeen Syllables*. One, "Death Rides the Rails to Poston," was written in 1942 at the request of Sus Matsumoto, editor of the *Poston Chronicle*, the mimeographed camp "newspaper." I guess he wanted something to feature besides the Administration announcements. If memory serves, he had to prod me every week to come up with the next installment. I see now that it records some of the details of that May day in 1942 when all Japanese from as far south as the Imperial Valley and San Diego, and from as far north as Laguna Beach, obediently converged at railroad stations in San Diego and Oceanside and filed into trains that took us to the Colorado River Relocation Center (Poston) in Arizona.

"Fire in Fontana" is based on my employment at the *Los Angeles Tribune*, the weekly newspaper that hired me fresh out of camp. I lied to get the job because I needed and wanted the job badly. Almena Lomax (then Davis), the editor, asked whether I could proofread and, mentally crossing my fingers, I indicated that I could. So I went home and boned up overnight on proofreading marks in my *Webster's Collegiate*. Painfully, in the two to three years of my employment, I came to realize that our internment was a trifle compared to the two hundred years or so of enslavement and prejudice that others in this country were heir to.

My own background is also the basis for "Eucalyptus." Although while I was going through it I was as wretched as I have ever been in my life, I learned a lot about myself. A fellow patient and I agreed that this time spent in the booby hatch was an experience not to be missed.

"Florentine Gardens" is based on my first trip to Europe. I have since been able to return to those same "gardens" in Tuscany, where our family will always have connections.

Hisaye Yamamoto
February 2001

Death Rides the Rails to Poston

A ten-year-old girl, in submitting a mystery entitled "Murder Story" to Collier's *magazine, appended this note apologizing for the confusion towards the end of her story: "I got so excited towards the end of the story, wondering who the murderer was, that I made a lot of mistakes, not understanding it very well myself." Maybe it would do well to use that excuse here, this being the author's first attempt at a mystery story.*

Everybody hates me," mumbled the little man as he stepped up into the train. Shu overheard him and laughed, "Persecution complex." Shu Shingu noticed in the morning that everyone was avoiding the little man. He seemed a little drunk—he had probably taken a last snifter to last him for the duration—but otherwise he didn't seem particularly obnoxious. The man was shortish, stout, and had a cherubic face with a tiny black wisp of mustache under his button of a nose. Though he had more than the average number of chins, they were all weak.

Shu was the last one aboard the last car of the evacuee train. It was much less filled than the others. He saw the little man sitting all alone with the seats across the aisle from him, behind him, and in front of him mysteriously and, it seemed, deliberately empty. Intrigued, Shu seated himself next to the man and by the time the train had begun moving out of the Oceanville station, he had struck up a fruitful conversation with the ostracized man. It didn't take much subtle questioning, the poor man was already talkative because of his intoxication and his loneliness.

"My name is Tsuyoshi Koike," the man said after Shu had introduced himself. "From Oceanville, all the people in this car are from Oceanville."

He pointed out the various evacuees from Oceanville's Li'l Tokio. "Would you believe that the old woman sitting there knitting in the corner and ignoring me is my mother? She hates me."

The pretty one opposite his mother was Pat Nori. She had had a civil service job in San Diego before the war broke out. The attractive young couple were only recently married, Mr. and Mrs. Joe Miyamoto. "Frances, that's Mrs. Miyamoto, used to be my fiancée once upon a time. She hates me now." His voice was bitter and self-pitying.

That good-looking, rather nervous woman up in front was Mrs. Kimi Ogata. That crutch beside her was necessary for her leg. She had had an accident a year ago and had to have it broken and set twice before it had started mending properly. Her husband was interned somewhere in North Dakota. She was hoping that he would be allowed to join her in Poston. She was expecting a baby in a couple of months. The little brat who kept running up and down the aisle, making friends with the M.P.'s, and getting paper cups of water for the passengers was Yoyo Nakamura. His mother and father and little baby sister were sitting in front of Mrs. Koike.

The moody-looking young man in the front of the car was Toro Nogawa. His parents had been teachers in Oceanville's Japanese Language School and were in a concentration camp in Santa Fe. They had written Toro that they would soon be released and would come to him.

There were two other families, both with what seemed innumerable little children. They had both farmed in Oceanville, on hilly, fertile plots overlooking the sea. These were the Muratas and the Sakamotos.

After every one-sided introduction Koike would add "He hates me" or "They hate me" or "She hates me," because it seemed that after the war began Koike had angled himself a job with the FBI and the local Japanese had been jealous of his authority. He had merely done his patriotic duty and accompanied FBI searchers into Japanese homes and helped to look for contraband and reported suspicious actions.

When the train pulled out, Shu was still listening while the man got a little maudlin and defended himself. Whatever emotions he felt, it was evident that his self-pity was the deepest.

"Hey, Yoyo, get me some water, too, and I'll give you a quarter," Koike said to the energetic little boy who kept wandering up and down the car.

"A quarter? Okay!" he said, and running up to the front of the car was soon back with a paper cup of water.

"What's your name?" Yoyo said to Shu Shingu. Shu told him. And the impish little boy laughed and said, "Knock, knock."

"What?" Shu knew what was coming and, with annoyance, tried to ward it off.

"You're supposed to say, "Who's there?" the little boy prompted.

Shu resigned himself to his fate. "All right."

"Knock, knock."

"Who's there?"

"Shu Shingu who?"

"Shu Shingu ra!" And the little boy laughed till he was forced to sit weakly down in the aisle and wipe his eyes. Shu grimaced politely.

Tsuyoshi Koike said something about the water on the train tasting funny—"Ought to have brought some water with me"—and soon fell into a deep, drunken sleep. Shu moved over to the seat next to the pretty girl who had been pointed out to him as Pat Mori. She was reading a book.

"*True Confessions?*" She ignored him. He looked at the title. *Man's Hope* by André Malraux.

"Wow! Deep little thing, aren't you?" She looked up at him and through him and then turned to look out of the window.

"That's right, better take a last look at the ocean. We won't be seeing that again for a long time." It took him quite awhile to get her thawed out, but after awhile she smiled at his persistence and began talking to him.

"I think I've seen you once or twice in Oceanville," she said.

"I taught at the college this last term. French. I never got around to knowing any of the Japanese except one boy who was in one of my classes."

When the long line of evacuee cars headed inland, they both turned their seats around to catch a last glimpse of the sea that stretched bluely and endlessly out until it met the paler blue of the sky.

"I'm going to miss the magenta and red bougainvillea that cover Doheny Ledge. And the row of hibiscus near San Clemente. And going grunion hunting. And the fog coming in from the ocean in the afternoon." She was sentimental about the same things that he was, Shu discovered. He decided that he liked Pat Mori very much.

Just before noon, the M.P.'s, helped by little Yoyo, passed out box lunches to everybody. It was then that one of them, trying to arouse Tsuyoshi Koike to make him take his lunch, found that his sleep was one from which he would never awaken. He was dead.

A unanimous horrified gasp hissed through the car. Pat, suddenly seeming to remember something, paled. Shu stood watching while the young train doctor said, "Heart attack or apoplexy," and the M.P.'s carried the still body out and into the M.P. car just ahead. The car was quiet with a puzzled silence, as if the people could not grasp the idea that one among them had died, and the comings and goings of the grey-haired nurse, the young doctor, and the M.P.'s were watched with morbid curiosity. A baby cried, sensing something frightening.

Then the rustle of lunch boxes being opened came to Shu's ears. He shrugged; even though a man died, the living must eat.

Something bothered Shu and a vague suspicion pricked him. He looked towards Mrs. Koike, the dead man's mother. It was evident that she was shaken, but she was not weeping. Her face was a stoic mask as it leaned over her knitting.

Shu went over and introduced himself. A few polite condolences, and then suddenly, "Was Tsuyoshi subject to heart attacks or apoplexy?"

She was puzzled, but she answered him. "No, but he drank too much, and I often told him he was weakening his heart, but he wouldn't listen to me." Despite her calm words, Shu saw the nervous needles in her hands dropping stitches and realized that his questioning was hurting her.

He tried to walk into the M.P. car but was stopped by one of the soldiers. "I want to talk to the doctor." The doctor came towards him, wiping perspiration from his brow with a handkerchief but unable to wipe away the frown of worry that had cut into his forehead.

"Doctor, I think it was murder."

"Murder? I examined him. He wasn't strangled or shot or anything. It's bad enough him dying without your trying to make a case of murder out of it. This is the first time anyone's died on an evacuee train."

"Everyone on the car hated him. They all had reason to kill. It could have been poison."

"You've been reading too many mystery stories."

"Sure, I have. It's my hobby. And one thing it's taught me is that a lot of so-called natural deaths are really perfect crimes."

The young doctor cursed, not wanting to believe him. But he was becoming interested. "And do you think you can solve the murder, if it is a murder?"

"Maybe. Do I have your permission to try?"

The doctor shrugged and sighed. "Go ahead. Do you want to examine the body?" He wasn't at all sure that he should be letting Shu interfere, but he was young and the more Shu talked the more he was convinced that there was something to what he was saying.

Koike still looked as if he were enjoying a deep sleep, except that his face was rather pale. It did seem a natural death, so natural that Shu would not have been too surprised if the man had suddenly turned over, muttering drowsily, "They hate me," and then gone back to sleep. He talked awhile to the doctor and then decided to do a little investigating.

Shu had had no experience in such matters. But he had read detective stories all his life—well, nearly all—and now he was going to put some of that gleaned knowledge to use. Besides, he had always had contempt for the way the storybook detectives always allowed a few more to be murdered before they solved the case. There would only be one victim here, that man now covered with a blanket and lying in the M.P. car, if he had anything to say about it.

He would begin by interviewing all likely suspects. Everyone with the exception of the baby and the children—though that little ghoul Yoyo was capable of anything, he thought—everyone was suspect. Even himself, he had to admit. Come to think of it, he had had the best opportunity to commit the crime because he was the only one who had associated with the fellow. If he weren't so absolutely positive that he hadn't done it, the first thing he would do would be to put himself under arrest.

"Did you kill the man, Shu Shingu?" he asked himself.

"Nope," he answered.

"I didn't think you did. But you're really sure?"

"Of course. Don't be so persistent."

"All right, then, you're eliminated."

"Thank God."

But the other passengers weren't going to get off as easily as that, he promised himself, and going over and seating himself beside the sullen young Toro Nogawa, he started in on his questioning. Koike had said that Toro hated him. Toro told Shu why. Koike had accompanied the FBI to the house of the Nogawas and helped them search the house. The Nogawas had been taken for possessing suspicious literature, the Japanese school textbooks. The FBI men did not read Japanese, but Koike had persuaded them that seditious material was printed in the books.

"How did you feel toward Koike?"

"I hated his guts."

"You admit that? Why did you kill him?"

The young man was calm. "I didn't. He died of a heart attack. You heard the doctor say that yourself. He wasn't worth killing, anyway. You don't know what that guy did. He used his new position to get petty vengeance on everybody for every real and imagined slight. He tried to convince the government men that everyone he had a personal grudge against was a saboteur-potential. They caught on to him and kicked him out and promised that the ones who had been sent to concentration camps because of him would get the first hearings. If someone killed him, more power to that someone. Leave him alone, he's a hero."

Shu saw that he wasn't getting anywhere. He asked a few more questions and then sighed. Stymied. He went over to Mrs. Koike.

"Did you hate your son?"

"Hate him? How could I? I'm his mother. I bore him, brought him up, watched him take his first steps, heard him speak his first words. Can any mother hate her son remembering him in childhood, no matter what a rotter he turned out to be?"

Shu was cruel. He felt he had to be. "Let's not get sentimental. The child Tsuyoshi was an absolutely different person from the man Koike who betrayed his friends for trivial, personal reasons. Did you still love him when he lied to the FBI?"

"He was always weak, not so much physically as morally. He was only doing what he thought right, the best way he knew."

"Would you have done these things?"

"No. I begged him to stop. He struck me and told me that it was for my sake that he was doing it. We never did have much money. And after the war began, he was able to get me nice things, like new linoleum."

"Your conscience let you accept them?"

"He loved me. It was the only way he had of showing it."

"You mean hitting you?"

"Please . . ." A quick spasm of pain contracted her face.

"I'm sorry."

The newlyweds next. When Shu explained his purpose in questioning them, the man was resentful, more so at questions directed at his wife than at himself.

"You were engaged to Koike before you met your husband?"

"It was sort of taken for granted when we were children. Our families were old friends. I didn't think much about it until I met Joe." Her husband took her hand then and pressed it.

"The doctor said Koike died of a heart attack or apoplexy," Joe Miyamoto protested.

"I have reason to believe he was murdered." Frances and Joe Miyamoto cast startled looks at each other.

"Did he annoy you after you and Joe began seeing each other?"

"Once he came over and tried to make me change my mind. He was drunk. I hated him then."

Her young husband spoke, "I caught him at it and threw the guy out. After she told me what it was all about, I wished I'd killed him. I'm not spilling any tears because he's dead. If someone murdered him, I'd like to shake the guy's hand."

Only an innocent man would dare to talk like that, thought Shu, when he knew that anything he might say would be used against him. But then it might be a clever bluff.

"Sure you wouldn't like to shake your own hand?"

"Do you think I'd admit it if I would?"

Shu shrugged, "Hope springs eternal in the human breast."

He questioned the other passengers, Mr. and Mrs. Murata, Sakamoto, and Nakamura. They all admitted having only contempt for the dead man, but none seemed too surprised to know that it might have been murder and none could or would give him any hints as to whom it might have been.

Mrs. Kimi Ogata was distraught when he spoke to her. Her hand dabbed a flimsy handkerchief around her nose and her mouth. His speaking to her was more to reassure her and lessen her evident fright than to question her. It was hot and stuffy and the M.P's had asked that the windows be closed and kept that way.

"It's so hot," she complained.

"Maybe the doctor will get you permission to keep your window open. Do you feel sick?"

"Just a little dizzy."

"And your leg, how's that?"

"Oh, my leg hasn't bothered me for quite awhile. Before it was set the last time, though, it hurt so much I had to have a sedative. But it's all right now." Her strikingly attractive face twitched nervously under its make-up, almost as if she had a tic.

When the doctor came around the next time, he opened the window for her and she seemed to relax.

Shu got permission to search the little bags that almost everyone had with them, besides their larger pieces of luggage in the baggage cars. He found paper diapers, baby bottles, candy, make-up kits, books and magazines, and other little necessities. He found nothing interesting until he came to Toro Nogawa's small, black, smooth-leather kit. Tucked away in a corner was a small glass bottle half-filled with strychnine crystals.

"Why is this in here?" he asked Toro, who looked uncomfortable and mopped his flushed face incessantly.

"I'd forgotten it on a shelf, and when I took a last look around the house I found it and put it in the bag because everything else was too much trouble to undo."

"How do you come to have strychnine in the first place?"

"Japanese school-teaching doesn't pay much. We had a fair-sized strawberry field, too. Some birds kept pecking at the berries as soon as they got ripe, and I got some strychnine at the drugstore to kill them with."

"How did you use it?"

"I dissolved it in water, then got some chicken feed and stirred it in till it got pasty, dried it, and spread it along the berry rows. But it didn't work. I was just trying it out and this much was left over, and I didn't want to throw it away so I just kept it. I put up some scarecrows instead of trying to kill the birds, and that worked lots better." He was scared but defiant.

"Thanks for the lesson in agriculture, Nogawa," said Shu.

Shu Shingu went back to the seat next to Pat and put his head in his hands. It looked like he had bitten off more than he could chew.

"Found the murderer yet, Shu?" Pat's question was casually put, but her voice had a tremor in it.

"Listen, why don't you confess so I can clear this mess and get it over with."

"But I didn't do it."

"Who do *you* think did?"

She hesitated, "I-I don't have the slightest idea and you know it."

"You almost sound as if you do know."

"Don't be silly." Her fingers fumbled nervously as she tried to turn the pages of her book.

"Versatile, aren't you?"

"What do you mean?" Pat was startled.

Shu pointed to the book in her lap. "When you read a book you don't just read it from cover to cover right side up, but upside down too."

"Oh." She reddened and then turned to the window, and after that she didn't answer when he spoke to her. He looked out too and saw the grotesque stone formations, the cactus, sagebrush, and the hot stretches of desert sand pass swiftly by them. After awhile he stopped trying to make her talk, and leaning back, he lit a cigarette and closed his eyes.

Suddenly he sat up. Could it be? Incredible! But it must be . . . the only one . . . and . . . He laughed softly and triumphantly so that Pat turned and looked at him queerly.

He stood up and made his way to the head of the car and motioned for attention. The doctor stood with him.

"Tsuyoshi Koike died this morning. The doctor here diagnosed it as a heart attack or apoplexy, but I wasn't satisfied. It was obvious that everyone thought they had a reason for hating him—he knew he was hated and I'm not saying that the hate and distrust were wrong, I'm not up here to discuss moral values, but I believed that a murder was committed because of this hate. I've had to intrude on your privacy because of this belief, and I'm sorry, but I think I know now who the murderer is because you allowed me to carry on my investigation. I examined Koike's body; he wasn't shot or strangled. He suffered no bizarre death by poisoned darts or anything like that. I concluded that it must have been poison."

Shu was aware that he was doing it badly. He promised himself he would never meddle in anything like this again. But he hadn't finished here yet.

"You all look at Toro Nogawa suspiciously. You think because I found strychnine in his bag that he was the murderer. But death by strychnine is a violent and frightening thing. The body becomes arched in an unnatural position. Am I right, doctor?" The tall, young doctor nodded. Eyes no longer stared at Toro Nogawa.

"Death came quietly to Koike. It was as if he fell asleep. It must have been some sleeping powder or some similar drug which was slipped unnoticed into something Koike ate or drank. An autopsy will determine just what drug, later. I was sitting next to Koike when Yoyo brought him some water. I remember that Koike complained of the water tasting queer. I know now that somebody must have put the drug into the water before he drank it. I think Yoyo can tell us if somebody stopped him when he was bringing it."

"He's asleep now, Mr. Shingu," Yoyo's mother spoke up.

"Oh." He was going to continue speaking, when he suddenly shouted. "What? Quick, doctor, look at him, he looks drugged!"

Frightened, Mrs. Nakamura said, "But he's only sleeping."

"That's what we thought Koike was doing."

The boy's mother screamed and collapsed.

The doctor and Shu carried the little figure to the M.P. car. Yoyo was still breathing faintly. "Stomach pump . . . hurry," Shu urged the doctor.

Yoyo's eyelids fluttered open. He knew Shu and smiled. "Shushingura, I don't feel so good."

"I know."

Shu went back to the car. "He's all right now," he told Mrs.

Nakamura. He watched her as she gave a sharp sob of relief and went to her son.

There was a slight commotion, and Shu turned around. Some woman's voice screamed hysterically, "She jumped out of the window . . . she jumped out of the window!" Someone pulled the emergency cord, and the train shuddered jerkily to a violent stop. A couple of soldiers ran back along the track to where a crumpled body was lying.

Shu watched the doctor examine the body and then roll it over onto one half of an army blanket and fold the other half over to cover the body. The doctor came up to where Shu was watching from the train doorway. "You were right. Look what was in the purse that was clutched in her hand." He held out a small brown glass vial. It was an empty bottle of quarter-grain hypodermic morphine tablets.

The train started up again, and the car was filled with excited but relieved conversation. Shu, setting fire to a cigarette, saw that his hands were shaking. "Lord, how I've bungled it. There must have been some way I could have worked it so that she wouldn't have killed herself and the unborn baby."

And then, because he felt he had to talk to somebody, he went over to Pat and began explaining to her while she kept her eyes on the text of *Man's Hope*.

"I don't think Mrs. Ogata hated Koike any more than anybody else did. It was just that she was more sensitive and neurotic than the others and more unable to control her hate. And the condition she was in, the hurried process of evacuation, the oppressing heat—everything combined in such a way that she was unable to stand it any longer, and her mind, already warped with worry about her husband and the coming baby, cracked under the strain. She put the morphine pellets into the water Yoyo brought to Koike. Those pellets were probably left over from the time she had to take a sedative for the pain she suffered in her leg. She must have distracted twice Yoyo's attention in some way and dropped the tablets in the water."

"I know," Pat said.

"What do you mean?" He was incredulous.

"I saw her stop the boy when he was taking Koike water and make him look at some yucca plants we were passing while she put the tablets in the water." She spoke in little gasps, as if she were breathless.

He was stunned. A mixture of anger and bewilderment overwhelmed him, and when he finally spoke his voice was unnaturally low and thick with controlled anger. "You're a cold-blooded number, aren't you? If you knew all about it, why didn't you speak up? She needn't have killed herself or tried to poison Yoyo."

Pat's face whitened. She began to cry quietly with huge tears rolling down her cheeks and making wet, shiny splotches on *Man's Hope*.

"Why?" Shu insisted more gently.

She shook her head. Her hands clutched tightly at the armrests of her seat. "I wasn't sure and I was afraid." How could she tell him that since evacuation had become a reality her life had somehow taken on the quality of a dream and that she felt numbed, as though nothing now were awakening her and that she was beginning to feel whole and alive once more?

Shu, who had stood up, sat down again. He sighed deeply and then put his hands over hers. He didn't quite understand, but he felt that he would soon. Besides, who was he to criticize anybody else's action?

After awhile she stopped crying, and by the time they had crossed the Colorado and were almost at Parker, *Man's Hope* had slid unnoticed to the floor, they were both smiling radiantly at each other, he was still holding her hand.

(1942)

Eucalyptus

Laurel and I have stayed in touch over the years, both of us more or less back in business, exchanging yearly cards and such. One day she even drives over for dinner—rice and chicken teriyaki—during which I ask if she heard from Mary of Van Nuys. I recall them getting along famously, Laurel admiring Mary's wry matter-of-factness. There isn't a city in the country you could name where Mary hasn't once lived—St. Louis, Wichita, places like that. When we line up for our medication, Mary always gets Metamucil along with her pills.

Laurel flabbergasts me by answering, "Toki, you're the only one I remember." How can this be? I can summon up so many faces, wondering to this day about their gnawing concerns. True, our cots are next to each other, and I always make it a point to seek her out because she seems perfectly fine to me. The urgent advice of my husband Saul, a pretty shrewd fellow, is to stick with the ones that are just about to go home, to get in on the secret of getting well. The only trouble is that everybody else in this place seems okay to me; I feel like the only sick one.

So, those hot July days on the broad patio, Laurel and I usually share the shade of the same bright-striped canvas swing. We light endless cigarettes, weave colored yarn onto plastic baskets, call it occupational therapy. We wait for our names to be called if it's our day to see the psychiatrist. When that horrible sensation of psychic imbalance overwhelms me, when I become Munch's anguished, O-mouthed woman at this end of the bridge, I lift my eyes towards the eucalyptus trees towering over the terraces behind the mansion, silently praying, O God above the eucalyptus trees . . . help me, heal me, make me whole. . . .

So when Laurel says she doesn't remember Mary, whose sweet, weatherbeaten face I would recognize anywhere in the world, it throws me for a loop. Then a possible explanation occurs to me: Laurel, impatient to get back to the land of the living, opts to stay on for electro-shock while I, willy-nilly, venture back uneasily to my place with my husband and children. Perhaps it is the electro-shock that has erased the memory of all the other women. There is a college student here who has undergone electro-shock and complains about the results. Her bed in the dormitory is surrounded by piles of books which she seems to be reading all at one time. Once I overhear her crying out to her visiting parents, "How would you like it if you lost your whole memory?"

This might be the cause of Laurel's forgetfulness. The treatment doesn't seem to hasten her discharge. After she gets back to her apartment and a less demanding job—part of her condition seems to be the result of stress at the workplace, where a superior without let-up demanded perfection. We keep tabs on one another by phone. "So how are you doing?" I ask. "Oh, you know," she says, "Comme ci, comme ça," which is exactly my condition.

There are others getting electro-shock, the idea of which terrifies me. One morning at the medicine counter, the nurse doesn't hand me my tiny fluted paper cup of the usual medications. "You don't get any today—you're scheduled for electro-shock."

My hair stands on end. "Nobody told me about it," I protest.

"Here's your name on the list," she says, turning the paper around so I can see for myself. "There. Amparo Martinez."

What a relief, "That's not me. I'm Toki Gonzales." Amparo's the only other Hispanic name in the place. I can't help an inward epithet about white people. Amparo, she's the one who's been weeping ever since she got here. When her bewildered husband, small and mild-mannered, tries to comfort her during his visits, she answers in wails and sobs. True, neither of them look stereotypically Hispanic, but neither do I, being Japanese and having acquired my surname through marriage.

Most of the staff and patients are white. But there is a sprinkling of us others. When I first get here, a young Chinese couple attend to me. It seems to be the middle of the night, and I undress and lie down on the examining table so they can attach any number of gadgets and wires to my body, which they hook up to machines. Are they husband and wife? Brother and sister? They go about their monitoring job efficiently, saying little. My rib cage reminds me of an old washboard. I've lost a lot of weight from not being able to eat. Solid food won't go down at all, so I've only had a few sips of milk in recent days.

The occupational therapist is also Chinese. She's usually in her office, so her assistant, a tall, young black girl from Minnesota, is the one seeing to our activities. She drags us to the terrace out back to play tetherball. I'm surprised to find myself enjoying it. She also comes out to the patio to check our handiwork on the plastic baskets. Arts and crafts are not my forte. My yarn work is pretty basic and mangy compared with the meticulous, imaginative productions of some of the others. It takes me forever to finish one, because I have to undo a lot of it and start all over again.

Then there's Phyllis, ah, Phyllis. We all flock around her when she's on duty. She is tender loving care in person. She sits with us and chats as though she has all the time in the world. She gives us a no-fail method for fixing corn-on-the-cob, for instance. When, after a day or two, I finally decide to take a shower, I ask her to stand by outside the stall because I'm still afraid to be enclosed by myself, afraid I'll go berserk. She obliges, like it's the most natural thing in the world. When one of the women curses a mite too much for Phyllis' taste, she takes her into the washroom and cleans her mouth out with soap, while we gather around and watch. The offender takes it in good humor, too. Phyllis is black and the only person on the staff we'd all do anything for.

The only black patient comes and goes twice during my stay of a month or so. The young woman is obviously distraught on both occasions, and her husband equally so. He does not really want her to be admitted, it appears; he wants her home where she belongs. But he doesn't know what to do with her at home, either. An auto accident has left her in this tortured state. No physical scars, but the psychic ones incapacitate her. The husband is not alone; men tend to respond to this kind of emergency with impatience and anger. They have been on the receiving end of care so long, taking for granted all the work that goes into a smooth-running household, that they cannot seem to grasp that they will just have to do without for awhile.

Later in the day I meet Amparo in the corridor. She's no longer crying, for the first time, but she doesn't seem to know where she is. I guide her to the other dormitory and help her find her bed. But she doesn't need any help after her second treatment the following week. She is suddenly transformed into another woman entirely, engaging in sprightly conversation, even clasping her hands in joy over the gain of a pound or two when we all go in for our weighing.

The shock treatment also works miracles for Anna, the tall blonde European who sits alone at the card table playing endless solitaire. After one treatment—the patient is first anesthetized here before the current is applied—she comes to life, bringing out her art supplies, large sheets of thick, grainy white paper and charcoal sticks. Nothing will do but I must sit for her; she has never drawn a Japanese before. However, as I oblige because I have nothing much else to do, I am alarmed to note that when the intercom comes on with its static buzz, she almost leaps out of her skin, as though the electrical residue in her is responding to the electricity in the speaker up there on the wall. She continues her quick sketching after each interruption, making no mention of this reaction. She says this is her second episode of depression, her first coming some years ago after the death of her brilliant husband. After a day or two, she is gone. The word is that "she came back too fast." After a short absence, she is back among us, a charming and witty conversationalist as she resumes her sketches in the "booby hatch," which is what she calls Hilltop House.

Amparo and Anna are not the only unforgettable people. There is a gorgeous young woman who goes out every weekday to a job, her face carefully made up and her head wrapped in a turban. It seems she cannot be trusted with scissors; she has a compulsion to cut off all her hair. Her latest barbering results when she borrows shears from a woman who keeps them to cut the yarn for her baskets. "I didn't know," the woman says. "When she asked to borrow them, I just handed them to her, like I would anybody else." The owner of the scissors seems hale and hearty to me; the only possible clue to her being here is when I overhear her saying, with rapture, "I just love pills!" As for the shorn beauty, the story is that her father had his heart set on a son instead of a daughter.

There is another well-dressed woman who comes out to the patio every morning and works a crossword puzzle. "I do it to make sure I'm not crazy," she says. But her wardrobe causes another young woman some distress, "That's why I'm sick, because I can't afford pretty clothes." We doubt her, but we do not plumb much more. She and her husband are from Kansas. He comes to take her back home to Menninger's.

Hilda is a plumpish woman who reads omnivorously. If she is not ensconced in one of the easy chairs in the spacious living room with a heavy tome in her lap (one seems to be the history of France), she is walking around with a couple more. I can't help noticing her in the dining room because her enjoyment of food is obvious. She grabs a couple pieces of dessert for herself before she sits down with the others at her table. Some months later, when I return for a group therapy session or two, I encounter her there looking emaciated. "She's been fasting," someone explains. "She says she doesn't deserve to eat." Another woman's arms are purple-raw. She has scratched them till they bleed. "I have blasphemed against the Holy Ghost," she says, "I have committed the unforgivable sin." We get to a Bible to check the passage, but she is not specific about the manner in which she has blasphemed. Someone brings up Saul who persecuted Jews, but who later became Paul the Christian missionary. Would she not say that if anyone had blasphemed, Saul surely had? Yet he was forgiven, even chosen to spread the Word. But she refuses to accept this premise. She is

Catholic, and one Sunday her family comes to take her to Mass, and she agrees to go.

This one has come here after the birth of a son. "I hate him," she says. "Everything would be all right if he would just go away." She already has a little daughter whom she loves dearly. There is a lovely young Britisher whom I meet in the library. We both have been unable to read. All the books look too demanding. She has dark hair cut short like a black cap and her eyes have a brooding look. She has bandages on both wrists. I find what looks like an easy book to read, by Henry Van Dyke, something about the three wise men. She lounges in a chair and gently answers questions in her clipped speech. We both agree we're smoking too much. Later, out on the patio, she has visitors. Her husband, a musician in a black combo, has brought fellow band members along to cheer her up, and there is much laughter as they converse.

One husband is indignant when he finds out that we can help out in the kitchen washing pots or whatever, as part of our therapy. "We're paying good money here—why should you have to wash dishes? That's ridiculous!" His wife has a semi-private room. She recalls that her mother attempted suicide once, after which she followed her mother around wherever she went. In her gentle voice, she tells us that she doesn't want to live any longer, but that she is afraid to die.

One day there is an intercom announcement about some of the patients going down to a nearby restaurant for lunch and coming back tiddly. We are reminded that drinking is strictly forbidden. I suspect my roommate to the right in the dormitory, the older woman who doesn't seem to belong here—there's nothing wrong with her that I can see. Probably she's here because of booze.

When I first get to Hilltop House, I am frightened by what might lay in store. In the dining room that night, I am seized with vertigo. The food on my plate, which I cannot eat, is a blur. I stare at the blur and am certain that this time, I am going over the edge into darkness from which I will never come back.

Somehow I am out on the patio in the warm evening air. A small group of young women, younger anyway than my thirty-eight, sit here and there about me. I hear their voices through my fog of sustained agony, and I cannot believe what I am hearing. They are like grizzled veterans of the emotional wars. They gaily accuse each other of having had to wear diapers back there at the county facility they've been transferred from. I dimly sense that they are, each and every one of them, interrupted suicides.

This is where Phyllis first appears. I hear one of the girls ask her,

"Don't you think he'll leave his wife and marry me?" And Phyllis shakes her head, "I wouldn't count on it."

The first hint that maybe I will get over this thing comes when the head psychiatrist interviews me. He diagnoses it as "anxiety." It feels good to have a definite name for it. He says others have been helped here.

The doctor in charge of my case is on the quiet side, bespectacled, and I blurt out everything in my life that I can think of that could possibly be a clue to my problem. One day we discuss a current magazine article about psychiatry. So how do I feel about the psychiatry I'm having, he asks. "I guess you're the ideal psychiatrist," I say, "bland, colorless, nonintrusive, but expertly guiding the patient."

At my next appointment, he's smoking a long cigar.

Another time I tell him about a friend up north to whom I've mentioned my illness. "Let me tell you about MY operation," the friend has written; it seems he has been suffering all along. "He's Jewish," I remember the yarmulke, "very devout." Such a slight movement backwards in his chair so I barely notice, as I go on, "God doesn't seem to sustain him, either." Afterwards, I remember. The instinctive recoil—ah, I did not mean; he must be—inadvertently have I caused the doctor pain?

As I grope my way towards health, I realize I am learning things. "I lost my girlish laughter" is a phrase now with new meaning, as is "The Age of Anxiety." Finally, too, I understand: "If the salt hath lost his savour, wherewith shall it be salted?"

The doctor gives me a sentence to live by, "There is nothing in daily life that is insurmountable." Even though I think to myself, it's not daily life; it's the accrual.

I tell him of days gone by when my heart almost burst with the joy of being alive, when even the dog crud along the sidewalk seemed right and proper. He suggests that perhaps I could learn to scale down this romanticism, that perhaps then I need not descend to feelings so low, reduced to a quivering mass of protoplasm by my "fear of responsibility." But I do see little ways in which I am getting better. The freeway noises no longer prevent my sleep. I am able to down food, even enjoy the chocolate cake baked by the rather hefty cook (she says she climbs the steep hill each day but cannot lose a pound). I even sit down at the grand piano in the living room and tinkle out the few bars I remember of "Für Elise."

Still, when I leave, I don't feel ready. I understand now why Molly, another patient, sneaks off without a word to anyone. She probably doesn't see that much improvement and is just going home to give it a try.

There has been a study of neurotics that is something to ponder. The

Eysenck Study, it is called, and it says that in patients undergoing psycho-analysis, there is a 44 percent improvement rate, in those undergoing psychotherapy, a 64 percent improvement rate. But there is a 72 percent improvement rate in those who receive no treatment whatsoever. What is one to make of such statistics?

It is good to be home and to have the children back. First, kind relatives and friends take them in, obliging me forever. When it looks like I might be awhile, friends arrange for the boy to go to the Japanese Children's Home. He loves it there because there is sushi every day—his favorite food. And the kids there are taken to a pool for swimming lessons. The girls, still babies, go to a foster home. The lady there loves babies and her three children, including an adopted half-Japanese daughter, are all in school now, so she has decided to care for other people's children. Her husband's work keeps him away from home a lot. But Saul is agitated by the children's absence and annoys the lady by calling constantly.

It takes me a couple of years before I finally have a really pleasant day. Meanwhile I return to Hilltop House for some group therapy meetings. One day when I arrive, Phyllis takes me aside and asks me to speak to a Korean woman who has just arrived. So I find in her another woman who, after an extremely difficult delivery, cannot accept her newborn son. She tells me of her symptoms, which are much like mine in the beginning, and I am able to assure her that she is going to be all right.

Hilltop House also phones when another Asian patient turns up. So I call her and learn that she is from Japan. I have to rummage in the back of my mind for words that I haven't used in years, but manage to get the information that she and her brother have come to this country together. They are getting on well until her brother falls in love with and marries a white girl. Whether from feelings of abandonment or not, she decides to kill herself. But she is fine, she tells me, she has already finished a whole slew of baskets. She certainly sounds chipper enough.

However, when I get over to the House the next time and inquire about her, she is gone. She has been transferred to a facility for more serious cases. "She sounded fine when we talked on the phone," I protest. "Some do that," I'm told. "They hide their real feelings and they're thinking of ways to do themselves in."

I remember one who is discharged and goes home. The news we get the next day is that she is dead. We are pretty subdued for the next few days. I don't know whether the group therapy helps or not. As we are partway through one session, the psychiatrist observes, "I know why everyone is so depressed." He says it is because he is going to be away for a couple of weeks. When he leaves the room, most of us express surprise. We had no idea he was going to be absent. This is the same doctor who lays down the dictum, "All depression is anger turned inwards." Which reminds me that I have heard it said that it is obvious in medical school which students are going to take up psychiatry.

Unwanted sons, intransigent married lovers, husbands and sons who treat us like dirt, father who wanted a son instead—this aggregate of female woe, are we all here because of what men do or don't? No, it is not that simple. Probably there are men in like places whose vulnerabilities stem from dealings with mothers, wives, women friends? Where do the roots of our malaise lie buried? In the ways we are nurtured or not nurtured? Or further back, when the first mother received news of her firstborn refusing to keep his only brother?

The echo of her howl comes to us without diminution across the tumult of the ages.

(1970)

A Fire in Fontana

Something weird happened to me not long after the end of the Second World War. I wouldn't go so far as to say that I, a Japanese American, became Black, because that's a pretty melodramatic statement. But some kind of transformation did take place, the effects of which are with me still.

I remember reading a book called *Young Man with a Horn*, by Dorothy Baker, which is said to be based on the life of Bix Beiderbecke, in which the narrator early wonders if his musician friend would have come to the same tragic end if he hadn't become involved with Negroes (in 1985, how odd the word has become!) and with one musician in particular.

In real life, there happened to be a young White musician in an otherwise Black band which played in such places as the Club Alabam on Central Avenue. His name was Johnny Otis, and the group became quite respected in jazz and blues circles. But his name was once Veliotis—he is of Greek heritage; in more recent years he has become the pastor of a church in Watts. I suppose he, too, arrived at a place in his life from which there was no turning back. But his life, as I see it, represents a triumph.

But I don't know whether mine is or not. Because when I realized that something was happening to me, I scrambled to backtrack for awhile. By then it was too late. I continued to look like the Nisei I was, with my height remaining at slightly over four feet ten, my hair straight, my vision myopic. Yet I know that this event transpired inside me; sometimes I see it as my inward self being burnt black in a certain fire.

Or perhaps the process, unbeknownst to me, had begun even earlier. Once, during the war, squeezed into a hot summer bus out of Chicago, my seatmate was a blond girl about my size or maybe a little taller, who started telling me her life story.

The young woman wore a bright-flowered jersey dress, swirling purples and reds and greens on a white background, and she chortled a lot. She said she was twenty-eight years old and married to a man in his sixties, a customer of where she'd been a waitress. Just now she had been visiting in Chicago with her married sister and she'd had a lot of fun, her brother-in-law pretending he was going to drown her in the lake where they'd all gone for a swim. She said in East St. Louis, where she lived, all the kids of the neighborhood would come around for her cookies. Her husband was very good to her, so she was quite content.

The bus was south of Springfield somewhere when suddenly, startling me, the girl sat bolt upright and began chortling. "I knew it! I knew it!" For some reason, she was filled with glee.

"See that nigger?" she asked. "He got off the bus and went into that restaurant to ask for a drink and they told him to go around outside to the faucet!"

Sure enough, the young fellow was bent awkwardly over the outside tap which protruded from the wooden building about a foot from the ground, trying to get a drink without getting his clothes sloshed.

"I knew they wouldn't give him a glass of water!" She crowed as though it were a personal victory.

Here I was on a bus going back to the camp in Arizona where my father still lived, and I knew there was a connection between my seatmate's joy and our having been put in that hot and windblown place of barracks.

Even though I didn't dare shove her out the window, I must have managed to get some sign of protest across to her. After awhile, she said doggedly, "Well, it's all in the way you're brought up. I was brought up this way, so that's the way I feel."

After the girl got off in East St. Louis, where (she had informed me) Negroes walked on one side of the street and White people on the other, the bus went through a bleak and dry territory where when one got off, there were large grasshoppers which clung to the walls like ivy and scrunched underfoot on the pavement like eggshells. The toilets were a new experience, too, labeled either Colored or White. I dared to try White first, and no one challenged me, so I continued this presumptuous practice at all the way stations of Texas. After I got back on the bus the first time, I was haunted by the long look given me by a cleaning woman in the restroom. I decided, for the sake of my conscience, that the Negro woman had never seen a Japanese before.

So the first job I got after coming out of camp again was with a Negro newspaper in Los Angeles. I really wanted the job badly, and was amazed when I was hired over a Nisei fellow who was more qualified since the ad in the *Pacific Citizen* had specified a man. Moreover, the young man, already a Nisei journalist of some note, had edited his own newspaper before the war and knew athletes like Kenny Washington and Woody Strode because he'd gone to UCLA with them. The idea of hiring a Japanese on a

Black newspaper was that maybe the returning Japanese businessmen would advertise and this would attract some Japanese readership, and maybe there would be the beginnings of an intercultural community.

It didn't work out that way at all, because I'm not one of your go-getters or anything. I did rewrites mostly, of stories culled from all the other Black newspapers across the country that exchanged with the *Los Angeles Tribune*, from the very professional ones like the *Chicago Defender* (with columnists like Langston Hughes and S. I. Hayakawa) and the *New Amsterdam News* to smaller ones like the primly proper Bostonian sheet with elegant society notes and the smudged weeklies from small towns in Mississippi and Oklahoma that looked to have been turned out on antiquated, creaking presses. Almost every week, I toted up the number of alleged lynchings across the country and combined them into one story.

The office was on the mezzanine of the Dunbar Hotel, where people well-known in the entertainment industry, as they say, would regularly stay. There was a spirited running argument going on almost every day of the week down in the foyer which the *Tribune* office overlooked. The denizens of the place, retired members of the Brotherhood of Sleeping Car Porters and such, were provoked to discussion regularly by one of the hotel owners, a Negro who looked absolutely White and whose dark eyes smoldered with a bitter fire. The inexhaustible topic was Race, always Race.

I got a snootful of it. Sometimes I got to wondering whether Negroes talked about anything else. No matter what the initial remark, if the discussion continued for any length of time, the issue boiled down to Race. Even the jokes were darkly tinged with a dash of bitters. More than once I was easily put down with a casual, "That's mighty White of you," the connotations of which were devastating.

But it was not all work. One Halloween Mrs. Preacley, the secretary, and I visited a nightclub to watch a beauty contest. Among the contestants flouncing about in their scented silks and furs across the platform were a couple of guys employed by the hotel. One young man, donning a mop of auburn curls, a pink sheath dress, and high heels, had turned into a young matron; another competed in a simple white gown, statuesquely, regally, as though posing for an expensive fashion magazine. Another time, the bosses took a visiting fireman out for a night on the town and a couple of us Nisei were invited along. At one Sunset Strip nightclub the waiter was slow in returning with drinks and the table chitchat suddenly turned into a serious consideration of what strategy to use if the waiter failed to return. But eventually the drinks came.

The office was frequently visited by a well-to-do retired physician, the color of café-au-lait, whose everyday outfit consisted of a creamy Panama, impeccable white suit, and cane. With his distinguished-looking goatee, all that was missing was the frosted, tall, tinkling glass topped with a sprig of mint. The young eager beaver sports editor–advertising manager rushed in and out at all hours, breathlessly, bringing in a new display ad or dashing off to interview a boxing contender.

Later he was to get an appointment to West Point from Rep. Helen Gahagan Douglas. There were glimpses of the sprinkling of showfolk who stayed at the hotel—Billy Eckstine, the recently married Ossie Davis and Ruby Dee, the Delta Rhythm Boys; and down on Central Avenue, the theater marquee would advertise live acts like Pigmeat Markham, Mantan Moreland, Moms Mabley, and Redd Foxx. A tall young police lieutenant, later to become mayor of the city, came by to protest the newspaper's editorial on police brutality.

One day when a new secretary named Miss Moten and I were in the mezzanine office, which was really three desks and two filing cabinets jammed into one end of the open mezzanine, with a counter separating the office from the subscribing and advertising public, a nice-looking young man with a mustache came up the stairs.

He said his name was Short. Urgently, he told us a disturbing story. He said he and his wife and two children had recently purchased a house in Fontana. They had not been accorded a very warm welcome by the community. In fact, he said, there had been several threats of get-out-or-else, and his family was living in fear. He wanted his situation publicized so that some sentiment could be mustered in support of his right to live in Fontana. He was making the rounds of the three Negro newspapers in town to enlist their assistance.

I took down his story for the editor to handle when she got in. After he left, I noticed Miss Moten was extremely agitated. She was on the tense side to begin with, but she was a quiet, conscientious worker and always spoke in a gentle murmur.

But now her eyes were blazing with fury. She spat out the words. "I hate White people!"

"What?" I said, feeling stupid. I'd heard her all right, but I'd never seen her even halfway angry before.

"I hate White people! They're all the same!"

Then, later the same week, there was a fire in Fontana. Dead in the blaze, which appeared to have started with gasoline poured all around the house and outbuildings, were the young man who had told us his story, his comely wife, and their two lovely children, a boy and a girl (one of the other newspapers had obtained a recent portrait of the family, probably from relatives in the city).

There was an investigation, of course. The official conclusion was that probably the man had set the gasoline fire himself, and the case was closed.

Among those who doubted the police theory was a White priest who was so skeptical that he wrote a play about the fire in Fontana. *Trial by Fire*, he called it. Not long after it was presented on stage, the priest was suddenly transferred to a parish somewhere in the boondocks of Arizona.

And that was the last time I heard mention of the conflagration.

It was around this time that I felt something happening to me, but I couldn't put my finger on it. It was something like an itch I couldn't locate, or like food not being cooked enough, or something undone which should have been done, or something forgotten which should have been remembered. Anyway, something was unsettling my innards.

There was a Japanese evangelist who, before the war, used to shout on the northeast corner of First and San Pedro in Little Tokyo, his large painting of Jesus propped up against the signal pole there, and his tambourine for contributions placed on the sidewalk in front of the picture. He wore a small mustache, a uniform of navy blue, and a visored military-type cap. So regular was the cadence of his call to salvation that, from a distance, it sounded like the sharp barking of a dog. "*Wan, wan, wan! Wan, wan, wan!*" until, closer up, the man could be seen in exhortation, his face awry and purple with the passion of his message.

A fellow regular about that time on the sidewalks of Little Tokyo was a very large boy in a wheelchair which was usually pushed by a cute girl in bangs or another boy, both smaller than their charge, both of whom seemed to accept their transporting job cheerfully, as a matter of course. The large boy's usual outfit was denim overalls, his head was closely shaven, Japanese military-style, and there was a clean white handkerchief tied around his neck to catch the bit of saliva which occasionally trickled from a corner of his mouth.

It seems to me that my kinship, for all practical purposes, was with the large boy in the wheelchair, not with the admirable evangelist who was literally obeying the injunction to shout the good news from the housetops and street corners. For, what had I gone and done? Given the responsibility by the busy editor, I had written up from my notes a calm, impartial story, using "alleged" and "claimed" and other cautious journalese. Anyone noticing the story about the unwanted family in Fontana would have taken it with a grain of salt.

I should have been an evangelist at Seventh and Broadway, shouting out the name of the Short family and their predicament in Fontana. But I had been as handicapped as the boy in the wheelchair, as helpless.

All my family and friends had already been feeling my displeasure when it came to certain matters anyway. I was a curmudgeon, a real pill. If they funned around or dared so much as to imitate a Southernly accent, I pounced on them like a cougar. They got so they would do their occasional sho-nuffs behind my back, hushing up suddenly when I came into the room.

And my correspondence suffered. When one fellow dared to imply that I was really unreasonable on the subject of race relations, saying that he believed it sufficient to make one's stand known only when the subject happened to come up, the exchange of letters did not continue much longer.

I even dared to engage in long-distance tilting with a university scholar who had been kind enough to notice my writing. Specifically, I objected to his admiration of Herman Melville's *Benito Cereno* as one of the most perfect short stories extant, to his citing of the slave Babo in the story as the epitome of evil. The professor replied that race was not the issue, and that, anyway, Melville was writing from assumptions prevalent in the culture of his time, and, furthermore, Negroes themselves had participated in the selling of their fellow Blacks into bondage. These *non sequiturs*, coming from such a distinguished source, dismayed me.

So I guess you could say that things were coming to a head. Then, one afternoon when I was on the trolley bus heading home to Boyle Heights, there was some kind of disagreement at First and Broadway between the Negro driver of the bus I was on, turning onto First, and the White driver of the other bus turning onto Broadway. The encounter ended with the White driver waving his arms and cursing, "Why, you Black bastard!"

The Negro driver merely got back on and turned the bus onto Broadway, but I was sick, cringing from the blow of those words. My stomach was queasy with anxiety and I knew Miss Moten's fury for my very own. I wanted to yell out the window at the other driver, but what could I have said? I thought of reporting him to management, but what could I have said?

Not long after, going to work one morning, I found myself wishing that the streetcar would rattle on and on and never stop. I'd felt the sensation before, on the way to my mother's funeral. If I could somehow manage to stay on the automobile forever, I thought, I would never have to face the fact of my mother's death. A few weeks after this incident on the street, I mumbled some excuse about planning to go back to school and left the paper.

I didn't go back to school, but after a time I got on trains and buses that carried me several thousand miles across the country and back. I guess you could say I was realizing my dream of travelling forever (escaping responsibility forever). I was in Massachusetts, New York, New Jersey, Maryland, and most of the time I didn't argue with anyone.

But once in Baltimore, I couldn't help objecting to a guest's offhand remark. This lady had been a patient in a maternity ward alongside a Negro woman and she mimicked the latter's cry, "Oh, give me something to ease the pain! Give me something to ease the pain!"

She gave me a pain, so I entered into a polite and wary fray, with the lady's husband joining in on his wife's behalf. "Edge-acated niggers," they said, what they couldn't support was the uppity airs of edge-acated niggers.

As the discussion continued, they backed down to allow as how Northern Negroes might be another matter. But I knew nothing had been accomplished except the discomfiture of those whose hospitality we were enjoying.

In Baltimore, too, I admired the industry of the lady owner of the rowhouse next door. Lovely enough to be in the movies, with softly curling dark hair, she spoke a soft Marylandese that enchanted me. In the middle of winter, I could see her cleaning her upstairs windows, seated precariously on the sill so as to face the windows from the outside. But, one day, happening to walk with her to do some shopping, I saw her spewing lizards, toads, and wriggling serpents: "It's them damn niggras!"

When I finally came back to Los Angeles I was married and set about producing a passel of children. But stuff kept happening. Our son in high school reported that his classmates took delight in saying "nigger" behind the back of the Black electronics teacher. A White electronics teacher, visiting his sister in the hospital in the same room where I lay, said that he knew it was wrong, but he didn't want Blacks moving into his neighborhood in Alhambra—no Moors in Alhambra?—because of the drop in property values that would ensue (I jousted feebly with him—well, I was sick—and later, on my return home, happened to be talking to someone who knew him, and found out that the teacher felt the same way about Japanese moving near him). When I objected to my children repeating a favorite word used by their playmates, one grandparent informed me that there was nothing wrong with the word nigger—she used it all the time herself. An attractive Korean lady friend and real estate agent put her children into Catholic schools because, as her daughter explained it, the public schools hereabouts were "integrated," while, on the other hand, she winsomely urged local real estate onto Black clients because, as she explained to me, "It's the coming thing," and her considerable profits ("It's been very good to me") made possible her upward mobility into less integrated areas.

So it was that, in between putting another load of clothes into the automatic washer, ironing, maybe whipping up some tacos for supper, I watched the Watts riot on television. Back then I was still middle-aged, sitting safely in a house which was located on a street where panic would be the order of the day if a Black family should happen to move in—I had come there on sufferance myself, on the coattails of a pale husband.

Appalled, inwardly cowering, I watched the burning and looting on the screen and heard the reports of the dead and wounded. But beneath all my distress, I felt something else, a tiny trickle of warmth which I finally recognized as an undercurrent of exultation. To me, the tumult in the city was the long-awaited, gratifying next chapter of an old movie that had flickered about in the back of my mind for years. In the film, shot in the dark of about three o'clock in the morning, there was this modest house out in the country. Suddenly the house was in flames and there were the sound effects of the fire roaring and leaping skyward. Then there could be heard the voices of a man and woman screaming, and the voices of two small children as well.

(1985)

Florentine Gardens

"To spend May in Florence is the foreigner's dream."
—Mary McCarthy

What is this odd quartet doing over here?

There's an older Latino fellow, a Japanese woman who is younger by a few years, a young man of Slavic forebears from the American Midwest, and a young Eurasian woman.

They're all from Southern California, and each has a separate purpose in being abroad. The young man, Bob Kovalak, is the one with official business here. He's a computer expert; his firm has sent him to a conference at European Community headquarters in Frascati. The others are tagging along. The young woman, Lisa Jauregui, is his co-worker and friend. The older couple, Al and Kimiko Jauregui, are her parents, whom she has asked along. The young people have taken care of all the travelling arrangements, by fax.

So everything is going pretty smoothly. One small glitch. The older man is the only one who has been here before, first as a paratrooper and then as a seaman. He still contains shell fragments from that first sojourn, so there's usually a problem when he passes through the airport metal detectors. He is taken to a side room, asked to divest himself of all metallic appurtenances. Then a hand-held detector is passed up and down, front and back, to pinpoint the offending shrapnel. Still, he's in remarkable shape, able to outdo some of the younger exercise brigades in the hills back home. Arriving at Rome airport, they are made uneasy by the sight of uniformed guards armed with automatic weapons (and reminded then of the massacre that took place here only a few years before). But they find ample peace and quiet at a pleasant *albergo* in a small mountain town on the outskirts of the city.

In between Bob's meetings and once his assignment is completed, the group gets a chance to visit Hadrian's Villa, the Vatican, the Colosseum and Palatine Hill, the Spanish Steps. They marvel at the gung-ho plunging into traffic of Italian drivers, note the laundry hanging from the apartment balconies above the Roman mercantile establishments which, block on block, extend for miles, and wonder at such graffiti as *ASSAD ASSAS-SINO* and *MILANO IN FLAMMA*. They're amused that the village teen-agers seem to have taken up, girls and boys alike, the wearing of blue jeans and other denims. They become adept at dodging the importuning of the hawkers (Arab? African? Pakistani?) of postcards and leather goods who display their wares on mats along the Roman sidewalks, and agile at work-ing their way around the scaffolding that props up a great deal of the city. They gaze, impressed, at the remnants of the Aqueduct and other ruins which stand here and there on the landscape amidst the dusky green olive groves and budding vineyards.

Then it's on to Florence, selected by the mother; thence to Venice, the young woman's choice. They will wind up in Paris for the father's benefit.

Kimiko Jauregui will accomplish that for which she has come, and this will both alleviate and exacerbate an old grief. Lisa wants to glide down the canals in a gondola in the moonlight, to the strains of a ser-enade. She will be so appalled by the olive-drab murk under the bridges that she will forego the ride and take consolation in gelati.

Al Jauregui likewise will find disillusion in the carnival atmosphere around Sacré Coeur. It is there he remembers resting on the sloping grass while on leave from nearby Lariboisiére hospital. To begin with, there's a small carousel at the bottom level. Then litter, litter, all the way up the curved path. On the first terrace a woman with a hand organ is singing Piaf-style songs. After the next flight of stairs, a mime in a clown costume is entertaining the crowd which sits on the step stairs leading up to the cathedral. Now and then the performer darts up the steps mimicking a climber, eliciting bursts of laughter. So even though the foxgloves grow tall in many colors along the sides of the lawns and the grass is generally respected, Al can't help wishing for the good old days. "Bad idea coming back here," he will mutter. "That was wartime," Kimiko will remind him, "Us tourists weren't here then."

The phenomenon of sitting people is to be encountered time and again. When the four wait on the Spanish Steps for Bob's colleague from work, they are among a vast throng which jampacks the stairs from bot-tom to top. The Steps might be the tiers of a stadium, with the crowd expecting some spectacle to begin momentarily. But they might just be resting from the rigors of touristry or this is a convenient place to meet. "I'll see you at three o'clock on the Spanish Steps!" Whatever, the sitters are seemingly content to just sit and be here.

They will come upon the sitters in Florence in front of their hotel, occupying the cracked stone stairs and looking out on the piazza. Later, too, at the pool adjoining the glass pyramid entrance to the Louvre, the sitters will make use of the pool edges while others will stand around as though awaiting their turn to be sedentary.

Al will still approve of the Paris Metro as a model of efficiency and cleanliness. "Isn't this great?" he will ask, as he leads her down, down into the lower depths. But she doesn't see that it's so different from Rome's underground transport. Finding breath hard to come by at that infernal level, she will decide that he must be associating this place with his youth and a wartime romance (wasn't there someone named Danielle?). Vendors will surround them here, too, in Montmartre, most looking to be from Africa. They will accept several business cards along the way which advertise the prophetic gifts of such as monsieur SQUARE, Grand Medium Africain who has *la solution sur tous vos problemes.*

On the Metro, Al will be struck by the appearance of a statuesque young African woman who sits across from them. Kimiko will agree that she must be one of the most beautiful women in the world, although she is apparently unaware of this distinction.

Bearing first-class Eurail passes, the foursome attempts to head north from Rome to Florence. It is not that simple, even with reservations. Finally, they virtually force their way into a second-class compartment, half-expecting to be ousted again. But the train pulls out without yet another challenge to their presence. While the others nod off, Kimiko looks out the window at the crimson poppies alongside the tracks and, sprinkled here and there in the fields of Latium, the neat vineyards and olive groves which cover flatland, hillside and valley, and, at intervals, the prosperous looking two-story farmhouses of rosy stucco with their red-tile roofs. Once into Tuscany, the agriculture becomes more various—could these be strawberry fields? She recalls her brother Tommy writing that the Italian countryside reminded him of Southern California. That would have been in the spring of 1944. Ah, that resemblance no longer exists. If Tommy could see it now, he would be staggered by the transformation of those bucolic spaces of alfalfa, orange grove and sprawling dairy into the concrete and stucco density of freeway, tract home and shopping mall. No more malt shops or soda fountains—McDonald's, Colonel Sanders and Burger King offer their instant victuals in every hamlet up and down the state (octopi whose tentacles extend here to Europe and the rest of the world). Come to think of it, the changes since World War II are mind-boggling: Japanese cars, TV, men on the moon, rock and roll, AIDS, Vietnam, Martin Luther King; the list could go on and on.

There is some of California that can still match this Italian scene—those northerly farms around Salinas and Watsonville of strawberry and lettuce, the vineyards, all of which she usually sees from the Coast Starlight. One spring, when there is still some rain in the state, she rejoices at the splendor of the green velvet mountains stretching forever, sprigged here and there with clumps of bright yellow mustard.

In recent years, the mountains have been green only in patches, the dirt and rock and bush clearly visible. There have been past years when the green velvet has turned tawny towards autumn, a furry sheath for the sinuous mounds, putting a body in mind of colossal sleeping animals.

These Tuscan mountains differ. Once laid bare, they say, by serial warfare, they are thickly wooded now with stone pine and cypress. She guesses they're not called Italian here as they are at home, where several cypresses in the front yard have grown so tall that Al regrets ever having planted them.

She's already seen spring arrive in the backyard where she keeps tabs on the seasons by the fruits and flowers. For instance, she has been overcome, as she is yearly, by the flowering of the apricot and nectarine, followed by the orange poppies and red flags. Now in May she will miss the ripe loquats. But when they explore the mountain village, she is astounded to see loquats aplenty, in the delectable open-air markets and the restaurant displays. What's more, they're gorgeous, all evenly enormous and plump and golden, evidently cultivated for market. Were the smooth, shiny brown pits brought home by the Polos? Later in Venice, she is to conjecture a like origin for the masses of mauve peonies in tall Oriental vases atop the tables in the hotel lobby.

Reaching Florence, the four trundle their gear from the station to their first hotel, named after an English poet, because their *loggiato* suite won't be available until the next day. But it's worth the wait. The second place is a former monastery and the rooms overlook the Piazza della Santissima Annunziata, where all of Florence appears to converge at one time or another.

There's activity from early in the morning until late at night. People going to work, walking dogs (some unseen presence tends to the results immediately, something devoutly to be wished for later on Giudecca, where sidestepping on the *fondamenta* is a gait quickly learned), riding bicycles, Vespas, Lambrettas, Fiats. Police cars use the piazza as a short-cut or turnaround, circling a fountain or the green-streaked bronze of Ferdinand Medici astride a horse. One evening a group of young men play a pick-up game of soccer; later on, a corner of the piazza becomes a parking lot for those spending the evening at one of the establishments down the street. On another evening the wide, worn steps of the ancient foundling home opposite become a stage for two groups of students in a singing competition. Nothing familiar, but the young voices rise sweetly. Then, suddenly, is a ringing *Guantanamera!* On Saturday a young bride trails her flowing white gown across the dust of the piazza and into the church. She and her intended stop for a quick kiss before entering with their arms around each other. On Sunday, the piazza is a painting by Brueghel: a Casa di Risparmo banner is stretched across an archway of the orphanage *loggia;* bright yellow-canopied stalls under Kimiko's window offer refreshments (quartered oranges and such). Gradually the square fills up. It's an awards ceremony of some kind. Trophies are handed out after each microphoned announcement, to shouts, claps, boos, banners waving above each uniformed school group in turn. Then it's over. The stalls are instantly dismantled, the piazza empties rapidly, to be abandoned to its more ordinary uses.

Kimiko is at the window every chance she gets. The young ones are off every day with the Michelin guide to cover as much art as they can. Bob photographs the Michelangelo David from a dozen angles. Both he and Lisa get acquainted with Tuscan cuisine. But Al is beginning to feel the effects of unaccustomed fare, so he and Kimiko find a Chinese restaurant which uses Kikkoman and Blue Rose rice, a taste of home. One evening as they are eating, a young Chinese girl rushes in, removing a motorcycle helmet as she heads for the kitchen. She must have arrived for work on the rear of a Vespa? Later in Paris they will frequent a Chinese auberge which advertises gourmet cuisine, but its noodles will suffer in comparison with those served up at the Florence ristorante.

Since coming to Florence, Kimiko has been examining the city map to find the U.S. military cemetery. She finally locates a *cimiterio americano* to the east of the city. She and Al go down to the reception cage for directions. The young woman speaks English fairly well and she gets excited when she finds out their destination. "No, no," she says, "the cemetery you want is down in Tavarnuzze."

By a happy coincidence, it appears that her co-worker here, who relieves her for the afternoon shift, is the daughter of the cemetery superintendent. She calls to find out the visiting hours. Kimiko and Al then go in hasty search of flowers, but it's siesta (a continental custom which they find both reasonable and exasperating), so they go back empty-handed to the loggiato. They inquire of the clerk whether there might be a florist open in Tavarnuzze by the time they get there. She comes to the rescue again, phoning to learn that the manager will be gone but that someone will be there to help with flowers.

So Kimiko and Al set out by cab on a pleasant drive over the Ponte alla Carraia, one of those that had to be rebuilt after the war, and down the Via de' Serragli through timeworn towns that look to have been there forever.

But the greying cabbie overcharges them at the cemetery. Al and Kimiko hear him telling the caretaker (that much Italian they understand) that it's because he has to go back empty. The attendant gives a what-can-you-do shrug at Al's pique, and then breaks into perfect Ameri-canese. It turns out he's a Latino from Modesto. The flowers? He's going to cut them a bouquet from the cemetery's rose gardens. As he leads them towards the graves area, he steps over the low hedge and darts here and there, snipping here a red bloom, there a pink one.

Kimiko and Al see that the place is quite grand. The immaculate white marble crosses and stars stand in ordered row on row on row on the acres of green grass, the whole park bordered by trees. A broad walk of small variegated pebbles, with leafy plane trees on either side, leads up to the monument at the far end. There a man can be seen hosing down the area, probably in preparation for Memorial Day.

The caretaker goes ahead of them and places the roses at the bottom of one white cross, and Kimiko is invaded afresh by a wrenching sense of loss, as though news of her brother's death forty-six years before has only just reached her. Now all the fantasies must be put away. No, he did not walk away from the war and hide out with some farm family (he would have been a good worker) for the duration, nor did he marry the daughter, have a family and decide to stay on. Why not? It is within the realm of possibility, easier to imagine than the other, certainly more acceptable.

But here is Tommy's name, engraved on the white marble cross.

Each year the family goes to Little Tokyo for a photo session in order to send pictures to both sets of grandparents in Japan. In this picture Tommy is probably not walking yet. He perches barefoot on a round stool, wearing rompers, a little round brimmed hat, his bright eyes staring at the camera. Kimiko, in a dark velvet dress with round flowers appliqued across the bottom, holds on to his arm and gazes frontward with a questioning air.

There's a story to the pippin apple in Tommy's hand. She almost remembers it happening because her mother recounts the anecdote more than once. The apple has been given to him by the mother of a little boy.

"Shall we ask for him and take him home with us?" the woman asks her son.

"No, he's too heavy to take!" the boy protests. "*Omotai kara mor-awan-yo!*"

And this picture where she is in a pale woolen dress, high-top shoes over long stockings. She is sitting in a little chair and he is standing alongside. He wears a short-sleeved top with button-on shorts, a visored cloth military cap, carries an American flag.

As more siblings arrive at two-year intervals, there are group pictures, the most elaborate being a large portrait of six, mother, father, herself, three brothers. About then the family acquires an Ansco camera and, except for another studio visit or two, the pictures that henceforth go to Japan are snapshots.

The family Hudson figures in the background of this one, the International truck in another prosperity, the pictures lie, as though each depression year is not a replay of the last, with the annual visit to the bank for a loan, the struggle to pay it back by growing strawberries on land her father can by law never own, the moves every couple of years, so that by the time they end up farming in view of the ocean, there have been about nine moves and changes of schools.

The kids fight like cats and dogs as they are growing up. Kimiko recalls one relative who says about his own several brothers, "We don't see much of each other any more. But we were good friends when we were small—we used to fight all the time!" So it is with her, Tommy, Timmy and Ray. When the boys are small, she is able to grab them by the shoulders with her two hands and grind her thumbs into them until they concede defeat, "I give up!" But she discards this ploy as the three pass her up in size and strength.

Every Wednesday night one year Kimiko and Tommy clash over whether the radio will be tuned to Jack Benny or the Lone Ranger. She turns the dial on the little domed Philco to the comedian and he changes it to the masked rider and his faithful companion Tonto. Back and forth they go, the words getting more vehement, until one night their mother steps in and turns the radio off, "Enough, enough!" Wails from them both, but Tommy turns on their mother, "Goddam you!" Kimiko is shocked to the core but the words roll off their mother because she doesn't comprehend their exact meaning (only that they represent anger—their father often says worse, *kottemu sanagabi'chi, kakisaka,* but he doesn't know what he's saying, either). Not long after this Kimiko gradually eases into another mode, that of making deals to gain her ends.

There is the sweater Tommy gets one winter. It's a simple woollen pullover, forest green, with a V-neck. She borrows it every chance she gets, in exchange for her share of this or that confection. At the time she is attending a high school where girls wear the mandatory navy blue or black skirt with the white middie, shawled with the large detachable navy collar. She wears it over her blouse, the collar outside, the black bow in the V, feeling like the best-dressed person in the world. Surprising to remember because she ordinarily doesn't pay that much attention to what she wears. In fact, she hates shopping so much that she wears anything her mother brings back from the store, whether it fits exactly or not. In despair, her mother takes to having dresses for special occasions tailored for her at the Japanese dry goods store. What so beguiles her about the sweater she cannot now recall, only that she covets it so much that she wishes she were a boy so she can own one just like it.

Their mother dies at age forty when Kimiko has just turned eighteen. So the three boys are much younger. For a while Kimiko goes off to the city where she gets mother's helper jobs, first for a doctor, his wife and dog (she is to take the dog to the vacant lot next door twice a day, urging, "Go, go!" then pat him off gently before bringing him back inside), then for a family with two children, a girl and a boy, who, when their parents are gone, chase her around the house trying to tickle her. She decides she is not meant for such irrelevancies and goes back home to the family.

In that short time, Tommy has become quite domestic. It is he who teaches her how to make strawberry jam with MCP pectin and tomato soup with bacon from the produce in the fields. She reciprocates by showing him how to arrange lettuce, cottage cheese and canned fruit cocktail as a salad, then is more or less content to takeover as chief cook and dishwasher. Her cooking is elementary, usually rice and *okazu*, or fish that their father regularly goes down to catch.

Even then, Kimiko and Tommy have their differences. Lordy, Lordy, what is it that so enrages him that he gets into her dresser drawers and, armed with scissors, snips some of her clothing at random? He comes outside with the scissors and announces his revenge with a triumphant grin.

He is in high school now, active in athletics, as are all the boys. He is proud of his friendship with the star athlete. He brings home the yearbook and points to the fellow's signature (Teutonic name, she notes) and the scrawl above, "You're a pretty good guy, for a Japanese." She feels fire flare in her gullet, but she realizes that Tommy has not taken offense. What if she had seized the opportunity then to begin infecting him with her own jaundice? What if she had not been so mindful of his feelings? Would she have prevented his death? Probably not. If the fact of their mass removal had not embittered him, then nothing would have.

Because Tommy does not get to graduate with his idol. The war comes, and with it the round-up of all Japanese in what is called the Western Defense Command. So Tommy and the rest of the scheduled Japanese graduates get early diplomas before being shipped off with their families and neighbors to a concentration camp in Arizona.

The last night, sleeping on the floor because secondhand dealers and other bargain hunters have bought almost everything that isn't nailed down, Kimiko lies awake acutely aware of the unyielding floorboards beneath her. She no doubt mentions her discomfort because she remembers Tommy advising, "Stop complaining and do like me—stop thinking about it and you'll be able to sleep."

In camp, he decides to go out as soon as he is permitted, with other fellows who are going to Fort Morgan, Colorado, to top sugar beets. Probably eighteen then. After the sugar beets are done, he goes to Denver where he finds a job washing dishes in a seminary. He is a faithful correspondent. He once mentions that there are some students who evidently consider their bodily functions to be rarefied accomplishments but that there are others who are pretty decent to the help. Then he gets a job candling eggs and begins night classes in accounting.

Suddenly he informs them that he has volunteered for the Army. Much to Kimiko's dismay—her incipient pacifism is grounded more in emotion than reason, but she also wonders at the irony of bearing arms for a country which uproots them for no good reason and plunks them in the middle of the desert.

She remembers writing a history paper in high school, "Who Won the World War?" No one had, she answers, citing encyclopedia figures for the casualties of each country involved. She is an 'A' student in the class—Mussolini and Count Galeazzo Ciano and his Edda for instance, are fascinating figures—but this paper is handed back with a C. She shreds the pages into little bits and drops the confetti into Miss See's wastebasket, right in front of her. Miss See watches this performance with a half-smile while some of the other students look on in puzzlement. Miss See has gone to college with Robert Taylor and refers to him as Spangler.

Anyway, Tommy's decision to join up while the rest of the family is in camp is a done deed. He ships his civilian clothes back to camp. In washing everything (by hand in a sink of the block laundry room) Kimiko finds a note in the pocket of a windbreaker. It's for a girl, he wants her to know that he has waited quite a while for her to show up as she promised. In his photo collection is the snap of a bright-lipped, lush-looking girl. Kimiko suspects this is the girl who stood him up. The same pocket has an ugly ineradicable stain in it. From a stolen egg? She surmises that he must have had trouble making ends meet on the outside.

Sworn in at Fort Logan, Tommy is shipped off to basic training in Mississippi where most of the Hawaiian and mainland Japanese troops are segregated. He gets one furlough that enables him to come to Arizona to visit. He looks burlier than when he left. That's the last time the family sees him.

Kimiko frets when her father gets a telegram that Tommy has been operated on for a hernia. As a small child he wore a truss; perhaps the toting of the cumbersome mortar—he sends a magazine picture of his equipment—has brought on the need for surgery. When he next writes, he says he is fine but that the Army doctor has told him that he has another hernia on the other side which might have to be tended to sooner or later. So why has he not been given a medical discharge?

Then a rather strange message comes. "I've changed, Kimiko," he writes. "Don't expect me to be the same guy I used to be." What does this mean—beer guzzling, carnal knowledge, the capacity to kill? He adds that some of the officers are so hated that they will definitely be among the early casualties. Hair-raising notion, but Kimiko decides he is quoting some tough among his fellow trainees. She writes back that whatever he means, she is not making any judgment. After that, as though relieved of a burden, he continues to write as before. Remembering that now, Kimiko finds it infinitely touching that he has found it necessary to inform her of his altered state. Whatever it was that happened, he must have been overwhelmed himself.

After that there is thin bluish V-mail as well as regular mail, an Algerian banknote picked up in Oran, sepia postcards of Il Colosseo, Maria Aracoeli church, the Vittorio Emanuele monument, the Palazzo di Giustizia. This is when he compares the Italian clime to Southern California's.

As they tread the grass above the graves and go up towards the monument, Al asks, "How did he die?"

"An 88-millimeter shell, full on the chest."

"Who told you?" He sounds as if he does not want to believe her.

"His two sergeants, or I guess they were second lieutenants by then—battlefield commissions that they had to give up after the war. They said the company was under attack so everybody was lying low in the foxholes. But for some reason Tommy stood up and that's when he got it. They said death was instantaneous."

Al is silent but Kimiko has an idea what a graphic scene his thoughts are conjuring. He knows exactly what that means. He has seen enough to have material for nightmares ever since.

Some there are who learn to rifle the medical packets of their dead comrades for morphine, in order to place what they are doing at a bearable remove. In winter snow, when troops have been instructed to stay awake at any cost, he has watched more than one die with a beatific smile. From time to time, he has taken out his rations and eaten meals amongst the carnage of mangled and severed bodies. Sometimes, a replacement coming in fresh from the rear goes rigid at the sight of the first corpse or becomes a whimpering blob; such a one has to be carted out, sent back to a stateside hospital.

Al also remembers a sergeant of his who is about to shoot an unarmed prisoner. He in turn takes aim at the sergeant daring him to carry out the unwarranted execution. Once, incredulous on the ground, they are deafened by a deep and endless thunder and look up to see wave upon wave of aircraft on their way to blast Dresden and its china (forewarned, but who listens?) to smithereens. And, when they at last approach Berlin they are brought to a standstill and ordered to cool their heels to allow Soviet troops to catch up on their end, as per Yalta agreement.

Tommy is killed at Grosseto and buried in Livorno. They are notified that some effects cannot be forwarded because of their condition. That would include his small harmonica, Kimiko is sure, the one he would whip out of his shirt pocket when he felt like making music. He always had to have one, and it always had to be a Hohner Marine Band.

A few years later, when they are back in California, a letter comes to her father offering the option of having the deceased sent home or having him buried at Arlington or in a permanent overseas cemetery.

The reality of what would be returned to them in a box is more than Kimiko can bear. Leave him there, she advises her father. But her aunt wants Tommy to come home.

"Do you know what would be coming back?" she asks her aunt.

"It's part of war," her aunt argues. "We must honor the dead."

"We would be crying again," Kimiko reminds.

"We want to cry!" her aunt assures her, "*Nakitai-no-yo!*"
So her father is being persuaded. Kimiko, under a demure de-
meanor, is a willful mule. Knowing his intense dislike of ceremony, Kimiko
incidentally mentions that another funeral will be in order. Considering this
prospect with a slow nod, her father reluctantly agrees, let's leave him
there then.

Kimiko and Al stop to read some of the markers before they get to
the far end. According to the cemetery pamphlet, there are exactly 4,398
buried here, with two headstones for two bodies "whose remains could not
be separated" and another one for three unknowns together. Only crosses
and stars, Kimiko notes—no Buddhist wheels, which would have been
more appropriate for Tommy.

What would I know about God, one letter says, I've never even been
to church. Has he forgotten the weddings and funerals at the Nishi Hongwanji and Higashi Hongwanji, the chanting priests, the incense? Maybe he
doesn't consider that church, because after every wedding and funeral
there is a huge restaurant feast of Chinese food—chow mein, egg foo
yong, pakkai, chashu, almond duck, pea chayu, egg flower soup with seaweed and those tiny little white globules that crunch.

The monument area is right up against the hillside. Polished and
engraved granite and travertine, a locked chapel, a pool with no water in it.
Lists on the wall of those, 1,409 of them, who have never been found.
Aircraft personnel, most of them seem to be. Marble, bronze, walnut, an
artistic intarsia map of the Italian campaign. Inscriptions abound, including
a quotation attributed to Pericles by Thucydides: *They faced the foe as
they drew near him in the stretch of their own manhood and when the
shock of battle came they in a moment of time at the climax of their
lives were rapt away from a world filled for their dying eyes not with
terror but with glory.*

Rapture, is it? Kimiko thinks not. She leaves off reading more; it is
only making her angry.

Kimiko has brought along some cheese and Al takes out some Ritz
crackers and the *acqua naturale* from his knapsack. They sit on a wooden
bench under the plane trees and eat, the white markers and green grass all
about them. Then, one more stop at Tommy's cross, with the roses at its
base.

"We have to come back tomorrow," Kimiko says. "Timmy and Lily
gave us money for flowers."

They find the man from Modesto gone, the superintendent back in the office, and accept his offer of a ride to the next town where the bus service is more frequent than across the street from the cemetery gate. Not that much more frequent—Al has time for a *cafe lungo* in a little shop run by a woman who sounds British. He has given up trying to get "a good cup of American coffee" and just asks for hot water to dilute the espresso.

The next day they leave the loggiato well before siesta time and buy tall-stemmed roses and carnations. They plan to go out by bus, Al figuring they've contributed enough to Florence's taxi service. He's not at all surprised to learn that Florence is a crime capital, with emphasis on drugs.

After making a half-dozen inquiries which don't seem to be understood, they finally locate the SITA bus that goes past the cemetery. Once there, they place the flowers against Tommy's cross but do not linger, except to share a *panino* and some cheese in the shade. Kimiko, looking at the pamphlet, learns that the United States maintains a number of these cemeteries around the world—Mexico, Panama, England, Puerto Rico, Tunisia, Alaska, the Philippines. France, of course. Wherever it has been decided that U.S. interests are at stake.

Well-tended gardens of stone, Kimiko thinks, glorified boneyards. What of those on the other side? No doubt they too have their shrines at home and on alien soil. Back there in one mountain town she had noted a Via Mario Intreccialagli and a monument to one Placido Martini, both martyrs in the struggle *contro gli oppressori Nazi*. In Paris, they will see at the hospital a plaque dedicated to a couple of dozen personnel—doctors, administrative staff, attendants—who *sont morts pour la patrie*.

They have to wait at least an hour pressed against the high stone wall on the further side of the road, inhaling the exhaust of the vehicles zooming north and south. Meanwhile they observe across the street a frail-looking woman being gently helped from a car by a somewhat younger couple and slowly guided towards the graves. The mother of a dead soldier come for a last visit? A widow?

A bus arrives at long last, but only to let out a passenger up ahead, so Al and Kimiko have to run to hail it. It turns back around and goes a brief stretch on the autostrade before heading back to Florence station. On their walk back to the hotel they buy some dried apricots at a stall in front of the station, another bottle of water, then make their way through the flea market, stopping for a few postcards.

In the end, the older couple see little of the wonders that tourists flock to Florence to experience. Not even the David at the Academy right in back of their hostelry, because on their last day in the city, when they decide to scurry around to see what they can, the Sunday museum guides decide to go on strike.

They do manage a brisk walk over to the Ponte Vecchio, where most of the jewelry shops are closed. The green waters of the Arno below (like those of the Greve, which runs alongside the cemetery) look toxic. It is a river which has periodically flooded and devastated the city. As high as twenty feet on these buildings the last time, according to one guidebook, with thirty-five dead, 16,000 cars lost to mud and water, irreplaceable art damaged, many homeless. But here and there people are fishing along the banks. Kimiko recalls a bus ride the year before along the Columbia River, and earlier this year the train crossing the Mississippi. There does not seem to be a clear, clean river anywhere on the globe. In Paris, from a room overlooking the Seine, she will echo this same lament. There will be an immense swimming pool enclosure alongside the river whose sign guarantees that its water does not come from the Seine.

They cross the Piazza della Signoria and its excavations. This is where Savanarola cremated the books, paintings, jewelry and other vanities of a repentant populace and where he himself was later burned at the stake. They see "the other David" there among the statuary. And what's this over here?—five shiny red and white ambulances are lined up, awaiting the heart attacks from the 464-step climb up to the Duomo, which Bob and Lisa report having made.

"We could have been here a year and still not seen everything," Bob says.

"You're both young," Kimiko says. "You can come back many times."

As the train pulls out of Florence from the *stazione termini*, the four of them settle into their hard-won compartment. Kimiko knows she, unlike Bob and Lisa, will not come this way again. *Addio, Firenze*; so long, Tommy, little brother—whether she has been right or wrong to leave him here is something she will never know. She reaches over for her raincoat and puts her hand in one pocket, feeling there the fistful of small smooth pebbles she has filched from the cemetery walk. When she arrives home, she will take them to where her mother and father rest under the palms and strew them around the bronze plaque imbedded in the ground. Once Al catches on to what she is doing, he will stoop down to where she is kneeling and help her tamp the pebbles into the earth. Both will work silently, solemnly, as though they are performing an age-old ritual fraught with meaning.

(1995)

SELECTED BIBLIOGRAPHY

Primary Sources

"An Abandoned Pot of Rice." *Rafu Shimpo* 22 December 1984: 6–7, 14.

"After Johnny Died." *Los Angeles Tribune* 26 November 1945: 20–21. Reprinted as "Life and Death of a Nisei GI: After Johnny Died" in *Pacific Citizen* 1 December 1945: 5.

"Appointment in Japan." *Rafu Shimpo* 21 December 1954: 12.

"Berlin Adventure." *Hokubei Mainichi* 1 January 1997: 1, 3.

"Bettina." *Rafu Shimpo* 21 December 1955: 6, 14.

"The Boy from Nebraska." *Crossroads* 23 December 1949: 6.

"Broccoli and Spinach." *Hokubei Mainichi* 1 January 1991 Supplement: 2.

"The Brown House." *Harper's Bazaar* October 1951: 166, 283–284.

"Christmas Eve on South Boyle." *Rafu Shimpo* 20 December 1957: 9, 18.

"A Day in Little Tokyo." *Amerasia Journal* 13.2 (1986–87): 21–28.

"Dried Snakeskins." *Rafu Shimpo* 22 December 1952: 15. Reprinted in *Where the Coyotes Howl and the Wind Blows Free: Growing Up in the West*. Edited by Alexandra R. Haslam and Gerald W. Haslam. Reno: University of Nevada Press, 1995. 146–148.

"Educational Opportunities." *Hokubei Mainichi* 1 January 1989: 6–7.

"Eju-kei-shung! Eju-kei-shung!: A Memoir." *Rafu Shimpo* 20 December 1980: 11–12, 16. Reprinted in *Into the Fire: Asian American Prose*. Edited by Sylvia Watanabe and Carol Bruchac. Greenfield Center, N.Y.: Greenfield Review Press, 1995. 187–195.

"The Enormous Piano." *Rafu Shimpo* 20 December 1977: 6, 31. Reprinted in *Going Where I'm Coming From: Memoirs of American Youth*. Edited by Anne Mazer. New York: Persea Books, 1995. 139–148.

"Epithalamium." *Carleton Miscellany* 1.4 (1960): 56–67.

"The Eskimo Connection." *Rafu Shimpo* 21 December 1983: 9, 17, 22, 38.

"Eucalyptus." *Gidra* [20th Anniversary Issue] (1990): 34–36. Reprinted in *Charlie Chan Is Dead: An Anthology of Contempo-*

rary Asian American Fiction. Edited by Jessica Hagedorn. New York: Penguin, 1993. 102–111.

"A Fire in Fontana." *Rafu Shimpo* 21 December 1985: 8–9, 16–17, 19. Reprinted in *Negotiating Difference: Cultural Case Studies for Composition.* Edited by Patricia Bizzell and Bruce Herzberg. Boston: Bedford Books, 1996. 779–786.

"Florentine Gardens." *Asian America: Journal of Culture and the Arts* 1 (Winter 1992): 10–25.

"Gang Aft a-Gley." *Rafu Shimpo* 21 December 1953: 13–14.

"God Sees the Truth But Waits." *Catholic Worker* February 1957: 6.

"Having Babies." *Rafu Shimpo* 20 December 1962: 21.

"The High-Heeled Shoes, A Memoir." *Partisan Review* October 1948: 1079–1085.

". . . I Still Carry It Around." *RIKKA* 3.4 (1976): 11–19. Reprinted in Cheung, ed., 69–70.

"In Search of a Happy Ending." *Pacific Citizen* 22 December 1951: 17, 24.

"Ingurishi Tsuransureishan." *Rafu Shimpo* 20 December 1958: 9.

"Japanese in American Literature." *Rafu Shimpo* 20 December 1971: 13, 28, 36.

"Kichi Harada." *Pacific Citizen* 20 December 1957: B11

"Las Vegas Charley." *Arizona Quarterly* 17 (1961): 303–322.

"The Legend of Miss Sasagawara." *Kenyon Review* 12.1 (1950): 99–114.

"Life Among the Oil Fields, A Memoir." *Rafu Shimpo* 20 December 1979: 13, 24–25.

"The Losing of a Language." *Rafu Shimpo* 20 December 1963: 7.

"A Man from Hiroshima." *Rafu Shimpo* 20 December 1956: 9.

"Miyoko O'Brien (Or, Everybody's Turning Japanese)." *Pacific Citizen* 20–27 December 1985: A46.

"The Month of the Peacock." *Hokubei Mainichi* 1 January 1994 Supplement: 6.

"Morning Rain." *Pacific Citizen* 19 December 1952: 46, 50.

"My Cousin Midori." *Hokubei Mainichi* 1 January 1996 Supplement: 1.

"My Father Can Beat Muhammad Ali." *Echoes* 4 (1986): 14–15.

"The Nature of Things." *Rafu Shimpo* 20 December 1965: 7, 9–10, 12.

"Nip in the Bud." *Rafu Shimpo* 20 December 1961: 9–10.

"The Other Cheek." *Rafu Shimpo* 19 December 1959: 9.

"Peter Maurin Farm." *Catholic Worker* June 1953: 3; December 1954: 3, 8; January 1955: 3, 7; February 1955: 3, 5; July-August 1955: 6.

"Pilgrimage." *Amerasia Journal* 19.1 (1993): 61–67.

"The Pleasure of Plain Rice." *Rafu Shimpo* 20 December 1960: 9, 10, 14. Reprinted in *Southwest: A Contemporary Anthology.* Edited by Karl Kopp and Jane Kopp. Albuquerque: Red Earth Press, 1977. 295–301.

"Reading and Writing." *Hokubei Mainishi* 1 January 1988: 5–6.

"A Really Good Bus Stop." *Hokubei Mainichi* 21 January 1990: 1.

"Reunion." *Rafu Shimpo* 12 December 1992: A14–15.

"Seabrook Farms—20 Years Later." *Catholic Worker* June 1954: 3, 6.

"Seventeen Syllables." *Partisan Review* November 1949: 1122–1134.

Seventeen Syllables: 5 Stories of Japanese American Life. Edited by Robert Rolf and Norimitsu Ayuzawa. Tokyo: Kirihara Shoten, 1985.

"Sidney, the Flying Turtle." *Rafu Shimpo* 18 December 1967: 15, 27.

"A Slight Case of Mistaken Identity." *Rafu Shimpo* 19 December 1964: 6.

"The Streaming Tears." *Rafu Shimpo* 20 December 1951: 22, 24. Reprinted in *Six Short Stories by Japanese American Writers.* Edited by Iwao Yamamoto, Mie Hihara, and Shigeru Kobayashi. Tokyo: Tsurumi Shoten, 1991. 25–30.

"Surely I Must be Dreaming." *Poston Notes and Activities* April 1943.

"La tante de ma plume." *Rafu Shimpo* 31 December 1982: 11, 19, 25, 33.

"Tomato Surprise." *Rafu Shimpo* 19 December 1966: 26, 31.

"Underground Lady." *Pacific Citizen* 19–26 December 1986: A15–A20.

"Wilshire Bus." *Pacific Citizen* 23 December 1950: 17, 22.

"Writing." *Rafu Shimpo* 20 December 1968: 14ff. Reprinted in Cheung, ed., 59–68.

"Yellow Leaves." *Rafu Shimpo* 20 December 1986: 36, 38–39.

"Yoneko's Earthquake." *Furioso* 6.1 (1951): 5–16.

Secondary Sources

Chan, Jeffery Paul, Frank Chin, Lawson Fusao Inada, and Shawn Wong, eds. *The Big Aiiieeeee! An Anthology of Asian American Writers.* New York: New American Library-Meridian, 1991.

Cheng, Ming L. "The Unrepentant Fire: Tragic Limitations in Hisaye Yamamoto's 'Seventeen Syllables.'" *MELUS* 19.4 (1994): 91–108.

Cheung, King-Kok. *Articulate Silences: Hisaye Yamamoto, Maxine Hong Kingston, Joy Kogawa.* Ithaca: Cornell University Press, 1993.

———. "Double Telling: Intertextual Silence in Hisaye Yamamoto's Fiction." *American Literary History* 3.2 (1991): 277–293. Reprinted in Cheung, ed., 161–180.

———. "The Dream in Flames: Hisaye Yamamoto, Multiculturalism, and the Los Angeles Uprising." In *Having Our Way: Women Rewriting Tradition in Twentieth-Century America.* Edited by Harriet Pollack. Lewisburg, Penn.: Bucknell University Press, 1995. 118–130.

———. "Interview with Hisaye Yamamoto." In Cheung, ed., 71–86.

———. "Reading between the Syllables: Hisaye Yamamoto's '*Seventeen Syllables' and Other Stories.*" In *Teaching American Ethnic Literatures.* Edited by John R. Maitino and David R. Peck. Albuquerque: University of New Mexico Press, 1996. 313–325.

———. "Thrice Muted Tale: Interplay of Art and Politics in Hisaye Yamamoto's 'The Legend of Miss Sasagawara.'" *MELUS* 17.3 (1991–92): 109–125.

———, ed. *"Seventeen Syllables."* New Brunswick, N.J.: Rutgers University Press, 1994.

Cheung, King Kok, and Stan Yogi, eds. *Asian American Literature: An Annotated Bibliography.* New York: Modern Language Association, 1988.

Chin, Frank, Jeffery Paul Chan, Lawson Fusao Inada, and Shawn Wong, eds. *Aiiieeeee! An Anthology of Asian-American Writers.* 1974. Washington, D.C.: Howard University Press, 1983.

Crow, Charles L. "Home and Transcendence in Los Angeles Fiction." In *Los Angeles in Fiction: A Collection of Original Essays.* Edited by David Fine. Albuquerque: University of New Mexico Press, 1984. 189–205.

―――. "The *Issei* Father in the Fiction of Hisaye Yamamoto." In *Opening Up Literary Criticism: Essays on American Prose and Poetry.* Edited by Leo Truchlar. Salzburg: Verlag Wolfgang Neugebauer, 1986. 34–40. Reprinted in Cheung, ed., 119–128.

―――. "A MELUS Interview: Hisaye Yamamoto." *MELUS* 14.1 (1987): 73–84.

Goellnicht, Donald C. "Transplanted Discourse in Yamamoto's 'Seventeen Syllables.' " In Cheung, ed., 181–193.

Hsu, Kai-yu and Helen Palubinskas, eds. *Asian-American Authors.* 1972. Boston: Houghton, 1976.

Kageyama, Yuri. "Hisaye Yamamoto: Nisei Writer." *Sunbury* 10 (1981): 32–42.

Kim, Elaine H. *Asian American Literature: An Introduction to the Writings and Their Social Context.* Philadelphia: Temple University Press, 1982.

Koppelman, Susan, ed. *Between Mothers and Daughters.* New York: Feminist Press, 1985.

Matsumoto, Valerie. "Desperately Seeking 'Deirdre': Gender Roles, Multicultural Relations, and Nisei Women Writers of the 1930s." *Frontiers* 12.1 (1991): 19–32.

McDonald, Dorothy Ritsuko, and Katharine Newman. "Relocation and Dislocation: The Writings of Hisaye Yamamoto and Wakako Yamauchi." *MELUS* 7.3 (1980): 21–38. Reprinted in Cheung, ed., 129–141.

Mistri, Zenobia Baxter. " 'Seventeen Syllables': A Symbolic Haiku." *Studies in Short Fiction* 27.2 (1990): 197–202. Reprinted in Cheung, ed., 195–202.

Nakamura, Cayleen. *"Seventeen Syllables": A Curriculum Guide for High School Classroom Use in Conjunction with "Hot Summer Winds."* Los Angeles: Community Television of Southern California, 1991.

Osborn, William P., and Sylvia A. Watanabe. "A Conversation with Hisaye Yamamoto." *Chicago Review* 39.3–4 (1993): 34–43.

Payne, Robert M. "Adapting (to) the Margins: *Hot Summer Winds* and the Stories of Hisaye Yamamoto." *East-West Film Journal* 7.2 (1993): 39–53. Reprinted in Cheung, ed., 203–218.

Rolf, Robert T. "The Short Stories of Hisaye Yamamoto, Japanese American Writer." *Bulletin of Fukuoka University of Education* 31.1 (1982): 71–86. Reprinted in Cheung, ed., 89–108.

Usui, Masami. "Prison, Psyche, and Poetry in Hisaye Yamamoto's Three Short Stories: 'Seventeen Syllables,' 'The Legend of Miss Sasagawara,' and 'The Eskimo Connection.'" *Studies in Culture and the Humanities* 6 (1997): 1–28.

Wong, Sau-ling Cynthia. *Reading Asian American Literature: From Necessity to Extravagance.* Princeton: Princeton University Press, 1993.

Yogi, Stan. "Legacies Revealed: Uncovering Buried Plots in the Stories of Hisaye Yamamoto." *Studies in American Fiction* 17.2 (1994): 169–181. Reprinted in Cheung, ed., 143–160.

————. "Rebels and Heroines: Subversive Narratives in the Stories of Wakako Yamauchi and Hisaye Yamamoto." In *Reading the Literatures of Asian America.* Edited by Shirley Geok-lin Lim and Amy Ling. Philadelphia: Temple University Press, 1992. 131–150.

About The Author

Hisaye Yamamoto was born in 1921 in Redondo Beach, California. Her parents were immigrants from Japan. She attended Compton Junior College, where she majored in French, Spanish, German, and Latin. She also attended Japanese school for twelve years. From 1942 to 1945, she and her family were interned in the concentration camp at Poston, Arizona. In 1944 she and two brothers were "relocated" to Massachusetts, but another brother's death in combat in Italy brought them back to camp. In 1945 she moved with her family to Los Angeles.

She has been writing for publication since the age of fourteen, including for the concentration camp newspaper, *The Poston Chronicle*. After the war she worked for three years for the *Los Angeles Tribune*, a Black weekly. In 1948 she began to publish her fiction and non-fiction in journals including *Partisan Review, Kenyon Review, Harper's Bazaar, Carleton Miscellany, Arizona Quarterly,* and *Furioso*. One of her stories, "Yoneko's Earthquake," was selected for inclusion in *The Best American Short Stories of 1952*. Three other stories: "Seventeen Syllables," "The Brown House," and "Epithalamium," also were chosen for the annual listings of "Distinctive Short Stories," included in the *Best American Short Stories* volumes. Her poetry and prose have been published in numerous Japanese American, Japanese Canadian, and Japanese publications including *Rafu Shimpo, Kashu Mainichi, Pacific Citizen, New Canadian, Rikka, Ashai Shimbun, Pan,* and *Hokubei Mainichi*. Her work has also been widely anthologized in textbooks and in collections for general audiences.

In 1950 she received one of the first John Hay Whitney Foundation Opportunity Fellowships. From 1953 to 1955 she participated in the work of Catholic Workers in New York and also wrote for *The Catholic Worker*. She is married to Anthony DeSoto and has five children, five grandchildren, and two great-grandchildren. She was the recipient of the 1986 American Book Award for Lifetime Achievement from the Before Columbus Foundation. She lives in Southern California.